# I
# REMEMBER
# EVERYTHING

Also by Brooks Eason

**Travels with Bobby**
*Hiking in the Mountains of the American West*

**Fortunate Son**
*The Story of Baby Boy Francis*

**Bedtime with Buster**
*Conversations with a Handsome Hound*

**Redemption**
*The Two Lives of Harry Brooks*

**The Scoutmaster**
*Lessons in Service and Leadership from an American Hero*

**Trigger Warning**
*Tales from a Life in the Law*

# I
# REMEMBER
# EVERYTHING

## a tale of friendship

### BROOKS EASON

WordCrafts Press

**I Remember Everything**
Copyright © 2025
Brooks Eason

Hardback ISBN: 978-1-967649-10-5
Paperback ISBN: 978-1-967649-11-2

Cover concept by Brooks and Carrie Eason.
Cover design by Mike Parker.



Published by WordCrafts Press
Cody, Wyoming 82414
www.wordcrafts.net

To friendship

# Part I

## End of a Friendship

# Chapter One

July 11, 2023

The Night That Changed Everything

The ballroom of the Westin Hotel in downtown Jackson was standing room only. Five days earlier, with a Category 4 hurricane gaining strength in the Gulf, the annual Mississippi Bar Convention was moved to Jackson from the Sandestin Resort on the Florida Panhandle. Three days later, the storm veered to the west, sparing Florida, but it was too late to move the convention back to the beach.

Sam shook the outgoing president's hand, stepped to the lectern, and looked out at the crowd. He was the center of attention, but he was used to it. He had rehearsed the speech half a dozen times—three times alone, twice for his wife Evelyn, and one last time for Jeff Freeman, his best friend. Jeff was an investment advisor, but he would have been a great trial lawyer. Sam's standard practice when he had a big trial was to present his opening statement and closing argument to Jeff and get his advice. Jeff had declined Sam's invitation to attend the banquet and speech, saying he was feeling under the weather, but he listened to Sam's final rehearsal, suggested no changes, and gave him two thumbs up.

But even after six rehearsals and nearly forty years of jury trials, Sam still used notes as a security blanket. He pulled them out and placed them on the lectern. He knew exactly what he planned to say, but the notes would be there just in case. He nodded and smiled at familiar faces, then began.

"Thank you for your excellent service to the Bar, Tom, and for your kind introduction. And many thanks to all of you for coming, even those who didn't vote for me.

"Lawyers don't have a sterling reputation. As my physician wife reminds me, people tell lawyer jokes, not doctor jokes. To some, the president of the Bar association is just the head pig in the pigpen.

"Our lousy reputation comes with the territory, at least for litigators like me. We spend our careers doing battle in an adversary system, trying our best so that our side will win and the other will lose. But trying our best and winning are not enough to make us popular. And some lawyers, it's sad to say, give the rest of us a bad name. We're not the world's oldest profession, but many believe ours is no better.

"But I don't believe it, and neither should you. I regard our profession as the most essential of all professions, and I'll tell you why. It's often said that we're a nation of laws and not of men. True enough, but without lawyers, laws would just be words on a page. They would mean nothing without men and women willing to do the hard work to bring them to life. Without lawyers—both those who serve as judges and those who come before them—laws would be empty promises.

"I have the deepest admiration for dozens of lawyers I've worked with during my long career. I opposed many of them in hard-fought cases, some that I won and some that I lost. I'm proud that we're members of the same profession. And I'm even prouder that you have chosen me to serve as your president for the coming year. To lead this organization is the highest honor of my professional life.

"As many of you know, my beautiful wife Evelyn is an accomplished pediatrician, the best in all the land so far as I'm concerned. As most of you probably don't know, Evelyn is a perfectionist. She wants everything to be exactly right. Not almost right. Exactly right. Tom and my other predecessors in this role have done a wonderful job serving all of us, and the state of our Bar is strong. But, as Evelyn often reminds me, there is always room for improvement. And so, I have identified four areas in which I hope the Mississippi Bar will improve during the coming year."

After laying out his plans to improve the Bar's pro bono programs, make its disciplinary system more transparent, and increase participation in its high school mock trial program, Sam came to his fourth initiative.

"Finally, and this is a new goal I've set for us, I want to improve the Bar's morale by celebrating our profession and our many outstanding members. I see many outstanding lawyers here tonight. Practicing law is stressful, and it always will be. Any lawyer who's stood in a courtroom and heard a judge ask if the jury has reached a verdict knows that all too well.

"But in recent years, as practicing law has become less of a profession and more of a business, as lawyers have bounced from firm to firm to firm, and as dollars have seemed to become the sole measuring stick of our worth, life as a lawyer has become even more stressful. These days I hear more and more lawyers say they wish they had chosen to do something else for a living. But this remains a great and essential profession, and we need to be reminded of that.

"So how will we improve our morale? How will we make ourselves happier about being lawyers and more satisfied that we chose this honorable profession? I will ask for suggestions from you in the weeks to come, but there's one thing I've already decided to do. Once a week, every week, I will send out an email to every member of the Bar celebrating a Mississippi lawyer.

"It won't just be lawyers who've prevailed in important cases against long odds or volunteered their time to represent convicts on death row and established their innocence. Those lawyers are worthy of celebrating, to be sure, and they will be. But I also plan to recognize lawyers whose heroism consists entirely of practicing law the way law should be practiced. By that, I mean lawyers who work hard, represent their clients zealously, and charge a fair fee. I mean lawyers who treat everyone well, from the justices on our Supreme Court who hear their appeals to the employees of their firms who make the coffee. I mean lawyers who take the time to teach young lawyers how it should be done. And finally, I mean lawyers who are so honest you could shoot craps with them over the phone, lawyers who, like John Prine's grandpa, are level on the level. If you don't know about John's grandpa, look him up. He was a carpenter, an honest one.

"Thanks to lawyers who have these qualities, long after most of us are gone, this will still be an honorable profession, and it will still be practiced by honorable men and women. I'm sure you know many lawyers who fit the bill. You're probably thinking of them now. I will ask for nominees.

"If it sounds like I've set ambitious goals for the coming year, well, I have. And as we all know, the road to hell is paved with good intentions. How will I turn my good intentions into concrete actions and achieve these goals? How will a busy member of the Bar find the time to write an email every week celebrating another member of the Bar?

"Well, I will end my talk tonight with an announcement. With the blessing of my family, my law partners, and my clients, I am retiring from the active practice of law"—Sam paused, looked down at his watch, looked up, and smiled—"this very minute. There. I said it, and I feel good about it. I plan to devote my time and energy during the coming year to the profession I love and that has been so good to me. After that, I will devote my time and energy to something I love even more—my wife, my children and, hopefully soon, my grandchildren. I also plan to spend more time sitting by campfires with my best friend.

"Thank you for your faith in me. I hope to prove you right."

As Sam turned to shake hands with the others on the podium, some in the audience stood and clapped. Soon the standing ovation included everyone in the room. Sam was the preeminent litigator in the largest firm in the state. That he was giving up a successful practice when he was still in top form astonished many, but those who were closest to him were not surprised. Since joining the firm in the 1980s, he had litigated many high-stakes cases, most successfully but not all. The ones he lost still haunted him. What could he have done differently? There is, as he just told the audience, always room for improvement. Sam may not have shown the stress, but he felt it. What he said was true; it felt good to be retiring.

Sam and Evelyn lived on a tree-lined street in a quiet neighborhood in Madison, a suburb north of Jackson. On the drive home, she complimented him on his speech and told him how proud she was. After he turned onto the unlit Natchez Trace Parkway, she reached over and put her hand on his thigh. "We've had a public celebration. When we get home, I think we need to have a private one."

Sam smiled but kept his eyes on the road. "Is that right? What exactly do you have in mind?" Like Sam, Evelyn was sixty-three, but she took very good care of herself and was still a beautiful woman. She squeezed his thigh.

"This is your special night, big boy. You decide."

"Hmmm. That's a lot of pressure. You want to give me some options?"

"Whatever you want, baby. But whatever you decide, just remember this: There is always room for improvement." Sam glanced over at Evelyn and smiled.

That's when it happened. There was a loud thud. Evelyn screamed. In an instant one life ended, and many more were changed forever.

Sam slammed on the brakes and pulled off the road onto the shoulder. "What was that? A deer?"

Evelyn looked like she'd seen a ghost. She was shaking. "No. A man."

"A man? My God. You sure?"

"Positive." Sam reached to open his door, but she grabbed his arm. "Let me go check first," she said. "I'm the doctor."

"No. Let me go."

"No. You stay here in case another car comes. I'll be back in a minute." She was out the door before he could stop her. Sam tried to watch her in the rearview mirror, but it was too dark to see. He was sweating, his heart and mind racing. What had he done? Was there anything he could have done?

The man was lying face down just off the road twenty yards behind them. A bicycle lay another ten yards behind the man, the wheels in the grass and the seat on the edge of the pavement. He wasn't wearing a helmet, but it could have been knocked off in the collision. Evelyn lifted his right arm and felt his wrist for a pulse. Nothing. She checked his neck to make sure. Still nothing. She returned to the vehicle, walking slowly.

"Is he alive? Please tell me he's alive."

"I'm afraid not. He was riding a bike. It was on the edge of the road behind him. Looks like he lost his balance and fell off in front of us. He must have been killed instantly."

"I don't guess you recognized him."

She shook her head. "Too dark, and he was face down."

Sam picked up his iPhone.

"What are you doing?" she asked.

"Calling 911."

Evelyn put her hand on his before he could enter the number. "Hold on a second."

He turned to face her. "What? Why?"

"How much did you have to drink tonight?"

"What are you saying? I'm not drunk. As you just said, he fell right in front of me."

"I know he did, but are you sure you could pass a breathalyzer test?"

"How would I know? I've never taken a breathalyzer test. But I know I'm not drunk."

"I know you're not too, but how much did you have to drink?"

"I don't know. Two Tito's and tonics, maybe three glasses of champagne. But we were there for three hours. I'm not even tipsy. I just gave a speech."

"You may not be tipsy, but I think we need to leave."

"What are you saying? I hit a man and killed him. I can't just leave him, Evelyn. I'm not drunk, and it wasn't my fault."

"I know it wasn't, but listen to me, Sam. The man is dead. We can't do a thing to help him. He'll be spotted at first light if not before. And no good can come from calling 911 or staying here until somebody sees us."

"But I can't just leave the man, Evelyn. I'd be fleeing from the scene of a crime."

"It's not a crime, Sam, but if you fail a breathalyzer test, you might just be charged with one."

"But leaving would be a crime for sure. I killed a man. I can't just drive away and leave a dead body on the side of the road."

"Staying here won't do that poor man any good, Sam. But it could be catastrophic for you. Let's go now before another car comes."

Sam thought about his late father, who always did the right thing. He wouldn't leave, that's for sure.

"Sam, listen to me. Let's leave now, before somebody sees us. Please."

Sam stared straight ahead. How could he leave? How could he just drive off into the night? But Evelyn was right. Other than sparing him the shame he would feel for the rest of his days, no good could come from staying. And though the accident was not his fault, he might be charged with a crime because of it. Five seconds passed, then five more.

Evelyn spoke again. Her voice was softer now. "Let's go, Sam. Please."

He banged his hands on the steering wheel, then pulled back onto the pavement. They rode home in silence. When they were in bed, Evelyn spoke for the first time. "It was the right thing to do."

"No, it wasn't. Maybe it was the smart thing, but it wasn't the right thing." He rolled over onto his side and stared at the wall.

# Chapter Two

July 12, 2023

A Priest and John Prine

Sam took a Melatonin at one in the morning, another at 3:30. When he woke up, he could tell it was mid-morning from the angle of the light. The other side of the bed was empty. He reached for his iPhone to check the time; it was 9:45. His first thought was that he was late for work, but then he remembered: He was retired; he wasn't late for anything. He spotted a note on his bedside table, picked it up, and read it twice.

*S –*

*I decided I should go on to the clinic. I will check on you at lunch.*

*You can read the paper and watch the news but don't search the Internet. Nothing that would leave a trace. Everything needs to be normal.*

*Your Explorer is fine. Looks like there might be a small dent, but there were plenty of old ones. There's nothing anyone would notice.*

*Maybe it wasn't the right thing, but it was the only choice we had.*

*I love you.*

*E*

*P.S. Tear up this note.*

After doing as instructed, Sam put on shorts and a tee shirt and went out to get the *Clarion Ledger*. He was sure there would be nothing about the accident in the morning paper, but reading it was part of his morning routine, and it might serve as a distraction. Lois Brantley, who lived down the street, came walking by with Zeus, her Labradoodle. Sam said good morning and squatted down to pet him.

"What on earth are you doing here? You're usually long gone to the office by now."

Sam stood up and forced a smile. "I'm retired. Today's my first day."

"Retired? Well, congratulations. I never would have guessed it. I figured you'd die with your boots on."

"A lot of people thought that, but I was ready. Tired of all the fighting and worrying."

"I know your partners and clients are disappointed, but if it's what you want, it's what you should do. I'm happy for you."

"Thank you, Lois. I suspect you'll be seeing a lot more of me and Buddy."

Buddy was the most recent in a long line of mixed-breed shelter dogs to join the Thompson family. As long as there were shelter dogs needing a good home, Sam and Evelyn would never have a fancy doodle dog.

"That will be great. Listen, did you see on the morning news about the cyclist on the Trace?"

Sam felt his face flush. "No. What happened?"

"A man on a bicycle was killed between here and the interstate last night. Hit and run."

"That's terrible. Do they know who it was? Who did it?" He wondered if he should have asked the second question.

"Sounds like they've identified the victim. The reporter said his name was being withheld pending notification of next of kin. They didn't find him until daybreak. No mention of a suspect. I can't believe somebody would hit a poor man on a bike and just drive off and leave him. You just don't know about people these days. Well, Zeus is tugging. You have a good first day of retirement, Sam."

"Thank you, Lois."

He walked back into the house with the paper. When the door closed behind him, he repeated Lois's words—"you just don't know about people these days"—and slumped into a chair. Leaving the man he killed was the worst thing Sam had ever done. He was not a perfect man by any means, but he always tried to be like his father and do the right thing. And now he'd done this.

He didn't blame himself for hitting the man, who fell right in front of him on a pitch-black section of the Natchez Trace. But he should have called 911, told the cops what happened, and let the chips fall where they may. If they had given him a breathalyzer test and he was over the legal limit, so be it. But he didn't call. Instead, he fled.

Sam didn't blame Evelyn. Her first instinct was to protect him. If she'd been driving, his first instinct would have been to protect her. But he should have stood his ground. When she said they should leave, he should have said no. But he didn't, and there was no turning the clock back now.

Sam prepared his standard summer breakfast, a bowl of Wheat Chex topped with blueberries and a fresh peach, peeled and sliced. He sat down at the table with the newspaper and was soon joined by Lady, the family cat and another rescue. She was more aggressive than usual, no doubt because she was used to being presented with the last half inch of Sam's cereal milk much earlier than this. He scratched her behind the ears and positioned the paper as a barrier between her and his bowl. Her time would come.

The *Clarion Ledger*, like other print newspapers, was struggling to compete with the Internet. Most news was now free; why pay for it? The paper became thinner and thinner as the years went by, but Sam still subscribed. Reading it had been a daily ritual since he moved back to Jackson after finishing law school and marrying Evelyn in 1985. He was a creature of habit and read the paper in the same order every day. The Cardinals were off the night before, but they'd beaten the White Sox two games in a row. They were still far below .500, but maybe there was hope for the season. When he finished the comics and his cereal, he folded the paper and pushed his bowl over to Lady. The milk was purple from the blueberries, but she didn't mind.

He walked to the bedroom and checked the time and weather on his iPhone. It was nearly eleven and eighty-eight degrees, four hours later and fifteen degrees warmer than usual for his morning walk in the summer. The heat would make it unpleasant, but he figured he deserved it. Buddy followed him to the bathroom and back, ready to go, but Sam decided it was too hot for his fur-covered dog. To trick him, Sam went out the back door instead of the front and waited to put on his shoes and socks until he sat down on the curb outside the gate. It didn't work; he heard Buddy barking as he walked down the hill.

Sam made a point of always speaking to everyone on the walking trail, but he walked past a man and then a woman without saying a word. Part of his regular route was on the paved trail in the Natchez Trace right-of-way. He was tempted to walk farther than usual and return to the scene of the accident, but there was no point in doing that. As always, Evelyn was right; everything needed to be normal.

He wished he could talk to someone other than Evelyn about what happened. He wanted someone to tell him this one terrible sin didn't make him a terrible man, that he would get past this and it would all be okay. His first thought was Jeff, but he didn't want to drag him into it and turn him into a co-conspirator. What if the truth came out and people found out Jeff knew all along? Telling him would be selfish. Sam had already been selfish enough. He didn't even get out to check on the man.

Then he thought of David Eldridge. Sam was not especially religious, but he and Evelyn attended church religiously. Other than when he was on a trip or in trial, they went nearly every Sunday. He wasn't sure how much Christian theology he believed—he often thought about lawsuits he was handling during the sermon—but he liked the music and the friends he saw on Sundays.

Sam and Evelyn were longtime members of the Chapel of the Cross, a beautiful old Episcopal church built a decade before the Civil War with slave-made bricks and oak floors hewn from trees cut down to clear the site. They enjoyed the quiet drive to the country church northwest of Madison when they joined in the 1980s, but the city had expanded since then. The road to the chapel was now lined with subdivisions and golf courses, and the drive was no longer quiet.

David was one of the priests at the chapel. He was in his eighties but still very active. He and Sam were close friends. Though they'd met at church, their relationship had nothing to do with Christianity. Now that Sam thought about it, he couldn't recall ever having spoken to David about religion.

They had instead bonded over their shared reverence for an American musical icon, the late, great John Prine. They loved both the man and his songs. The two professionals with advanced degrees marveled at the genius of the singing mailman who never attended a day of college. John's melodies, played by fingerpicking on his old Martin guitar, were beautiful, but it was mostly his words. Yogi Berra said you can observe a lot by just watching, and John excelled at watching. He painted pictures of the human condition in his songs and revealed profound truths in a single line—about lost love, an exhausted marriage, the loneliness of old people, and a thousand other things.

Once a month, when Evelyn went out with friends, Sam would invite David to grill steaks and have a John Prine night. They had decided years earlier that each Prine night would be devoted to just one of John's songs, and they took turns choosing it. They would listen to the song several times, often different versions by John and sometimes covers by other artists. Bonnie Raitt's version of "Angel from Montgomery" and Nancy Griffith's of "Speed of the Sound of Loneliness" were favorites. They played recordings from before and after the throat cancer that nearly killed John, lowered his voice by an octave, and made it richer. Then they would analyze the lyrics, line by line, closing their eyes and picturing the imagery. They almost certainly spent more time thinking about the words than the man who wrote them did.

Evelyn would come home and find them in the study or on the screened porch, immersed in the song and sipping a single malt Scotch. After rising to greet her, they would sit back down and return to the subject at hand. Still standing, she would listen a while, then smile and say goodnight. If David stayed too long and sipped too much, Sam would make him stay the night.

After the great songwriter died of COVID in April 2020, the

two friends spent more time together and became closer. For a time, they had a Prine night once a week, and Sam invited Jeff and other friends who loved John's music to attend. They changed the format, one week debating John's best song, the next his best lyric.

Nominees for best song included "Sam Stone," which tells the sad story of a wounded veteran who comes home from the war addicted to morphine, "Illegal Smile," which fans mistakenly believed was about smoking pot, and "Souvenirs," which John made up while driving his '65 Chevelle to play a show at the Fifth Peg in Chicago when he was first performing. The cover charge was fifty cents. The Fifth Peg got one quarter; John got the other.

Most of the nominees for best song were half a century old, but the last song on John's last album, "When I Get to Heaven" from *The Tree of Forgiveness*, was also one of the picks. It wasn't really one of his best songs, but it was fun to imagine John's arrival at the gates of heaven. In the song, he takes the place by storm. After shaking God's hand, he opens a nightclub, starts a rock 'n'roll band, has a vodka and ginger ale, and smokes a cigarette nine miles long.

The men ultimately chose as John's very best song "Hello in There," his magnificent ballad about the loneliness of old people. John had great empathy for old people when he was still very young; he wrote "Hello in There" when he was only twenty-two. The song pairs a beautiful melody with timeless, unforgettable lyrics about a couple who lost a son in the Korean War and still don't know what for.

Funny lyrics were nominated for John's best, including the line claiming the topless lady in "Spanish Pipedream" has something up her sleeve and the one in which the woman from "In Spite of Ourselves" becomes aroused from watching convict movies. They debated whether convict movies made the topless lady in the other song horny too but decided she would have plenty of opportunities without watching a movie.

Most of the choices for best lyric were from sad songs. Comparing the morphine injected by the veteran in "Sam Stone" to gold rolling through his veins like a thousand railroad trains was one choice, and wondering how a man could go to work in the morning, come home in the evening, and have nothing to say from "Angel from Montgomery" was another.

After a lengthy debate that lasted through three rounds of drinks, the group settled on a revealing line from "Far from Me" as Prine's very best because it said the most with the least. The song is about the first girl who broke John's heart, and the line—the girl still laughed with him but waited a second too long—is classic Prine. Short and sweet, but it says it all.

Like their songwriting idol, David was a kind, caring man. He wouldn't judge Sam or condemn him, and he would understand why he and Evelyn left the scene of the accident. And David would probably have a mandatory legal obligation not to disclose anything Sam told him. Sam had never had a case involving the priest-penitent privilege, but he thought it would probably apply if he chose to confide in David. And Sam might feel better if he did. On the other hand, did he really want his close friend to know he'd killed a man and left his body on the side of the road?

He was still undecided when he finished his walk. He checked his iPhone again before he went inside. It was noon and ninety-one degrees. His shirt was soaked with sweat. He opened the door and was welcomed by Buddy and the AC. When Sam squatted down, Buddy licked the sweat from his face. Buddy wasn't angry that he'd been left behind. Like David, Buddy wouldn't judge him.

# Chapter Three

July 12, 2023

The Worst News in the World

The local news at noon mentioned the fatal accident on the Trace but said nothing about the identity of the victim or a suspect. Sam jumped when his cell phone rang. He was used to getting at least a dozen calls a day, but now the prospect frightened him. He checked caller ID. It was Evelyn.

"Hey."

"How are you, Sweetie?"

"I'm okay," he lied. "You?"

"I'm fine. We'll get through this. What time did you get up?"

"A little before ten."

"Wow. You've never slept that late."

"I didn't fall asleep until four something."

"I'm sorry. What have you been doing?"

"I read the paper and had my cereal, then went for a walk. Just got back a few minutes ago."

"It wasn't too hot for you and Buddy?"

"I made him stay here. He wasn't happy about it."

"I bet not. What are you gonna do this afternoon?"

"Try to take a nap. I took a melatonin around one and another one at three something. I'm still groggy."

"Well, call me if you need anything."

"Listen, I think I may want to talk to David. I think it might help."

"I'm not sure that's a good idea, Sam. Can we talk about it when I get home?"

"Sure. It can wait till then."

Sam never took naps, but he'd never been retired either, so he decided to give it a try. After showering, he closed the bedroom curtains, set the noise app on his iPhone to *Rain on a Tent*, and pulled a quilt over him. Buddy gave him an odd look—he'd never seen Sam in bed during the day—but jumped up and joined him. Sam tried to sleep, but he couldn't get the dead man off his mind. After half an hour with his mind racing, he gave up and turned on his bedside lamp. Buddy woke up, yawned and stretched, then resumed his snoring. Sam was envious; he wished he could sleep like a dog.

When Sam met with Jeff to rehearse his investiture speech, Jeff had loaned him *The Caretaker*, a new novel by Ron Rash. He said it was wonderful. Sam opened the book and started. After four pages, he realized he couldn't remember a word he'd read, so he gave up on that too. He pulled out his iPhone and looked up David in his directory. He started to call, then remembered he'd promised Evelyn he would wait.

He decided to pass the time by inspecting his Ford Explorer in the sunlight to make sure there was no visible damage. With Buddy in the passenger seat, he drove north on the Trace nearly twenty miles to the picnic area at River Bend on the Pearl River. He pulled in and found a secluded spot where no one could see him or the vehicle. While Sam inspected the front end of the Explorer, Buddy entertained himself by chasing squirrels. Evelyn was right. The eight-year-old SUV already had plenty of dings and scratches. If there was anything new, no one would notice.

Sam found a tennis ball in the back of the Explorer and played fetch with Buddy, but they didn't last long in the heat. Before heading home, Sam walked out to the bank of the river. He and Jeff had spent many days and nights on the Pearl—canoeing and camping, fishing and exploring. Maybe they could have more good times on the river now that Sam was retired. He hoped his decision to call it quits would encourage Jeff to follow suit. He thought about the day forty-five summers before when they had promised each other on a mountaintop in Maine that one day they would hike the Appalachian Trail from end to end. Families and careers had prevented them from keeping the vow, but maybe they could keep it now. It would take longer than it would have in the past, but he figured they could still do it. And they could have campfires from Georgia to Maine.

But first he would have to get past this, and it wouldn't be easy. It wasn't his fault, he kept reminding himself, but there was no escaping the fact that he'd killed a man, then driven off and left his body on the side of the road.

When Sam was alongside the Ross Barnett Reservoir on the drive home from River Bend, his cell phone rang. He checked caller ID, then answered.

"Marsha, how are you? How are Bob and the baby?" Marsha was Jeff's daughter. She stayed in Oxford after graduating from Ole Miss, married Bob two years later, and was now a real estate agent. Oxford was the hottest housing market in the state, but it was still tough to make a living. It seemed that half the town's residents were realtors.

"I have terrible news, Sam." Her voice trembled. She tried to continue but couldn't. Sam could hear her crying.

"What is it? What's wrong?"

She took a deep breath and answered. "Daddy's dead."

"What? That can't be. I just saw him day before yesterday. He said he wasn't feeling well, but he seemed okay. What happened?"

"He was killed." Her crying was louder now.

"Oh my God. How?"

After another deep breath, she broke the worst news in the world. "He was riding his bike last night on the Trace. Hit and run. Driver just left him there."

Waves of nausea came in a rush. Just like the night before, Sam slammed on the brakes and pulled off the side of the road. This time he opened the door and got sick.

"Sam, are you there? Sam?"

"I need to call you back." He hung up before she could respond, leaned out, and got sick again.

He started to shake. When the shaking and nausea subsided, he realized he couldn't stay where he was. If a park ranger stopped and asked what he was doing, he might say something stupid. He pulled back onto the Trace, turned into the scenic overlook near the south end of the reservoir, and parked facing the water. He needed to call Marsha back, but first he had to collect himself. When he felt he was ready, he pressed her number. She answered on the first ring.

"I'm sorry. I was driving and needed to find a place to pull over."

"I understand."

"I can't believe it."

"I can't either."

"What do you know?"

"No more than what I told you. I just found out a little while ago."

"What do you need?"

"Just be there for Eric and me." Eric was Jeff's son. He was in law school at the University of Virginia but was working at a firm in D.C. for the summer. "We're going to need you."

"Of course."

"And you'll probably need us too. You've loved him longer than we have. Longer than anybody."

They were both crying now. Sam decided to try to stick to business. "When are you coming to Jackson? Is there anything I can do before you get here?"

"I'm driving down in the morning. I do have some favors to ask."

"Anything."

"Can you call Daddy's friends in Jackson and the people he worked with?"

"Of course." Sam wasn't sure he could manage it, but he couldn't refuse. "Does your mother know?" Jeff and Olivia had divorced six years earlier.

"She and I just got off the phone. She's going to see what she can find out. You were my third call after Eric and Mama."

"I'll make a list of people to call as soon as I get home. I'll handle it. What else?"

"Can you go to Daddy's and check on Josey? He has a pet door, but he might need food and water." Josey was Jeff's well-loved golden retriever, a gift from a woman he dated after he and Olivia divorced. Jeff had named him for Clint Eastwood's character in *The Outlaw Josey Wales.*

"Sure. I have a key. I'll bring him to our house." Josey and Buddy loved spending time together. Sam and Jeff had taken the dogs when they went camping in May.

"Thank you. Eric booked a flight while we were on the phone. He gets in tonight at 8:30. I'm not sure he should be driving. Could you pick him up and take him to Mama's?"

"Of course. What else?"

"One more thing. I don't have a time scheduled yet, but Eric and I will need to go to the funeral home tomorrow to make arrangements. Will you go with us? Bob has a meeting he can't cancel. He won't make it to Jackson with Jeffery until tomorrow evening."

"Sure. Just let me know when."

"Thank you. I can't believe he's gone."

"Me either."

"How long have y'all been best friends, Sam?"

"Fifty-five years last month. Since the day he rang our doorbell in 1968. We became best friends the day we met."

"I know all about the day of the doorbell. I heard Daddy tell the story at least half a dozen times. I loved hearing it, but he loved telling it even more. I just didn't remember the year. We had a Zoom call last night so he could see Jeffery. Daddy insisted on calling him Jeff. I loved him so much, Sam."

"I loved him too. He was the best friend a man could have. Tell Eric to expect me at 8:30."

"He's already expecting you. I told him I'd let him know if you couldn't make it, but I knew we could count on you."

When they hung up, Sam stepped out of the car and walked halfway down the hill. There was a John Prine song for every occasion, even this one, and the words of "Speed of the Sound of Loneliness" came to him as he stared out at the water. *What in heaven's name have you done?* he asked himself. The person breaking the speed of the sound of loneliness was out there running just to be on the run. Sam wished he could run too, but there was no running away from this.

He walked back up to the Explorer, pulled back onto the Trace, and headed home. He couldn't bear the thought of walking into Jeff's house just yet; he would get Josey later. He missed the Old Canton Road exit, which he'd taken at least a thousand times, turned around at the Parkway Information Cabin, and made his way home. Once inside, he lay down on the floor with Buddy and cried.

After thirty minutes, he decided he couldn't just lie there until Evelyn got home. He retrieved a legal pad from his study and began making a list of the people who needed to be told, starting with Jeff's assistant at the investment firm where he worked. He listed their mutual friends and camping buddies, Jeff's golf group, and two women he'd dated recently. He would ask those he reached to spread the word. He already had some of their numbers in his iPhone and searched the Internet for others. Working on the list gave him an excuse not to call anybody.

In less than an hour, he had twenty-five names and numbers. He would no doubt come up with more after he started making calls. He stared at the first number on the list. Jeff's longtime assistant, Jane, had worked with him for two decades at three firms. She was competent and efficient and could be trusted to notify Jeff's colleagues and clients.

Sam started to enter the number but then sighed and put the phone down. He walked to the bar and poured himself a Tito's and tonic, stronger than usual. When Evelyn walked in forty-five minutes later, he was on his third.

She put down her purse in the kitchen. "Sam, I'm home. Where are you?"

"In here," he answered from the den.

She found him slumped in his recliner. All the lights were

off. She kissed him on the top of his head, turned on a lamp, then stepped back and studied him. "You don't look good. You feel okay?"

He looked up. His eyes were red. "It was Jeff."

"What was Jeff?"

"The man I killed. It was Jeff. I killed my best friend."

"Oh my God. How do you know?"

"Marsha called."

"I can't believe it. What was he doing out there?"

"I have no idea. She wants me to tell everybody who needs to know. I made a list, but I haven't called anybody yet. I tried, but I couldn't."

"I'm so sorry, Sweetheart."

"I killed him and just left him there." The sobs came. She wrapped her arms around him.

"It wasn't your fault, Sam. And he was dead. There's nothing we could have done for him."

When Sam was able to speak again, he said, "I told her I'd pick Eric up at the airport tonight and bring Josey to our house. I guess I better put this drink down. I don't want to kill his son and his dog too." He leaned back and closed his eyes.

"I'll go with you. I'll drive. When does Eric get in?"

"Eight-thirty. Thank you."

"Let me fix you some dinner. You'll feel better."

"No, thanks. I can't eat anything. I got sick when Marsha told me. But would you do me a favor?"

"Sure. What?"

"Would you call the people on my list?"

"Of course."

Evelyn had been the one to get out and check on the man who turned out to be Jeff, and now she would be the one to tell Jeff's friends he was dead. Sam followed Evelyn to the kitchen to listen to her side of the first conversation. She tried Jeff's assistant, but it was after hours and the call rolled over to voicemail. She left a message saying she would call again in the morning and went to the second name on the list.

"Robert, this is Evelyn Thompson."

"I'm fine, thank you, but I have some terrible news. Jeff Freeman was killed on the Natchez Trace last night. He was riding a bike.

"No. It was a hit and run.

"No leads that I know of. Sam just found out from Jeff's daughter a little while ago.

"His son is flying in from Washington tonight. No arrangements yet.

"Very hard, I'm afraid. They were best friends for more than fifty years.

"He sure was. A wonderful man. Listen, could you do me a favor? Sam made a list of people who need to be told, but I'm sure he didn't think of everybody. If you think of somebody, please tell them. Better for them to hear it twice from Jeff's friends than to read it in the *Clarion Ledger.*

"You're welcome. I'll tell him. Goodbye."

Sam walked to the bedroom, lay down, and closed his eyes. What in heaven's name had he done?

They left to get Josey and Eric at 7:30. It was strange to walk into Jeff's home and not find him there. Nothing was out of order, and there were no clues to explain why he was riding his bike on the Trace the night before. Josey jumped into the back seat of Evelyn's car when Sam opened the door, and they headed to the airport. She dropped Sam off outside baggage claim and waited in temporary parking while he went inside. What should he say to Eric? What could he say? After a few minutes, he spotted Eric on the escalator. He looked just like Jeff at the same age. He saw Sam and managed a weak smile. They hugged, but neither one spoke. After ten seconds, Eric broke the silence. "I just have this carry-on. I didn't check a bag." Like Sam, he would try to stick to business.

"Evelyn just dropped me off. Let me call her." When they saw her car pull up to the curb, they walked out into the hot July night, Sam's arm around Eric's shoulder.

Eric climbed into the back seat and buried his face in Josey's fur.

Evelyn did not stick to business. "We're so sorry, Eric, so sorry. It's hard to believe. He was such a wonderful man."

"Thank you, Dr. Thompson. It's hard for me to believe too. I just talked to him last night."

"How was your flight?"

"Fine, but too long. Too much time to think. I can't believe the bastard just drove off and left him. What kind of person would do that?" Sam winced.

"We're so sorry," Evelyn responded. "I've been trying to think about how Jeff lived, not how he died. He was a wonderful friend to us and a wonderful father to you and Marsha."

"I remember when he called from the hospital the night you were born," Sam said. "It was two in the morning, but he didn't care and I didn't either. He and your mama could have found out if you were a boy or a girl, but they decided to let it be a surprise. And when he called, he was on cloud nine. I remember his first words. He said, 'It's a boy. You have a son, and now I have a son too. And they're the same age, just like us.'"

On the rest of the drive to Olivia's house, Sam and Eric swapped stories from their camping trips with Jeff and Jason, the Thompsons' son. Evelyn had heard them all before, most more than once, but she didn't interrupt. They were fond memories and a good way for Jeff's son and best friend to grieve.

Olivia still lived in the home in the Belhaven historic district where she and Jeff had raised Marsha and Eric. The Thompsons had not remained close to Olivia after she and Jeff divorced, but they were still on good terms. As divorces go, the Freemans' was amicable. They were a decade apart in age, and as their kids grew up, they grew apart. That was about all there was to it. And when Eric left for Ole Miss in 2017, they decided to call it quits. But neither had remarried, and they still got along. They shared two children and doted on Jeffery, their first grandchild.

Eric walked in, followed by Josey and the Thompsons. Sam and Evelyn waited while Olivia hugged Eric. When Olivia saw her son was crying, she brushed away his tears and started crying too. Then Evelyn, followed by Sam, hugged Olivia. None of them had much to say. The Thompsons had enjoyed many wonderful times with Jeff and Olivia, but reminiscing with his ex-wife didn't seem like the thing to do.

As they were leaving, Sam said, "Marsha told me she would call me in the morning about meeting at the funeral home. If either of you needs anything before then, anything at all, please call me. If it's four in the morning, call me." He hugged them both again. As he opened the door, Sam had another thought. "We were going to take Josey home with us, but y'all may want him to stay here."

"That would be great," said Eric, "but Mama's allergic."

"I'm so sorry," Sam responded. "We shouldn't have brought him in with us. I forgot." Jeff had said one of the benefits of the divorce was that he could now live with someone who loved him unconditionally. He could live with a dog.

"No apology necessary. A few minutes won't hurt me, but he doesn't need to spend the night."

They were silent on the drive home until they pulled into the garage. Then Sam turned to Evelyn and repeated Eric's words. "I can't believe the bastard just drove off and left him." He knew he would hear the same message over and over in the coming days. And he would deserve it.

# Part II

## Building A Friendship

# Chapter Four

June 13, 1968

Day of the Doorbell

Jeff climbed the steps and stared up at the second floor. It was the grandest house on the street, with four tall white columns in front. He rang the doorbell and waited. Seconds later, a beautiful woman opened the door and smiled.

"Good afternoon. Well, aren't you a handsome young man. Whom do I have the pleasure of addressing?"

"The pleasure of what?"

"Addressing. That's a fancy way of asking what your name is."

"I'm Jeff Freeman. Me and my mama just moved in down the street."

"My mama and I."

"Your mama and you what?"

"My mama and I is the correct grammar."

"My mama's always correcting my grammar."

"Good for her. That's one of our jobs, you know."

"What's your name?"

"I'm Sara Thompson. I live here."

"I figured that."

"It's nice to meet you, Jeff." She stuck out her hand, and he shook it. "Did you just stop by to introduce yourself, or are you a traveling salesman?"

"I didn't come to introduce myself, and I don't have anything to sell. My mama kicked me out of the house."

"Goodness. Why on earth would she do such a thing?"

"She said I was driving her crazy. She says I talk too much."

"Well, do you?"

"I don't know. I just talk when I have something to say."

"An admirable quality. You haven't been kicked out permanently, I hope."

"No, ma'am. Just till dark. Mama told me to go find somebody to play with. Do you have anybody here?"

"I just might. Are you looking for a boy?"

"Yes, ma'am. That would sure be better than a girl."

"About your age?"

"Yes, ma'am. Or older. I don't like playing with little kids."

"And just how old are you?"

"I'll be nine on my next birthday. Ten the year after that."

"When's your birthday?

"May the 19th."

"So you turned eight last month."

"Yes, ma'am."

"I see. Well, it just so happens I have exactly what you're looking for. My son Sam is a little younger than you are but not much. He'll turn eight a week from today. He's upstairs watching television. You want to come in and watch with him?"

"No, thank you, ma'am. I don't much like TV. I'd rather be outside."

"Goodness. I thought all children loved television. What exactly do you like?"

"Lots of things. Frogs. Lizards. Fish. Owls. I love owls. You think Sam would go exploring with me? I found a creek down the hill behind our house. I want to see where it goes."

"That's a grand idea. In fact, that's such a grand idea I'm going to do what your mother did and kick Sam out of the house. He spends way too much time watching TV or with his nose in a book. Come on in; I'll go upstairs and get him."

Jeff had never been in such a home. Along one wall of the living room, walnut bookcases filled with hardcover volumes stretched from floor to ceiling. The other walls were decorated with oil portraits, one of a Confederate general, and the hardwood floors were covered with the most beautiful rugs Jeff had ever seen. Sam and his mother soon descended the winding staircase that connected the two floors. Sam stuck out his right hand.

"Hi, I'm Sam Thompson."

"Jeff Freeman. Nice to meet you."

They shook hands like grown men, with firm grips and eye contact. Their fathers had taught them well. Sara smiled and clasped her hands in front of her mouth.

"You want to go exploring? There's a creek down the hill. I want to see where it goes. My daddy says creeks go to rivers and rivers go to oceans."

"You're going to an ocean?"

"I won't make it that far today. I have to be home by dark, but I'll go as far as I can. Want to go with me?"

"May I go, Mama?"

"Sure, Sam." She tousled his hair. "But y'all be careful. And make sure you turn around in plenty of time to get home by dark. I don't want to have to send out a search party."

"We will. I promise."

"Hey Sam, who's the Rebel general in the painting?"

"That's my great-great-grandfather. He was wounded at Shiloh."

"I've been there. My daddy took me. He taught me all about the Civil War. He's a Marine."

"My daddy's a doctor."

"Let's go. We can talk on the way."

"Mama, Mama, you're not gonna believe what we saw!"

"I don't believe what I'm seeing right now. May I ask, young man, why you're standing here in the living room in your underwear?"

"My clothes were muddy. I took them off in the carport."

"That's good, I suppose."

"Where's Daddy?"

"He had to work late."

"He always has to work late." Dr. Thompson was a heart surgeon. "We followed that creek to this big river."

"Goodness. You made it all the way to the Pearl?"

"I guess. It was huge. Jeff's got this net. We caught lots of stuff. Frogs, tadpoles, fish, turtles. Even a snake."

"A snake?"

"It wasn't poisonous."

"How do you know?"

"Jeff told me, but his daddy says snakes aren't really poisonous; they're venomous. We came back through the woods and saw two baby armadillos and a whole bunch of deer. When they heard us coming, they held their tails up and ran away. Jeff said they were white-tailed deer. And you can't believe all the birds, Mama. There was this huge bird as tall as I am with wings out to here." He spread his arms wide. "A great blue heron. He took off and made this loud squawk. And we watched an egret fishing in the creek."

"I didn't know you knew about herons and egrets. Armadillos either."

"I didn't until today."

"So how do you know what they were?"

"Jeff told me. He knows everything."

"That's impressive. How does he know so much?"

"He and his daddy used to spend all their time in the woods. Camping and canoeing, hiking and building campfires and stuff."

"You said used to. Why did they stop?"

"His dad's in the Marines. He flies a helicopter. He got sent to Vietnam. That's why Jeff and his mom moved here. To be close to his grandparents."

"Goodness. I hope Jeff's dad is safe."

"He's not worried. He says his dad's the best helicopter pilot in the world. So we were wading in the creek and came around this curve. Jeff was in the lead. He turned around and held his finger up to his lips for me to be quiet. We sneaked up on two ducks—he said they were wood ducks—and got as close as from here to there." He pointed to the front door. "Then Jeff said *boo*, and the ducks jumped straight up out of the water and flew away. Just like that, they were gone."

"Sounds like you had fun."

"The most fun ever! Just before dark, we heard a weird bird call.

I'd never heard it before. He said it was some kind of woodpecker. Starts with a p."

"Pileated?"

"That's it. We spotted him on the trunk of a tree. Looked just like Woody Woodpecker. And then we heard a bird Jeff said was a barred owl. The owl would call, and Jeff would call back. And Mama, you're not gonna believe this, but the owl would then call back to Jeff. The owl thought Jeff was an owl!"

"Amazing."

"May I go back out after supper? Please."

"Goodness. To do what?"

Jeff says we can catch lightning bugs and run behind the fog machine."

"The fog machine?"

"You know, that truck that sprays out that white smoke for mosquitoes. And if we can find some other boys, we're gonna play kick the can."

"You know how to play kick the can?"

"I do now. Jeff told me."

"What about girls? Can't they play too?"

"I guess. If we can't find enough boys."

Thus it began. From that day forward, the boys were inseparable. They explored every inch of the creek and the floodplain along the Pearl, searched the woods and water, and caught anything that moved. They lured crawdads from their holes with bacon, put them on the ground facing each other, and tried to get them to fight. Jeff was an only child. Sam had one sibling, a sister who was five years his senior. Neither had a brother, but soon they were as close as any brothers. And so they remained for the next fifty-five years.

# Chapter Five

September 8, 1969

Death of a Hero

A green sedan crept past the Thompsons' home. The man at the wheel was in no hurry to reach his destination. He passed another house, then pulled up to the curb and stopped.

"Mama, there's a car outside Jeff's house."

She came to the window. A Marine in full-dress uniform and a man wearing a clerical collar were walking slowly up the sidewalk to the front door.

"Oh, no."

"What is it, Mama?"

"I don't know. Let me go find out. You wait here."

"I'm coming with you."

"You wait here, Sam. I'll come tell you as soon as I know."

"But Mama—"

"Wait here, Sam."

"Hurry, Mama."

He looked out the window as she rushed up the street to the Freemans'. She turned up the walk that led to the front door, then stopped. She paced up and down beside the car with her arms folded across her chest. Sam waited and watched.

The two men came out after fifteen minutes and spoke to Sara. When her shoulders heaved, Sam knew she was crying. After the men left, she took a deep breath and marched up the sidewalk, opened the door, and went in. Sam stayed at the window. After a few more minutes, the door opened again, and his mother trudged slowly back home. Sam was waiting and opened the door for her. She hugged him and collapsed into a chair.

"What is it, Mama?"

"Jeff's dad was killed in a battle, something called Operation Idaho Canyon."

"How?"

"I don't know. I didn't ask, and you shouldn't either. They'll tell us when they're ready."

"I need to go see him."

"You're his best friend. He's going to need you."

"Yes, ma'am."

"Mrs. Freeman said she wanted to be alone for a while. I'm going to call the neighbors to tell them and make supper for Jeff and his mother. You go ahead. I'll come when the food's ready."

"What should I say to him, Mama?"

"There's really nothing you can say, Sam. But that's okay. You don't need to say anything. Just be there. Talk about whatever he wants to talk about."

"Jeff said his dad was the best pilot in the world."

"Come over here before you go." She hugged him again, longer and harder this time. "I love you, Sam."

"I love you too, Mama."

The door to the master bedroom was closed, but Sam could hear crying coming from inside. Jeff's room was empty, so he returned to the closed door. He started to knock but decided to speak instead.

"Mrs. Freeman."

"He's out back, Sam."

"I sure am sorry."

"Thank you. Thank you for coming."

Jeff's dad had built a treehouse in the huge red oak in the back-yard when he was home on leave in the spring. Sam spotted a pair of legs dangling from the edge and climbed up the ladder. Jeff had a vacant look, but he wasn't crying. The boys nodded to each other but didn't speak. Sam sat down beside him. It was quiet until katydids and crickets signaled that the day was coming to a close. Tree frogs soon joined them. From the east, in the direction of the river, they heard a barred owl call. Jeff called back, then turned to face Sam. It was almost dark, but Sam could see he was smiling.

"The man from the Marines said Daddy was a hero."

"I bet he was."

Jeff turned back toward the woods behind the house but kept talking. "He was rescuing some wounded men in his Huey and got shot. But he kept flying, and he made it all the way back to the field hospital. The man said he set that bird down nice and easy too."

Jeff looked at Sam again and said, "Daddy was the best pilot. The man said the medics came and got the wounded men out, but Daddy was still sitting in the pilot's seat, so they came back to check on him. He was gone by then. That man said Daddy made sure those other men were safe before he died. He saved their lives."

Jeff began sobbing. Sam put his arm around Jeff's shoulder, but neither of them said another word. Half an hour later, Sam's mother came out and told them supper was ready. Jeff was no longer crying, but Sam's arm hadn't moved.

After Mrs. Thompson finished washing the dishes, Sam pulled her aside. "Mama, may I spend the night here? I think I should. I think Jeff needs me to."

She hugged him for the third time.

Chapter Six

August 4, 1970

Snake in the Classroom

Nineteen seventy, the year Sam and Jeff turned ten, was a time of great turmoil in education in Mississippi. The Supreme Court had ruled that separate schools for white and black children were inherently unequal in 1954 and ordered the nation's public schools to desegregate with all deliberate speed the following year. But in Mississippi and many other states, the decade and a half that followed was marked by far more deliberation than speed.

Neighborhood schools were tried, but nearly all the white students were assigned to schools in white neighborhoods and nearly all the black students to schools in black neighborhoods. There was also freedom of choice. Parents could send their children to the schools they preferred, but very few parents chose schools where nearly all the students were of the other race. The schools were no longer segregated by law, but they were still segregated in fact. And they were still unequal.

The federal courts finally lost patience and ordered immediate and complete desegregation. A mix of white and black teachers and students were assigned to schools that had been racially segregated since the day they opened. In many cities, including Jackson, white parents responded by establishing private academies so their children could continue to attend all-white schools.

Jackson Academy and Jackson Preparatory School were two of the largest private schools in the city. JA was established a decade earlier to teach children how to read by using phonics, but the opening of Jackson Prep, like most private academies in the state, coincided with the desegregation of the public schools in the fall of 1970.

Before Jeff could sit down, Sam broke the news. "Daddy and Mama are sending me to JA. They're sending Sis to that new school, Jackson Prep. I tried to get them to let me stay at Spann, but they said no."

"I figured that was coming."

"Why? I thought they would let me stay. They're not racists."

"Mama says every family that can afford it is moving their kids."

"I guess you're staying."

"Sure. There's no way Mama could afford JA."

"I'm sorry."

"Don't worry about it. I'll be fine. I went to school with Negroes before we moved here. They don't scare me. They're not all that different from us. Just darker and different hair."

"But we won't get to go to school together."

"Yeah, but we can still walk home together. I'll come down the hill from Spann, or you can walk up the hill from JA. And we hardly ever had any fun at school anyway. Whenever we did, we got sent to the principal's office."

Sam laughed. "You're right about that."

It happened twice. The first incident was in the third grade, Jeff's first year at Spann after moving to Jackson. During recess, he and Sam found a blue jay chick that had fallen out of its nest and brought it inside. It fluttered around the classroom, landed on Miss Gregory's desk, and relieved itself on a stack of test papers. She told the kids to open all the windows. After five minutes of trying to herd the terrified bird toward them, it fluttered out a window and disappeared. Miss Gregory demanded to know who was responsible, and the boys raised their hands. They were mischievous, but they were not dishonest. She marched them down to Mr. Jameson's office. He was more amused than angry but gave them a stern lecture about not bringing birds inside.

The second incident, the following year, was more serious. It involved a different animal and a girl in the class Sam and Jeff didn't like. Alice Wendleken was a know-it-all and a busybody and was always tattling on some other student for one thing or another. Again at recess, Jeff caught a speckled king snake about thirty inches long and put it inside his shirt to hide it. Then he found Sam on the playground and pulled him aside.

"What are you grinning about?"

Jeff reached between the two shirt buttons just above his waist and pulled the snake's head out. Sam grinned too.

"What you gonna do with it?"

"Put it in Alice's desk."

"Great idea. Let's do it."

They sneaked back into the school, checked to make sure the coast was clear, and returned to their classroom. Recess would last ten more minutes, so Mrs. Cheney was still in the teachers' lounge taking a well-deserved break. While Sam stood guard at the door, Jeff opened the lid of Alice's desk, deposited the snake, and closed it. They were back on the playground in seconds.

When the class returned to the room, Jeff and Sam tried not to look at Alice or each other while they waited for the action to begin. They didn't have to wait long. Alice lifted the lid, screamed, and ran to the front of the room. Everyone soon learned why. The snake raised its head, studied its surroundings, then dropped to the floor and slithered in the same direction Alice had run. Now there was screaming all around. Mrs. Cheney stood on her desk chair and shrieked. A baby bird was one thing, but a snake, even a harmless king snake, was a whole 'nother thing. Jeff and Sam looked at each other for the first time. They were thinking the same thing: Maybe this wasn't such a good idea.

To mitigate the damage from the incident and the consequences sure to follow, Jeff sprang into action. He trailed the snake up the aisle and followed it into a corner. He had caught it once and would catch it again. He reached down and grabbed it on the first try.

He was only nine, but he was already an experienced snake catcher. Without a word, he raced out of the classroom, down the hall, and out the door. He released the snake where he'd found it, then took a deep breath and walked back in to face the music.

Mrs. Cheney was no longer standing on her chair, and a semblance of order had been restored. But now there was the matter of accountability. "Thank you for saving our lives, Jeff. Now we all know that snake didn't come inside and get into Alice's desk all by itself. Somebody brought it in here during recess. And if someone in this class did it, I intend to find out who it was."

Jeff raised his hand. When Mrs. Cheney nodded to him, he confessed. "I did it, Mizz Cheney."

"And can you tell us why, Jeff?"

"I thought it would be funny."

A few boys laughed. Mrs. Cheney silenced them with a stare.

"And now that you've done it, do you still think it was funny?"

"Yes, ma'am." More laughter and another stare. Jeff was mischievous but not dishonest.

"And just why do you think it was so funny?"

"You know how Alice is, Mizz Cheney."

Now all the boys and a few of the girls laughed. Mrs. Cheney stared them down for a third time.

"Let me ask you this, Jeff. Did you do this all by yourself, or did you have an accomplice?"

"A what?"

"An accomplice. Somebody who helped you."

"No, ma'am. I caught the snake all by myself. It was my idea to put it in Alice's desk. I'm the one who put it there. Nobody else even touched it."

There was no reason to put Sam in the crosshairs too. But Sam wasn't going to let Jeff take the fall all by himself. He raised his hand.

"Sam, do you have something you wish to say?"

"Yes, ma'am. I helped. I guarded the door."

"I should have figured as much. Two peas in a pod. Okay boys, come with me. The rest of you get to work on your math problems. And no cutting up."

She grabbed each boy by an ear and marched them down the hall to Mr. Jameson's office. She told them to wait outside with his secretary, Mrs. Woods, then went in and closed the door. Mrs. Woods looked up from her typing and asked what they'd done this time. When Jeff told her, she shook her head and resumed her work. Mrs. Cheney came back out, wagged her finger at them, then returned to her classroom. Mr. Jameson motioned for the boys to come into his office. After he closed the door and the three were seated, he spoke.

"So the two outlaws who seem to want to turn our school into a zoo are back to see me again. And this time, or so I'm told, it was not just a bird. Mrs. Cheney, who is an honest woman, has told me what you did, but I want to hear it from you. Jeff, I understand you were the ringleader. Tell me what you did, please."

"Yes, sir. We were out for recess, and I saw something moving in the grass by the edge of the woods. I went over to see what it was. It was a king snake, so I caught it."

"Of course you did. And how big was this snake? How long?"

"I'd say a little over two feet. It was long enough to wrap around my waist."

"And how do you know that?"

"I put it inside my shirt to hide it."

"Of course you did. Then what?"

"I decided it would be fun to put it in Alice Wendleken's desk."

"Why Alice?" He knew, but he asked anyway.

"You know how she is, Mr. Jameson."

"And how is that?" He knew that too, but he wanted to hear what Jeff had to say.

"She thinks she's better than everybody, and she's always running to Mizz Cheney to tell on somebody for something."

"She's the worst," Sam added.

"So, gentlemen, I don't agree that Alice is the worst." He did agree, but he couldn't say so. "But let's say she is the worst. Do you believe putting a snake in her desk will make her change?"

Jeff spoke before Sam could. "I don't think anything will make Alice change," he conceded.

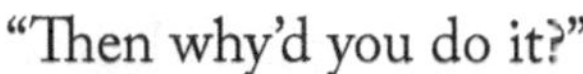

"Then why'd you do it?"

"Because of how she acts. And because it would be funny. It was just a king snake. It was harmless."

"Let's talk about that, Jeff. You and Sam know a king snake is harmless. I know it too. But do you think Alice Wendleken knows? That Mrs. Cheney knows?"

"I figured everybody knew."

"Well, you figured wrong. To a lot of people, especially girls and women, a snake is a snake. They're terrified of all of them."

"They sure acted scared," Jeff admitted.

"I'm sure they did. Imagine lifting up the lid of your desk and finding a snake inside."

Jeff had a ready answer for that. "We don't have to imagine, Mr. Jameson. We saw it."

Mr. Jameson covered his mouth to hide his grin. "Jeff, I understand you told Mrs. Cheney you didn't have an accomplice."

"It was all me. I caught the snake. It was my idea to put it in Alice's desk, and I put it there. All Sam did was stand guard. He never even touched it. And I wasn't about to tell on him."

"Is that right?"

"Yes, sir. That's something Alice would do." Jeff was right about that too.

"But Sam, I understand you confessed."

"I wasn't going to let Jeff take all the blame. When he showed me the snake and told me what he was thinking, I said it was a great idea."

"So you thought it was a great idea. You saw how much you scared Alice and your teacher. Let me ask you this, gentlemen. Jeff, you said you did it because you thought it would be funny. Now that you're sitting here in my office and I'm deciding what your punishment should be, do you boys still think it was funny?"

"Yes, sir," they answered simultaneously. Jeff continued. "You should have seen it, Mr. Jameson. Alice was screaming her head off and running up to the front of the room. The snake was chasing her. Mizz Cheney stood on her chair and screamed too. Yes, sir, it was funny. Real funny."

Mr. Jameson covered his mouth again. He sure did like these boys. They weren't bad, just spirited, and they were honest to a fault. They were going to turn out just fine. As for Alice, he wasn't so sure. Maybe a few more snakes in her desk would do her some good.

"Let me ask you one more thing before I decide what your punishment will be. Was it worth it?"

"Yes, sir," Jeff answered immediately.

Sam was more circumspect. "It depends," he said.

"On what?" asked Mr. Jameson.

"On what our punishment is."

"Fair enough. Well, here's what I've decided. I'll give you a choice. You can have detention for an hour after school every day for a week. I'll put you to work cleaning up the campus. Or, if you prefer, I'll give you a paddling right now."

Jeff didn't hesitate. "I'll take the paddling."

"Me too," said Sam.

They both stood up, turned around, and bent over. They were facing the other way, so Mr. Jameson didn't have to cover his mouth now. He opened his desk drawer and pulled out his paddle. He gave them two licks apiece, but his heart wasn't in it.

"Now rub your backsides and sit back down. I want to tell you a few things before you go. First, don't be smiling and laughing when you get back to class. If you do, I'll find out from Mrs. Cheney, there will be another paddling, and I'll swing a lot harder. Second, you need to apologize to her and Alice, and you better mean it. I know you think it was funny, but I promise you they didn't know the snake was harmless. Finally, and I'll say this only once, don't you ever, I mean ever, bring any animal back inside this building. Not a worm, not a bird, not a snake. Not a dog or a cat, not anything. If you do, it definitely won't be worth it. Do you understand?"

"Yes, sir," again simultaneously.

When they were gone, Mr. Jameson walked out to speak to Mrs. Woods. "They brought a king snake inside and put it in Alice Wendleken's desk."

"I know. They told me."

"But I still love them. I can't help myself. I love those boys."

"You wish you could be one of them, don't you?"

"Maybe so. Maybe I do."

# Chapter Seven

May 30, 1978

Road Trip

Sam and Jeff attended different schools from the fifth grade through the twelfth, private for Sam, public for Jeff. Sam went to JA, then Jackson Prep. After Spann, Jeff went to Chastain for junior high, then Murrah for high school. But when the boys weren't in class, they were always together. They played Little League baseball on the same teams and joined Boy Scout Troop 1, the oldest in the state, on the same day.

They loved being Boy Scouts. They learned all the knots, and the outdoor merit badges—Canoeing, Swimming, and Lifesaving in the water, Camping, Hiking, Bird Study, and others on land—were fun and came easy. The troop went camping nearly every month, and Sam and Jeff often went by themselves. Their favorite spot was under a grove of beech trees along the Pearl they discovered the summer they met. It was a short walk from home, but it felt like wilderness. For many years, they made a point to return at least once each fall when the leaves turned to gold.

Jeff thought the merit badges requiring book learning were boring, but Sam stayed after him to finish them. When the time came, they helped each other with their Eagle projects. Sam built and put up twenty-five birdhouses in the neighborhood, and Jeff cleared and cleaned the trails in the woods along the Pearl. They were awarded their Eagle badges on the same day at Saint James Episcopal Church, which sponsored the troop.

For his sixteenth birthday, Sam's parents gave him a ten-year-old red Mustang convertible with a stick shift. It was the coolest car in the Jackson Prep parking lot and served as the boys' principal means of transportation until the end of the following summer, when Jeff bought an old Ford pickup with money he earned by mowing yards six days a week.

On long drives on the backroads of Madison County, with the top down in the Mustang or the windows down in the pickup, the boys drank beer and listened to music. Their older friends had good taste in music, so they did too. Favorites included the Allman Brothers, Jackson Browne, Bruce Springsteen, and Warren Zevon. They also loved two dark-eyed beauties, Emmylou Harris and Linda Ronstadt. For weeks after the plane crash in south Mississippi that took the lives of Ronnie Van Zant and his bandmates Steve and Cassie Gaines in late 1977, the boys listened to nothing but Lynyrd Skynyrd. They loved "Free Bird" and "Sweet Home Alabama," the band's biggest hits, but their favorite was "Tuesday's Gone." They would turn up the volume and sing along at the top of their lungs. Whoever was in the passenger seat would accompany pianist Billy Powell by playing air keyboards. John Prine was not yet on their radar. When Sam discovered him in their freshman year of college, he called Jeff immediately to share the news.

The principal topic of conversation on their drives was girls. Jeff was the more confident and adventurous of the two. He explained to Sam how to French kiss and, as time went by, how to do other things. They kept no secrets from each other.

Both were good but not great athletes. Sam was the point guard and captain of the Jackson Prep basketball team. He didn't score a lot, but he called the plays and led the team in assists. When Jeff was a sophomore, he realized he couldn't run and jump like the black players on Murrah's basketball team, so he switched to tennis. Sam went to Jeff's matches and Jeff to Sam's games, and they were there in the bad times as well as the good. In their senior year, when Sam missed a free throw that would have sent the private-school championship game into overtime, Jeff was waiting in the Thompsons' living room when he got home. Six weeks later, when Jeff lost in the semifinals of the public-school state tennis tournament, Sam took him to dinner at Scrooge's and said at least he didn't double fault on match point.

On consecutive nights in May 1978, they went to each other's graduation ceremonies. Sam finished second in his class at Prep and gave a short speech. Jeff's scores on standardized tests were higher than Sam's, but Sam's grades were better. Jeff had taught Sam to love the outdoors, but Sam still kept his nose in a book most of the time.

Other than the car, the truck, and their camping gear, the boys cared little about material things. In lieu of graduation presents, they asked for money so they could take a long road trip. On the Tuesday after Memorial Day, they loaded up their gear in the Mustang and headed north. Their goal was to escape the heat by driving to New England, camping, hiking, and canoeing along the way. They had five hundred dollars between them. If they avoided hotels, bathed in lakes and streams, and ate on the cheap, they figured it would last nearly a month.

When the money ran out and they had to come home, they would work the rest of the summer before starting college. Sam had chosen Millsaps, a small liberal arts college in Jackson; Jeff would attend Ole Miss. Their eight years of going to different schools would extend to twelve. Both were awarded scholarships, Sam thanks to his stellar grades and leadership, Jeff based on his ACT and SAT scores. Before receiving the scholarship, Jeff's plan had been to live at home, work a year or two to save money, then go to college. With the scholarship and a part-time job in Oxford, he wouldn't have to wait.

The first stop on their trip was the Sipsey Wilderness in northwest Alabama. The Sipsey was less than 250 miles from Jackson but seemed a world away. There were steep cliffs and caves with bats clinging to the ceiling, and the Sipsey River was nothing like the slow, muddy Pearl. The clear water spilled over rapids on its way to Smith Lake, one of the deepest and clearest bodies of water east of the Mississippi. They camped two nights beside the river and hiked ten miles on the day in between.

They broke camp on the third morning, hiked out to the trail-head, and headed east. After a six-hour drive, they pitched their tent beside the Chattooga River, which forms the border between Georgia and South Carolina northeast of Atlanta. Whitewater streams in the Appalachians often have highways or railroad tracks running alongside them. The Nantahala in North Carolina has both. But not the Chattooga, which was designated a National Wild and Scenic River four years earlier. Encroachment and development were prohibited. The only sounds came from the birds, the wind, the water, and the boys' campfire. It was the first day of June, but it was just cool enough to have one.

Parts of *Deliverance,* which was released in 1972, were filmed on the Chattooga. When the boys launched their canoe the next morning to paddle Section III, Jeff told Sam to keep his ears open for a different sound. "If you hear 'Dueling Banjos,'" he said, "paddle hard. We don't want to wind up like Ned Beatty."

The Chattooga has some of the biggest and best whitewater in the South, and Section III was the most challenging day of canoe-ing Sam and Jeff had ever experienced. When they neared the end, they came to a sign directing paddlers to pull over to the bank to scout Bull Sluice, the dangerous rapid up ahead. On a plaque on the boulder overlooking it, the boys read the names of paddlers who'd perished running the rapid and saw that one of the dangers was called Decapitation Rock.

Pointing out that discretion is the better part of valor, Sam suggested they portage around the rapid. Jeff would have none of it and called Sam a wimp. Sam capitulated, as teenage boys do when their manhood is challenged. They walked back to the canoe, adrenaline flowing, and ran Bull Sluice successfully. Safely beyond it, Jeff dove into the river to celebrate.

After they returned to their campsite, they walked down to the river, each with a book in one hand and a beer in the other. They climbed atop a boulder, where they drank the beer, read the books, and listened to the river as the day grew short. Sam was reading *A River Runs Through It* by Norman Maclean, Jeff *Desert Solitaire* by Edward Abbey. The boys loved books about the outdoors.

When a pileated woodpecker called from across the river, Jeff looked up from his book. "I sure love these trees," he said, "but the sunsets in the desert must be spectacular."

"Life is all about trade-offs," Sam observed. "That's what Daddy says. If the sunset stretches all the way across the sky, you'd probably have a hard time finding firewood."

Sam volunteered to walk back up to camp and get two more beers. After another half hour, the sun dropped below the trees, and the temperature dropped with it. The boys decided it was time for the warmth of a fire and returned to camp. They had burgers and more beer for dinner, then s'mores for dessert. It was a perfect ending to a perfect day.

They drove to North Carolina the next morning and canoed the Nantahala, which was child's play after the Chattooga. They spent the next three days and nights hiking and camping in and around Great Smoky Mountains National Park. For part of a day, they went to the Joyce Kilmer-Slickrock Wilderness. Naming the old-growth forest for the man who penned the poem "Trees" was appropriate. The boys hiked a loop trail among enormous hemlocks and tulip poplars, including some of the tallest trees in the eastern United States, and walked along a creek underneath more towering giants. The ground was littered with huge chestnut trees that died in the blight of the 1930s but had not yet turned to dust. As they were leaving, they saw on a plaque that Kilmer, like Jeff's father, gave his life for his country. He was killed in 1918 in the Second Battle of the Marne.

After their time in the national park, the boys continued north on the Blue Ridge Parkway. They took their time, climbing to the top of Mount Mitchell, the highest point east of the Mississippi, and stopping often to hike and enjoy the views. They remained on the parkway until they saw the sign for Interstate 64, which would take them east to Charlottesville and Monticello, Thomas Jefferson's home.

Sam was a history buff, and Jeff had read several books about the

Lewis and Clark Expedition. Both wanted to see Monticello, but when they learned the price of admission from the woman at the entrance, they hesitated. After caucusing, they told her they better not. She looked around to make sure no one was watching and waved them in. Two handsome, polite young men with Southern accents can get away with a lot. The boys were the same size —six feet tall, 175 pounds—and were often mistaken for brothers. Those who thought so invariably assumed Sam was older because he was the serious one. Jeff was the prankster, always smiling like he knew some inside joke.

Sam was fascinated by the architecture of Jefferson's home and the many gadgets on the property, including dumb waiters, a spherical sundial, and a copying contraption, in which a second pen made an identical copy while someone wrote with the first. Jeff was more interested in the garden, the grounds, and the views from the "little mountain," which is what the Italian *Monticello* means in English. As always, Jeff wanted to be outside.

After they descended from the little mountain, he offered his assessment. "Old Tom was a smart guy, wasn't he?"

"Brilliant," Sam agreed, "but he was smart long before he was old. He was just thirty-three when he wrote the Declaration of Independence."

"I didn't see that. Was it on a plaque or something?"

"I didn't see it either. It's just something I read somewhere."

"I should have known."

"Here's something amazing. Our second and third presidents, John Adams and Thomas Jefferson, not only died on the same day, but it was on July 4, 1826, the fiftieth anniversary of the signing of the Declaration of Independence."

"That is amazing, but I'm not amazed you know it. You're not as bad as you used to be, but you're still a nerd."

"Am not. I'm just curious. And well-read."

"You're a curious, well-read nerd."

Sam had spent countless hours reading the encyclopedia and knew a great deal of American history. He wasn't a know-it-all or a show-off like Alice Wendleken, but he loved sharing interesting facts with Jeff, who was impressed with his encyclopedic knowledge but teased him about it. He even gave him a nickname: Britannica.

The next four days would be the Civil War section of the trip. The boys planned to visit five sites in three states where seven battles took place. Their first stop was fifty miles south of Washington in Fredericksburg, the site of a resounding Confederate victory in December 1862 over Union forces commanded by General Ambrose Burnside. Robert E. Lee, seeing the advantage that came from occupying the high ground, reportedly said, "It is well that war is so terrible, or we should grow too fond of it."

The boys went up to Marye's Heights and saw the Sunken Road and the stone wall alongside it that shielded the Confederates as they slaughtered Union infantrymen attempting a futile assault from below. Jeff studied the wall, looked down the hill, and said, "That Ambrose guy sure wasn't as smart as old Tom Jefferson. Even I, a public-school grad who doesn't own a gun, can see how dumb this was."

They left Fredericksburg and drove west to the site of two battles that took place exactly a year apart. Chancellorsville, which spanned a week in the spring of 1863, was another decisive Southern victory. The second, The Wilderness, was fought to a bloody draw, though the Federals suffered far more casualties.

Though the Confederates prevailed at Chancellorsville, the battle may have cost them the war. While scouting with his staff in the dense forest, Stonewall Jackson, Lee's brilliant but eccentric general, was mistaken for the enemy and hit by friendly fire from a North Carolina regiment. He died eight days later. Historians have debated whether his leadership in the crucial battles to come could have changed the outcome of the war. As always, what might have been can never be known, but Jackson's replacement, Richard Ewell, made critical errors at Gettysburg two months later that cost the Southern forces the battle and the chance to win the war.

While reading the plaque near the site where Jackson was

wounded, Jeff had an epiphany. "Stonewall is the coolest name ever. If I have a son, I'm gonna name him Stonewall."

"Your wife might have something to say about that," Sam countered.

"Who said anything about a wife?"

"It's customary to have a wife before you have a son."

"Then I'll make it a condition of my proposal. 'Will you marry me and let me name our son Stonewall?' All or nothing."

"Good luck with that."

The next morning, they drove through the countryside with the top down to the site thirty miles southwest of the District of Columbia where two more battles were fought a year apart. The Federals named them for Bull Run, a stream near the battlefield; the Confederates called them First and Second Manassas for the adjacent town.

In the first battle, the two inexperienced armies clashed in July 1861, just three months after the Confederates fired on Fort Sumter. In the decisive victory for the South, General Thomas J. Jackson became known as Stonewall when another general observed him standing like a stone wall as the chaos of the battle swirled around him.

The Union retreat toward the capital was impeded by carriages filled with government officials and civilians who had ventured out of the city with picnic baskets and opera glasses to watch the expected Union victory. Sam was appalled at the notion of war spectators. "I can't believe people went for a ride in the country to watch men shoot each other."

"Doesn't surprise me," Jeff responded. "There were big crowds at public hangings and when gladiators fought to the death. And people love ice hockey and NASCAR."

"Hockey and NASCAR?"

"Sure. People go for the fights and the crashes."

Before the First Battle of Bull Run, many in the North had thought the Confederacy would call off the rebellion in a matter of weeks and the war would end quickly. But after nearly a thousand men were killed in the battle, both soldiers and civilians knew the war would be neither quick and easy nor a spectator sport.

The second battle on the site, in August 1862, was another convincing Southern victory, which led Lee to march his army into Maryland. The boys followed Lee's route north to the site of the single bloodiest day in American history. The day was September 17, 1862, and the location was Sharpsburg, Maryland. The battle was Antietam, again named for a creek, in which more than 20,000 men were killed or wounded before the fighting ended. Though the Union army suffered more casualties and Lee's army fought the Federals to a standstill, the battle was still of significant benefit to the Union and President Lincoln. It ended a string of victories for the South and gave Lincoln the political capital needed to issue the Emancipation Proclamation, which persuaded England and France not to recognize the Confederacy as a separate nation.

While the boys walked among the monuments dedicated to the soldiers who fought there, Sam gave Jeff another history lesson. Lincoln freed the slaves, Sam said, but only in the states that had seceded and were still fighting against the Union. Slavery was legal in Delaware, Kentucky, Missouri, and Maryland, but they had not seceded and were exempt from the proclamation, as were Tennessee, which had seceded but was now under Union control, and the counties in Virginia that would soon become West Virginia.

"Every day with you is like a year of college," Jeff declared. "You should write a book."

"But a book about the Emancipation Proclamation has already been written. I've read it."

"Then write another one."

Sam smiled. "Maybe I will."

The boys spent the next day in Gettysburg, the small town in southern Pennsylvania that was the site of the three-day battle in July 1863 that marked the high point of the Confederate invasion of the North and turned the tide of the war in the Union's favor. While Sam was driving, Jeff had been reading aloud *The Killer Angels,* Michael Shaara's Pulitzer-winning masterpiece about the battle, and the boys were excited to see the landmarks Shaara had described. They viewed the battlefield from the top of Little Round Top and Cemetery Hill, walked through Devil's Den, and retraced the route of Pickett's Charge, the ill-fated Confederate infantry assault on the last day of the battle. More than a hundred summers had passed since 12,000 Confederate soldiers, some younger than Sam and Jeff, marched three-quarters of a mile across an open field toward the center of the Union line.

As the boys walked the same ground, Sam marveled at the extraordinary courage of the men and boys under Pickett's command. "Can you imagine what it took to do it? To march straight toward the enemy line while soldiers all around you are getting blown to bits by cannon fire? While thousands of soldiers with muskets are just waiting till you get close enough for them to mow you down? How on earth did they keep marching? How?"

"Beats me," Jeff said. "I would have called in sick or scheduled a hair appointment."

General Ewell made two key mistakes that sealed the Confederate defeat at Gettysburg. He first disobeyed Lee's orders and engaged the Union army on McPherson's Ridge, which led the Federals to retreat to Cemetery Hill, aptly named because the South's hopes for victory in the war were buried there. Then he allowed the North to secure the position. His subordinates urged him to attack before the Union could dig in, but he refused. Lee then ordered Ewell to attack "if practicable," but he again declined.

When faced with an enemy occupying such a commanding position, Stonewall Jackson likely would have attacked before they could secure it. He might not have succeeded, but the failure even to try assured the Federals of victory. The friendly fire that struck down Jackson at Chancellorsville may have been the key to preserving the Union.

The defeated Confederate army retreated after Gettysburg and went no farther north, but Sam and Jeff kept going. Their route led them to the Finger Lakes in central New York, then east to the Adirondacks, where they visited Lake Placid, which was preparing for the 1980 Winter Olympics. The Miracle on Ice would take place twenty months later in an arena that was still under construction when the boys saw it. They bathed the next day by skinny-dipping in Saranac Lake with a bar of soap. From there they rode a ferry across Lake Champlain to Vermont, then continued east to the White Mountains of New Hampshire.

On their third day there, they counted their dwindling supply of cash and realized their trip would have to come to an end. When they went into North Conway after their daily hike, Jeff stopped at a newsstand to look at the headlines in the local paper. There was nothing momentous, but he noticed the date on the front page. It was the twentieth of June, Sam's eighteenth birthday. If Sam realized it was his birthday, he hadn't let on. Jeff immediately broke into a rousing version of "Happy Birthday to You," and the man running the newsstand and a couple walking past joined him.

That night the boys splurged on pizza and beer. They would head home the next morning with just enough cash for gas and food for the 1,500-mile trip. They had already decided to drive straight through, taking turns driving and sleeping. The trip north had lasted three weeks. The trip south would take less than thirty hours.

# Chapter Eight

June 20, 1978

## Fortune in the Glove Compartment

Sam and Jeff said little during dinner. Their trip was ending, and melancholy had set in. When the beer and pizza were almost gone, Sam remembered something. His dad had put an envelope in the glove compartment of the Mustang the morning they left Jackson and told him to open it on the 20th. It was presumably a birthday card. He went out to the car and retrieved it.

Inside the envelope were two more envelopes, one with Sam's name on it, the other with Jeff's. Jeff opened his first. Inside were a graduation card and a check for five hundred dollars. There was a note on the card: "I know you're planning to start work as soon as you get home. I hope this will cover your losses. I'm proud of you. Dr. Thompson."

The boys looked at each other. Losses? What losses? What was he talking about? Maybe the contents of the other envelope would make sense of it. When Sam opened it, he broke into a wide grin. Inside there were five hundred-dollar bills and another note. "Get a load of this," Sam said. "'Stay till it runs out. Love, Dad.'"

"Hot damn," said Jeff.

"Scalding hot damn," Sam agreed.

"Where should we go?"

"Maine. The border's only a few miles from here. There are lots of great things to do there. I've read about them."

"Of course you have. What?"

"Acadia National Park on the coast is supposed to have terrific hiking. We can head north from there and climb Mount Katahdin. Then we can canoe the Allagash. It goes almost to Canada."

Feeling rich, they ordered a second pitcher of beer. They drove to Portland the next morning and saw the Atlantic Ocean for the first time. Sam's parents had taken them to the Gulf of Mexico half a dozen times, but neither had ever laid eyes on the Atlantic.

From there they wound their way up the coastline, arrived in Bar Harbor in time to dine on their first-ever lobster rolls, then spent the next three days hiking and camping in Acadia. It seemed strange for there to be mountains on the edge of the sea.

Based on a recommendation from a hiker they met on Cadillac Mountain, they drove farther north to explore Beals Island, the site of a tiny fishing and lobstering village. After it was settled in the 1600s, the island remained isolated from the mainland for the next three centuries. The first bridge connecting the two was not built until 1958. Two decades later, residents still retained the Elizabethan speech patterns of their ancestors. When Sam tried to imitate them, Jeff was not impressed. "Give it up," he said. "I don't know if they have hicks in London, but you sound like one." After stuffing themselves with more lobster, Sam and Jeff turned inland and continued north. Their first destination was Baxter State Park, their second the Allagash Waterway.

They spent several days in Baxter, hiking and exploring the park by day and sitting by their campfire at night. One night they walked down the hill to a meadow, where they lay down in the grass and gazed up at the heavens. They saw far more stars than they ever saw at home. The Milky Way painted a bright swath across the sky. They spotted the Big Dipper, Little Dipper, North Star, Leo, and Cassiopeia, and they counted shooting stars until the chill drove them back to their fire, which Sam poked and brought back to life. Jeff was the owl caller, Sam the fire poker.

The next morning, based on another hiker's recommendation, they rose before dawn and walked to the shore of Sandy Spring Pond. They counted half a dozen moose in the shallow water—two bulls, two cows, and month-old twins. The calves weighed thirty pounds at birth and would soon outweigh the boys. By Christmas, they might top four hundred.

"They have a face only a mother could love, that's for sure," Jeff declared. "I'm thinking a horse and a camel had too much to drink, started making out, one thing led to another, and nine months later the first moose was born."

"Maybe so," Sam said. "They've sure never won a beauty contest."

On their last day in Baxter, they climbed to the top of Mount Katahdin, a steep ascent of more than 4,000 vertical feet. The view from the top in all directions was magnificent. A sign marked the summit as the northern end of the Appalachian Trail. If they turned south and averaged fifteen miles a day, they could make it to the southern end in Georgia by Thanksgiving. They had other plans but promised each other they would hike the whole thing one day.

The next morning marked the start of the grandest adventure of their young lives. They would canoe the Allagash Waterway from beginning to end through the wilderness of Maine's North Woods. After driving to Fort Kent on the Canadian border, they stocked up on enough food for the next ten days. They decided that buying less and counting on catching fish to supplement their diet was too risky. The boys ate like trenchermen. If the fish didn't bite, they would go hungry. They wouldn't chance it. They bought nothing to drink other than coffee. Even with the fortune Dr. Thompson left in the glove compartment, there wasn't enough cash for beer. They would get by on river water.

Sam had called an outfitter from Bar Harbor to arrange a canoe rental and shuttle. The driver would take them and the canoe south to Chamberlain Bridge, which crossed the Allagash just south of the huge lake for which the bridge was named. After the outfitter dropped them off, the boys would paddle north on the lakes and river of the waterway and camp alongside it. If all went according to plan, the Mustang would be waiting when they arrived in the town of Allagash on day ten.

The cost of groceries, canoe rental, and shuttle used up most of the rest of their money. They would have barely enough to make it home. The boys wondered if they were making the right call, but they agreed by the end of the trip that the Allagash was more than worth it.

The first part of the trip was the lakes section of the waterway. They paddled the length of three huge lakes, Chamberlain, Eagle, and Churchill. It was hard work when there was a headwind, but the scenery was beautiful and the wildlife abundant. Below a dam on Chamberlain Lake, a beautiful stream with a swift current connected it to Eagle Lake. The boys rounded a curve, and Jeff pointed out a huge bull moose, much larger than the ones in Sandy Spring Pond. The moose was watching them from near the shore, unconcerned by the intruders and grazing contentedly on water lilies. He weighed nearly ten times as much as the boys, and his antlers were almost as wide as they were tall. Armed only with paddles, they were no threat to the moose.

Where the stream entered the lake, Sam spotted a pair of bald eagles on a high branch in a hemlock. Pointing up, he declared, "Look, it's eagles on Eagle Lake." Seeing eagles in the wild was always a thrill, but they saw so many on the Allagash they lost count. People were scarcer. They saw a grand total of two in ten days, a couple who paddled by one of their campsites one evening. They were too far away to speak, and yelling would disturb the glorious peace and quiet. They settled for waving.

They camped in pristine campsites in stands of cedar, tamarack, white pine, maple, and birch. Like their favorite spot along the Pearl River, there were also American beeches, with slick gray bark tempting carvers to defile them. The beeches looked just like the ones at home, but their leaves would turn to gold and fall a month sooner.

There were familiar sounds as well—the call of red-winged blackbirds, pileated woodpeckers, and barred owls. Jeff answered the owls just as he did at home. One flew into the boys' campsite, landed on a branch in a white pine, and stared at Jeff when he performed his imitation. The owl twisted its head from side to side, looking less wise than usual, then flew away.

They were entertained several nights by another familiar sound from camping in Mississippi. Coyotes began howling after dark, and other packs soon joined the chorus. The boys were being courted by fraternities at Ole Miss and Millsaps. They agreed the coyotes sounded like frat boys having competing keg parties.

Their favorite sound on the trip was a new one for them. It was the unique, mournful wail of the common loon, which sounded like nothing they'd ever heard and was something they would never forget. They heard loons every night and never grew tired of them.

There is very little in all the world better than sharing a campfire with your best friend, and the weather on the Allagash was perfect for campfires. Sam and Jeff talked about girls they'd dated and girls they wanted to date. Only one was on the want-to lists of both boys. Sam flipped a coin to see who would get to ask her out first. When Jeff won, Sam figured he'd never get a shot. Girls liked Sam, but they loved Jeff. Like the man in Carly Simon's "You're So Vain," all the girls dreamed that they'd be Jeff's partner.

They talked about the future and what they would do after they finished college. They had to decide on a major soon and wondered how they were supposed to pick one. Sam was thinking he might go to law school, Jeff that he would probably go into business or sales of some sort. But how were they to know what they should do for a living? Or whether they would be any good at it? They were eighteen years old.

They knew the importance of earning a good living from their own lives. Thanks to his dad's successful medical practice, Sam had a comfortable life. He'd just graduated from an expensive private school and drove a Mustang convertible that, until ten days before, had five hundred dollars in the glove compartment and a check for five hundred more. Jeff went to Murrah, drove a beat-up old pickup bought by mowing yards, and his mother was a widow who lived from paycheck to paycheck.

The boys had memorable wildlife experiences every day of the trip. Chipmunks invaded their campsite and tried to steal their food, as did birds they later identified in a field guide as Canada jays. A porcupine waddled past one night, secure in its coating of quills, and one morning they saw a red fox, sunlight lighting up its orange coat. The fox reminded Jeff of another fox, a gorgeous redhead a class behind him at Murrah. One afternoon they spotted two river otters taking turns sliding down the bank into the water and having a blast. Jeff christened them Sam and Jeff.

On a narrow section of the river, Jeff saw something large and brown moving in the bushes on the shore. He motioned for Sam to be quiet, and they pulled in close to get a better look. When they were twenty feet away, a black bear stood up on its hind legs and huffed at them. They paddled hard to get away and didn't look back until they were a safe distance downstream. The bear was still standing there.

One morning they saw two raptors catch fish within ten minutes of each other. The first was a bald eagle. It was gliding slowly no more than fifty feet from the canoe when it cupped its wings, dropped to just above the surface, and snatched a small brook trout with its talons. As it flew over, the magnificent bird transferred the fish to its beak, spun the fish around with its talons, and swallowed it whole.

The second incident was more dramatic. While the boys were still talking about the eagle, Jeff spotted an osprey hovering far above the water, looking down. Suddenly the bird dropped into a dive and landed headfirst with a splash. When the osprey rose to the surface and lifted off, like the eagle, it had a fish in its talons, this one a smallmouth bass.

On the morning of their next to last day, Sam spotted movement on the west side of the river. The boys were hoping to add to the list of wildlife they'd seen, but this animal didn't qualify. A face came into view looking back from the bank. It belonged to a small, skinny, black and white lop-eared hound. As they approached, they could see that the dog was a female, but her age, breed, and provenance were indeterminate, as they would remain for the rest of her life.

When they reached the shore, the pup didn't hesitate. She leaped into the canoe and landed on the pile of gear in the middle. She gathered herself and looked around, first at Sam in the bow, then at Jeff in the stern. Evidently satisfied that her crew of Eagle Scouts was trustworthy, she turned in a circle three times, lay down, and fell asleep.

Sam looked over his shoulder at the sleeping dog and declared, "Jeff, my boy, it appears we have a passenger."

"A passenger and a refugee," Jeff added.

They were running low on food, but Jeff made a third sandwich when they stopped for lunch. The dog wolfed it down in three bites, so he made a fourth one but tore it into pieces to make her pace herself. The boys sat leaning against a log and talked for a while. The pooch lay down between them, and they took turns scratching her behind the ears. When they walked back down to the river, she raced ahead and jumped into the canoe.

The threesome portaged around forty-foot-high Allagash Falls that afternoon. Running the falls, unlike Bull Sluice, was not an option. The hound wasn't any help carrying the canoe or their gear, but she raced ahead to make sure the coast was clear and came back with her tail wagging.

They camped the last night near the takeout point. The boys split their last dinner into three parts. After eating, their new friend lay down beside the campfire and slept like the dead. What was her life like before today?

Do a good turn daily is the Boy Scout slogan. Sam ran his hand along her back and said, "She was our good turn for the day. What will we do with her?"

"We can't very well just leave her in Allagash. She might belong to somebody, but there's no way to find who."

"I agree. I think we need to take her home and turn her into a Southern dog."

"But what then? We're going to college in less than two months. We can't take her with us."

"I don't know. Daddy says we already have too many pets." The Thompsons had a German shepherd, a calico cat, and two hamsters named Laverne and Shirley.

That's what Jeff wanted to hear. "Can we give her to Mama? She loves dogs, and she's been talking about how lonely she'll be with me in Oxford. Is that okay with you?"

Sam looked down and smiled. The dog was snoring. "I will consent to your request on one condition. I must be present for the introduction."

"Deal. What should we name her?"

"I don't know. Let's sleep on it."

When they were ready to turn in, the pup was still fast asleep. They thought about waking her up and inviting her into the tent but decided to let a sleeping dog lie. They added some wood to the fire to keep her warm and left the door of their tent open so she could join them if she woke in the night.

Long after midnight, a noise awakened the boys. The dog was barking. They figured an animal was in the campsite, maybe a bear, and they crawled out of the tent to investigate. The dog was down at the riverbank, looking downstream to the north and barking like crazy. No other animal was in sight. Sam and Jeff walked out from under the canopy of trees down to the river, and there they were: the Northern Lights. The boys had never seen them before.

Colorful lights danced across the sky, pulsating globs and rippling curtains of red, green, blue, and purple. They looked like magic. The boys said nothing, and the dog stopped barking. They sat down on either side of her, and the three of them watched the show.

After fifteen minutes, the colors began to fade. The boys retreated to their tent and this time were joined by the dog. After they crawled back into their sleeping bags and the pup squeezed in between them, Jeff declared, "Well, I've slept on it."

"Slept on what?"

"Her name."

"Let's hear it."

"Aurora Borealis Freeman."

"I like it, but that sure is a fancy name for a dog who looks like that."

"We'll call her Rory for short."

They rose early the next morning. After they loaded their gear in the middle of the canoe, Rory jumped onto her spot atop it without waiting for an invitation. They paddled the last three miles to Allagash and found the Mustang where they'd left it. They were on their way by ten a.m. with Rory curled up in the back seat.

They stopped at the same grocery store in Fort Kent, but this time their list was shorter and the bill much less. They bought Pop-tarts, a loaf of bread, chips, soft drinks, a bag of dry dog food, ice, and a pound of baloney. They still had mayo and mustard from the river. Jeff went into the hardware store next door and bought a six-foot length of rope to use as a makeshift leash.

After they were back on the road, Sam cited another in his limitless supply of nerdy but interesting facts. "We're in America," Britannica said, "but at this very moment we're farther north than most of the people who live in Canada."

"What about dogs? Are we north of most of them?" Jeff asked.

"Probably," Sam guessed.

"Well, we're not north of Rory. We're headed south, and she's in the back seat."

"But she's not in Canada."

As planned, they drove straight through to Jackson, though the trip was 350 miles longer than it would have been from North Conway. They took turns at the wheel, stopping only for gas and bathroom breaks, and made it from the Canadian border to Jackson in thirty-six hours. When they pulled into Jeff's driveway at ten p.m., they had six dollars and change, a quarter of a tank of gas, and neither a drop to drink nor a bite to eat. The bag of dog food was empty.

Jeff had a plan. "Go in and make Mama sit down and close her eyes. Open the door when it's time."

Sam did as he was told. When Mrs. Freeman asked why, he played dumb. "Jeff didn't say why. He just told me to tell you to sit down and close your eyes."

She did as she was told, and Sam walked to the front door and opened it. Jeff and the dog came in, and Rory walked over to Mrs. Freeman and licked her hand. She squealed and opened her eyes. "What on earth? Whose dog is this?"

"Yours," Jeff said. He leaned down and hugged his mother. In his eighteen years, they'd never been apart for this long.

"Mine?"

"Yes, ma'am. I can't have a dog in the dorm at Ole Miss. Sam can't have one either, and the Thompsons already have Chief and Puff and those dumb hamsters."

"Where'd he come from? Does he have a name?"

Jeff corrected her. "She, not he. We found her on the side of the Allagash River in Maine. She rode with us in the canoe the rest of the way and in the back seat of the Mustang all the way home. Her name is Aurora Borealis Freeman."

"What kind of name is that?"

"A perfect name. We saw the Northern Lights because of her. On our last night, she woke us up barking her head off. We got up to see what was wrong. She was barking at the Northern Lights. You should have seen them. Amazing. I've got an awful lot to tell you."

"I can't wait to hear all about it." She smiled down at the dog, who had curled up at her feet. "Aurora Borealis Freeman," she repeated. "That's an awful big name for such a little dog."

"We've been calling her Rory," Sam said.

"Rory. That's better. Welcome home, Rory."

# Chapter Nine

April 15, 1979

## The Parrot and the Power Plant

It was 6:30 on Easter Sunday evening. Jeff rose from his seat at the table to answer the phone. Sam had stopped identifying himself years before. He started with a question. "You're not tired yet, are you?"

"What do you think? I can barely lift my fork."

"Want to get even tireder? The tiredest ever?"

"I don't think tireder's even a word. Tiredest either. And the answer is no."

"C'mon, they need us. It will be another good turn. We won't have to do another one for a month."

"I'm whipped. I almost fell asleep in the shower. The minute I finish eating, I'm crashing."

"We'll get to work with inmates."

"Inmates? Really?"

"It'll be like working on a chain gang. Like working with Paul Newman in *Cool Hand Luke*."

"But I don't want to work with anybody. I want to sleep."

"C'mon, Jeff, don't be a wimp. It's not like you. It's unbecoming." Jeff had called him a wimp at Bull Sluice the summer before, and turnabout was fair play. "It'll be something new. You love new things." To close the deal, Sam sang a line from the Sam Cooke song "Chain Gang."

"So now you're singing to me? And I thought I was supposed to be the crazy one. What's this chain gang doing?"

"I'll tell you on the way. Finish your dinner and pick me up. We better take the truck where we're headed, not the precious Mustang."

"Okay, okay. I never should have answered the phone. Give me ten minutes."

"Great. Put your dirty clothes back on."

Sam was nearing the end of his first year at Millsaps, Jeff his first at Ole Miss. He had come home to Jackson to spend Easter with his mother and Rory, but the weekend wasn't turning out as planned.

The weather on Easter Sunday was clear, but the days before had been anything but. Heavy rainfall had swollen the rivers in north Mississippi. The Pearl rose to fifteen feet above flood stage, and by the weekend much of Jackson was under water. More than 17,000 residents of the metro area were forced to evacuate, and the flood ultimately caused $500 million in damage.

The Thompsons and Freemans lived in the hills east of Spann Elementary. Their homes were high and dry, but many Jacksonians who lived nearby were not as fortunate. The boys worked late into the night on Saturday, helping families move their belongings to second floors if they had them and higher ground if they didn't. They went to bed at midnight and woke up at six. After breakfast they met in the Thompsons' backyard, where Sam's canoe was resting on a pair of sawhorses. They picked it up and headed down the hill toward the floodwaters to the north. A boat would come in handy.

Before they'd gone far, the boys heard a noise behind them. Rory was running at breakneck speed to catch up. "I thought I'd gotten away without her noticing," Jeff said to Sam. "Rory, you can't come with us," Jeff said to the dog.

Jeff headed back up the hill and called for Rory to come. He took ten steps, then turned around. She was standing in the middle of the canoe. Sam was standing beside it, laughing. Jeff bent over, slapped his thighs, and called again for her to come. He punctuated his command with a whistle. Rory didn't budge. She punctuated her refusal by sitting down. She was an obedient dog for the most part but not when it came to a canoe ride. Jeff walked back down the hill, scooped her up, and carried her home.

During the night, the water had continued to rise. As they walked down the hill, a great, brown sea of roiling water stretching away to the northeast came into view. Tops of houses were visible above the surface. Several residents were sitting on their roofs or their second-floor porches. One was reading a book. Another saw the boys, smiled, and tipped what looked to be a Bloody Mary in their direction. A beachball, then a basketball, floated past, coming from the direction of the river. To the west, they could see Jackson Academy inundated by the waters of Hanging Moss Creek. The current was going the wrong way. Instead of flowing downhill to the Pearl, the water was backing from the river into the creek.

It was quieter than usual. All the cars had either been moved, or it was too late to move them. Then they heard a motor. A twelve-foot john boat, powered by a small outboard, came around the corner of a house. The pilot flicked a cigarette into the water, waved, and nodded. They were on the same mission.

The boys spent all day rescuing those who hadn't left in time. They paddled through streets and yards on which they'd ridden bikes and played kick-the-can years earlier. They made dozens of trips, ferrying people and their pets and belongings to higher ground. Their shoulders ached.

At five o'clock they decided to make one last trip. They would go from house to house to make sure everybody was out. An elderly woman they'd rescued earlier in the day from her home on Sheffield Drive had a special request. She'd left behind her beloved African Grey Parrot named Mr. Kelly. She'd thought there was no way the water could reach his cage, but now she wasn't so sure. The boys promised to find him and bring him to her.

They found no more people, but locating Mr. Kelly was a piece of cake. When they waded through the chest-deep water into the woman's house, they could hear the angry bird in the den, cussing a blue streak. The woman had not only abandoned him, but she hadn't bothered to open his cage so he could escape the rising water by taking flight. The bird was making his feelings known with a string of polysyllabic vulgarities. The boys were impressed; Mr. Kelly spoke fluent profanity. They wondered where he'd learned it. The lady seemed so nice.

Jeff lifted the cage from its stand, returned to the canoe, and put the bird in the middle between the thwarts. He smiled at the absurdity of it all. He'd come home for Easter to spend time with his mother and their dog but was paddling a profane parrot through the neighborhood where he grew up instead. Sensing that his circumstances had improved, Mr. Kelly asked the boys politely for a cracker. They didn't have one.

Sam saw an orange tabby cat pacing back and forth on the roof of a flooded house. Jeff steered the canoe to the house, and Sam stood up in the bow, picked up the cat, and placed him beside the bird. Mr. Kelly was safe inside his cage.

On their way back to where the bird's owner was waiting, they spotted a Doberman swimming in circles in the muddy water. With Sam leaning left to balance the canoe, Jeff leaned right, lifted the dog by her collar and docked tail, and plopped her down beside the cat. On the short trip to dry land, the dog left the cat alone, and the cat left the bird alone. The boys wondered if the truce would hold after they disembarked.

As they neared higher ground, Mr. Kelly's owner saw the bird in his cage, jumped up and down, and clapped. A young boy started yelling and went running to get his parents. The dog and cat were both theirs. No wonder they got along. Neither could be found when the boys brought the family out earlier in the day, but now they were all back together again. Jeff sang a line from a new song by Peaches and Herb: "Reunited and it feels so good."

When Jeff handed the birdcage to Mr. Kelly's owner, he complimented her on the bird's vocabulary. Jeff was a freshman at Ole Miss, he said, and thought he'd heard it all. But he'd learned some new expressions from Mr. Kelly he'd never heard before. The woman's face reddened—she knew her bird—and she claimed she bought him from a sailor. Jeff smiled and said, "That's what I figured. I knew he didn't learn all that from you."

As the boys trudged up the hill with the canoe, Sam asked a question. "You really think she bought that parrot from a sailor?"

Jeff laughed. "Hell, no. Bird cusses like a sailor cause the old lady cusses like a sailor. I bet she's been blaming it on a sailor for years. You know what would be perfect?"

"What?"

"If Mr. Kelly ratted her out and said he learned how to cuss from her."

After they put the canoe upside down on the sawhorses in Sam's backyard, the boys shook hands and parted ways. Sam went inside, and Jeff walked down the street to his house. They were muddy, famished, and exhausted. It was time to shower, eat, and sleep. They were good Boy Scouts. They had done far more than one good turn on Easter Sunday.

The boys had worked through Sunday dinner, so their mothers were prepared to feed them double at supper. Mothers take pride in feeding their families, especially their hungry sons. Sam's mother piled his plate high with fried chicken, mashed potatoes and gravy, green beans, and cornbread. When there was nothing but bones left on his plate, she brought him a big slice of hot apple pie with two scoops of ice cream on top.

Jeff's mom had baked a dozen homemade rolls and cooked a pot roast with potatoes, carrots, and onions. She kept it on low simmer all afternoon while she waited for her son to come home, checking often as the gravy got richer and thicker. She'd already eaten but sat at the table while Jeff did. Watching her only child enjoy her cooking was one of her greatest pleasures. When his plate was nearly clean, she asked if he wanted dessert. He was sopping his last bite of roll in his last drop of gravy, looked up, and smiled.

"No thank you, ma'am, but I think I'll reload."

Jeff was telling his mother about Mr. Kelly and finishing his second plate of food when the phone rang. He picked up Sam ten minutes later. Sam climbed into the passenger seat and said to drive slow so he would have time to digest. He directed Jeff to turn south on

Ridgewood, then west on Meadowbrook. When they crossed I-55, they could see that a section of the interstate north of Lakeland Drive was under water. The flood had transformed Jackson into another world.

Jeff turned south again on State Street and headed downtown. Along the way, Sam told him the plan. One of his KA fraternity brothers had called. Millsaps students had been asked to volunteer to help save the power plant on the east end of Tombigbee Street. If the station flooded, much of the city would be left without electricity. The water was still rising, and time was running short.

As they neared their destination, water closed in from the east and west. They were on a peninsula that narrowed to a few blocks wide. The fairgrounds and coliseum down the hill to the east were flooded. They could see where State Street dipped below the surface to the south. The water was level, but the street went downhill.

Jeff pulled into the parking lot next to the Hinds County Courthouse. The water would have to rise six more feet to reach the truck. They walked toward the plant but first came to the site on Pascagoula Street where crews were filling sandbags. Dump trucks came and dropped the sand. Men filled up the bags with shovels and loaded them into the beds of pickup trucks, which took them a block downhill to the plant. Sam hesitated. The men were all black and all wearing prison stripes. There wasn't a single KA in sight.

But Jeff was used to being in the minority from his years in public school. He marched right in, spotted a huge black man who looked to be running things, and asked what they could do. The man turned to face him, looked him up and down, and said, "Lookie here, I think we got us some fresh meat. Some fresh white meat."

Jeff didn't flinch. "I prefer dark meat myself, and I'm afraid we're not very fresh. We've been rescuing people all day in my buddy's canoe. I'm Jeff. He's Sam."

"A canoe, you say."

"Sure. You mean you don't have a canoe?" The man leaned on his shovel and smiled. Jeff continued. "We rescued a pissed-off parrot. Bird cussed like a sailor."

"No shit?"

"If I'm lyin', I'm dyin'. I bet that bird could outcuss any man here. The sweet little old lady who owned him said she bought him from a sailor, but I didn't buy it. I think she taught him every word. What you need us to do?"

"I'm Freddie. Get two shovels and some of them bags, and you and your buddy start fillin' 'em up. The warden told me and the guy in charge of the crew down at the plant he'd give us an early release if we save it from flooding. Maybe I'll get me one of them canoes if I do."

"It sure came in handy today. We'll get to work."

A few minutes after they started, Sam wiped the sweat from his brow, leaned on his shovel, and smiled at Jeff. "You're my hero, you know," he said.

By midnight, they could barely lift their arms. They'd paddled for nearly twelve hours and been filling up sandbags for almost five. They were fading fast. Jeff volunteered to find Freddie and ask for relief.

"Freddie, my buddy and I paddled his canoe all day, and we've been filling up sandbags since we got here. We're whipped. We want to help you get your early out, but can we do something else for a while?"

"Sure. Guys down at the plant are fading fast. You can help stack bags and build the dam."

"Got it, boss. Who's in charge down there?"

"Ask for Freddie. Can't miss him. He's bigger than me."

"But you're Freddie."

Freddie smiled. "Him too."

The boys couldn't see the plant while they were filling sandbags. When they topped the hill, it was like they'd walked onto a movie set. An army of at least a hundred men, nearly all black inmates, was engaged in a desperate effort to save the plant. Three white prison guards with rifles stood off to the side smoking cigarettes. The scene was illuminated by the headlights of pickup trucks and klieg lights on poles.

There weren't any of Sam's KA brothers here either. Even the one who'd called looking for volunteers was nowhere to be found. But some other Millsaps students, a bunch of Kappa Sigs, soon came charging down the hill, screaming like banshees. One told Sam they'd been promised they could skip Monday classes if they helped at the plant. It wasn't an early release from prison, but it was enough to get them to help.

A wide earthen berm had been built around the downhill side of the plant, but the water kept rising. The berm wasn't tall enough, so the men were now building a sandbag wall on its outer edge. Pickup trucks crept along on top of the berm. Men in the trucks handed the eighty-pound sandbags to the stackers, who lifted them to the top of the wall. The wall was getting higher, but so were the floodwaters. It was man against nature and a race against time. Only the guards took smoke breaks.

As they walked toward the berm, Sam and Jeff saw one of the pickups on top roll over onto its left side and slide down into the plant. Sparks flew. The driver had gotten too close to the inside edge of the berm, which had given way. A dozen men jumped down, lifted the left side of the truck, and tilted it back onto four wheels. The driver, a skinny white guy whose lit cigarette survived the accident, was able to open his door and get out. His window was shattered, and he was bleeding from his left arm and forehead, but he didn't appear to be seriously injured, and the truck was still running. He thanked the men, brushed the glass from his hair and clothes, and headed back for another load.

Jeff spotted a mountain of a man working and giving orders at the same time. He had to be the other Freddie. Jeff walked up to him.

"Freddie?"

"That's me."

"My friend Sam and I are reporting for duty. Little Freddie sent us."

The man grinned. "Little Freddie. I like that. Take a spot on the line. We need all the help we can get. If you need a break, swap out with two of the guys in the back of a truck."

"Little Freddie told us y'all are gonna get out early if you save the plant. We're gonna help."

"*Shh.* It's just me and him. The others are just gonna get like a steak dinner or something."

From the top of the berm looking east over what had been dry land just a few days before, there was water as far as the eye could see. The surface was only a foot or two below the top of the wall but far higher than the floor of the plant. If the water pressure ruptured the dam, the workers might get crushed by the sandbags or swept away by the rushing water.

The boys stacked sandbags until their backs and shoulders were cramping. If Sam hadn't been there, Jeff might have quit. If Jeff hadn't been there, Sam might have quit. But they were both there, and neither one was about to quit. Plus they now had two missions: save the plant and free the Freddies.

At 2:30 they swapped places with two inmates handing out sandbags from the back of the trucks. It was just as hard but used a different set of muscles. The wall and the water continued to rise.

At 4:30 they heard a cheer from the man Big Freddie had put in charge of monitoring the water level. The floodwaters had stopped rising. If the dam held, the plant would survive. Freddie gathered the men around him. All of them, Sam and Jeff included, laughed and high-fived each other. They had bonded through a long night of hard work. There were no slackers among those who were still standing.

Freddie spoke to someone on a walkie talkie. When he finished, he called for quiet. "Okay, men, looks like we've saved the plant. The big boss says they'll put a nice note in our files." Some of the men laughed; others booed. "But he said one more thing. We gotta add one more course of bags just to make sure." More men booed, but they were smiling. It was almost over.

On their drive back up State Street, the boys could see the first light in the east. They'd seen the first light walking down the hill with the canoe the morning before and had gone from one sunrise to the next without sleeping. Sam asked Jeff the same question he'd asked nearly twelve hours earlier. "You're not tired yet, are you?"

"You're lucky I'm too tired to whip your ass."

"Wouldn't take much."

When they pulled up in front of Jeff's house, Sam asked, "What you gonna do today?"

"I'm gonna take a long, hot shower while Mama makes me bacon and waffles and fries me four eggs over easy. After I eat, I'm gonna climb into my rack and sleep till Thursday.

"What about classes?"

"Classes can wait. Sleep can't. What about you?"

"I'll take a shower while Mama makes me a big breakfast too. I'm thinking pancakes and sausage and grits. Then I'll go to class. I have an eight o'clock."

"You're going to class? And I'm supposed to be the crazy one."

In his four years at Millsaps, Sam didn't miss a single class. When he graduated in May 1982, he was awarded the Founders' Medal for having the highest GPA in the senior class and receiving a grade of Excellent on his final comprehensive exams. He again gave a speech at the commencement ceremony, and Jeff was again there to hear it.

Chapter Ten

June 7, 1985

The Toast

Jeff tapped a spoon on his champagne glass and rose to offer a
toast. He'd asked to be the last to speak, and Sam's parents had
honored his request.

Jeff was wearing a white dinner jacket for the first time in his life.
Sam was seated beside him. They were at the head table in the enormous dining hall in the finest home either of them had ever seen. Five
beautiful crystal chandeliers, a massive one in the center, illuminated
the room. They hung from sixteen-foot ceilings with medallions atop
the chandeliers and ornate crown molding around the perimeter.
An enormous Persian rug covered the heart-pine floors. There was
ample space for the four dozen guests. The windows with views of the
lush courtyard were ten feet tall. The mansion, paid for with riches
generated by slave labor, was built before the Revolutionary War.

Jeff had returned to Jackson after graduating from Ole Miss and was
in his third year building a career as a stockbroker. It came easy to
him. People were drawn to him, both men and women, and wanted
to entrust him with their savings. He was not yet twenty-five but
already had an impressive stable of clients.

Jeff's income grew, but his bank account did not. He never had
much money growing up, and in short order he bought a nice
home in the Belhaven neighborhood with a mortgage at fourteen
percent and traded in his old pickup for a new BMW 320i. The

truck would never do for one of the most eligible bachelors in town. Jeff was a better-than-average golfer and used the sport for client development. He joined Jackson Country Club, then Annandale, a fine new club in Madison with many well-heeled members and a course designed by Jack Nicklaus.

Jeff also bought his mother a car, the first new one she'd ever owned. He enlisted one of her friends to find out what she would choose if she could ever afford one. Her dream car was a white Chevrolet Caprice Classic. Hardly a BMW, but it's what she wanted. After she went to bed on Christmas Eve, Jeff parked it in front of her house and decorated it with red and green ribbons. When she looked out the window the next morning, she cried. Jeff, who had spent the night in his old bedroom, cried too.

Sam graduated from Vanderbilt Law School three weeks before Jeff rose to offer his toast and three months after Sam called from Nashville with some important news. Sam was not the excitable type, but Jeff could tell he was excited from the tone in his voice. After thirty seconds of small talk, Jeff learned why.

"I've found her, Jeff. I've found the one."

Jeff laughed out loud. "Hold on a minute, big guy. How many times have you said that? How many times have you called me and used those exact same words?"

"I don't know how many. But this really is the one. I can tell."

"Well, I know how many. Four, and you said all three of the others were really the one too."

"I'm older and wiser now."

"You're older than you've ever been, there's no denying that, but I don't know that you're any wiser. I remember the first time you said you'd found the one. Susan, the girl in the class ahead of you at Millsaps. You sounded just like you do now. She was definitely the one, you assured me. Brilliant, funny, she introduced you to the music of John Prine. Whatever happened to her?"

"She transferred to Princeton after her sophomore year to study international relations. That was the end of that."

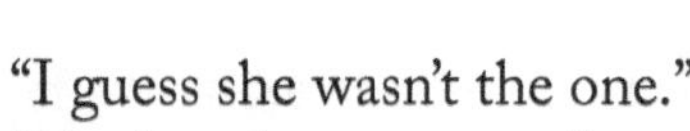

"I guess she wasn't the one."

"No, but she was great."

"I guess the magnificent Jessica, the gorgeous blonde with the perfect body, wasn't the one either."

"That was more lust than love."

"No surprise there. And Jennifer, the tennis player with the great legs, not the one either, I suppose."

"No, but she was great too."

"Notice a pattern here, Sam?"

"No, what?"

"Every time you sleep with a woman, you decide she's the one."

"Not true. I've slept with other women, and I never said they were the one. Never thought they were either. And I haven't slept with Evelyn."

"So Evelyn is the new one and only. How can you possibly tell she's the one if you haven't slept with her?"

"When you know, you know."

"But you said you knew with all the other ones too. Why haven't you slept with her? You haven't become a prude, have you?"

"She's not the type to hop into bed on the first date. Second or third either. And I'm not going to push it. She's too special. We'll go at her pace, but I sure wish she would pick it up. I can say this much: She's a great kisser."

"Wait a minute. Are you saying you've had only three dates with her?"

"That's right."

"Seriously? So you've gone out with this Evelyn a grand total of three times, y'all haven't gotten naked, and yet you know you want to spend the rest of your life with her. Is that really what you're telling me?"

"That's exactly what I'm telling you. She's the one; I'm sure of it."

"Sam, I think you need to hold on a second and listen to your old friend Jeff. You need to tap the brakes and hold your horses, to use two expressions that come to mind. You're not a patient man, as your track record demonstrates."

"I know, and I've been telling myself that. But she's the one."

"Okay, tell me why. You'll soon be a member of the Bar. Make your best case. Convince me she's the one. Start with looks."

"She's beautiful. Takes my breath away. Dark brown hair, almost black. Sea-green eyes that never look away. Perfect skin. A smile that lights up her face. Lights mine up too."

"What about her body?"

"She looks great in clothes, and my imagination tells me she looks even better out of them. She's short, maybe 5'2", but formidable. She's not a woman to be trifled with."

"What else? Or is it just looks and lust like it was with Jessica? Where's she from?"

"From an old-money family in Charleston. Her last name is Drayton. Could have made her debut, stuck around, and had her pick of all the rich Ashley Wilkes types. But she went to Princeton and studied pre-med instead. She and Susan were friends there; they graduated together."

"Small world. So she's a year older than we are too."

"Nope. She skipped a grade in elementary school. Her birthday is May the 29th. She's younger than you but older than me."

"Cool."

"She was accepted by Harvard and Columbia for med school—she's brilliant—but was tired of the winters and wanted to come back to the South. She says people here have better manners, and she likes the way we talk. She's in her last year of med school at Vandy."

"What will she do after med school?"

"She's gonna be a pediatrician. I can't wait for you to meet her."

"What about her sense of humor? Is she funny?"

"I laughed for two hours when she was making fun of Charleston high society the other night."

"You sure you didn't think she was funny just because you were staring at her and imagining what she looks like naked?"

"We were on the phone."

"Fair enough. Bring her to Jackson. I need to make sure you haven't gone off your rocker."

"She's the one, I promise."

Four weeks later, Sam called again. He sounded even more excited this time.

"I'm bringing Evelyn to Jackson to meet you and Mama and Daddy."

"Great. When?"

"Ten days from now. The second week of March. It'll be my last spring break ever. I'll sure miss spring break. We're spending the first half of the week in Charleston."

"What are the dates you'll be here?"

"The 13th to the 16th. We fly back to Nashville on Saturday afternoon."

"Damn. Don't tell me that. I'll be at a conference in Scottsdale."

"Cancel it. This is more important."

"I can't. Command performance. I'm getting an award as the leading producer under thirty in our region."

"Good for you. I hate you won't be there, but you'll meet her soon enough. You have your calendar handy?"

"Sure."

"Get a pen."

"Got one."

"Turn to June and block out four days, the 6th through the 9th."

"I'm free then, but what are we doing? Going camping, I hope."

"Nope. You're flying to Charleston on Thursday, and we're going to a party that night. On Friday morning there will be a fancy brunch. That evening you'll offer an eloquent toast to Evelyn and me at our rehearsal dinner. Make it good."

"I'm doing what?"

"Let me finish. On Saturday you and Daddy will serve as my best men in our wedding. On Sunday I guess you'll fly home, but you can stick around if you meet a gorgeous bridesmaid. We'll be flying to the British Virgin Islands for our honeymoon. You're not invited. Sorry."

"Damnation! Congratulations, but I protest. I haven't even met her. I haven't approved. I haven't even been consulted."

"You'll approve, I promise."

"Are you sure about this? It's been so fast. What, two months?"

"I'm positive. She's going to do her pediatric residency at University Med Center. She could have gone anywhere in America, but she's coming to Jackson."

"June sure makes for a short engagement."

"That's what she wanted. She says if we waited longer, her mother would have made the whole thing bigger and fancier. Evelyn would rather elope, but that would never do. She's the only daughter."

"I hope you've at least slept with her by now. You don't want to find out the sex is lousy on your wedding night."

"It's not, I assure you."

"I'm relieved. How good is it?"

"Unprecedented. Off the charts."

"Really? Better than the fair Jessica?"

"Light years better."

"That's hard to believe. Give me the details. I want to hear all of it, from start to finish."

"Nope."

"What do you mean, nope? We've never kept any secrets from each other."

"There's a first time for everything, Jeff, and I'm not telling you the details of my sex life with the woman I'm going to marry."

"Why not? You've told me everything about all the others, and I've sure told you everything about all the women I've dated."

"True, but I don't think Evelyn would want me to share the details of our sex life with anybody, not even you, and I'm never going to do anything she doesn't want me to do."

"You really are in love, aren't you? You say you'll never do anything she doesn't want you to do. What if she doesn't want you to go camping with me?"

Sam and Jeff hadn't gone on another trip that could hold a candle to the road trip to New England seven years before, but they'd managed to get away to the woods for at least a long weekend every year since then. They had come home every time smelling of campfire smoke, with their batteries recharged, and with new stories to tell.

"She has a strong opinion about our camping trips, as she does about most things," Sam said. "But she's in favor, not opposed. She knows all about you and the places we've been, and she can tell how happy our trips make me. She says she's going to make us keep going, and if you ever try to stop, you'll have hell to pay. And if you get married and your wife tries to make you stop, she'll have hell to pay too. I don't know what she has in mind, but you and your future wife don't want to find out. As I believe I've told you, Evelyn's a formidable woman."

Jeff began his toast by raising his glass to Evelyn, who looked radiant at Sam's side. "I first want to toast the bride. Here's to Evelyn, a beautiful, wonderful, extraordinary woman. You have made my best friend happier than I've ever seen him, and that makes me happy too. For that, I thank you and drink a toast to you."

He took a sip, then turned to face the guests. "Even a blind man could see that Evelyn is beautiful, but as some of you know, I just met her for the first time last night. So, it's fair to ask, how could I possibly know she's wonderful and extraordinary? Well, I know for two reasons. First, Sam told me she is, and he's never lied to me. But that's not all. I also know Evelyn's wonderful and extraordinary because my best friend, the best friend a boy or man could ever have, asked her to marry him.

"Let me tell you some things about Sam Thompson you may not know. When I was eight years old, my wonderful mama and I moved to Jackson." He turned and raised his glass to his mother, who was seated beside Sam's parents at the other end of the head table. Jeff had flown her with him to Charleston for the wedding.

"The next day Mama kicked me out of the house because I was getting on her nerves and told me to go find somebody to play with. I rang the Thompsons' doorbell, and his wonderful mother answered the door." Jeff now turned to Sam's mother and raised his glass. "I told Mrs. Thompson what I was looking for, and she climbed the stairs, got Sam, and brought him down. He and I explored the creek that ran from our neighborhood to the Pearl River that day, got home at dark, and have been best friends ever since. One day and we both knew. I believe Sam knew about Evelyn in less than an hour.

"I've been Sam's best friend for seventeen years, and he's been mine. We've worked hard together. During the Easter flood in Jackson six years ago, we worked twenty-four hours straight with a short break so our mothers could feed us. We rescued a profane parrot—ask me later if you want details; I can't repeat what the bird said in mixed company—and worked side-by-side till dawn with prison inmates to save the power plant in downtown Jackson.

"We've also played hard together—we paddled Section III of the Chattooga and saw a bald eagle and an osprey catch fish on the Allagash River in Maine. We didn't rescue a bird on the Allagash, but we rescued a dog. She woke us up barking to show us the Northern lights, we brought her home and gave her to my mama, and they've been best friends ever since."

Jeff then turned to Evelyn's parents. "Mr. and Mrs. Drayton, congratulations on adding Sam to your family. Your wise daughter has chosen wisely. I would do anything for Sam, and I know he would do anything for me. I would trust him with my life and, I promise, you can now trust him with Evelyn's. I am delighted and honored to be here with you this weekend to celebrate this wonderful, extraordinary couple."

Jeff turned back to Sam and Evelyn. "I drink to you, Evelyn, my new friend, and to you, Sam, my best friend. May you live happily ever after. I look forward to all the wonderful times we'll spend together and to telling stories about them fifty years from now."

Jeff took a final sip of champagne and sat down. After a few seconds of silence, a woman started clapping. Others joined her. One person stood, then everyone but Jeff, Sam, and Evelyn rose to their feet. Jeff then stood and lifted his glass again. When everyone sat back down and the room was quiet, Dr. Thompson rose and thanked the guests for coming. He said brandy would soon be served, and there would be cigars in the courtyard. He concluded by saying he was glad he let Jeff give his toast last. He would have been an impossible act to follow.

# Chapter Eleven

July 12, 1991

The Upper Missouri

Six years after the wedding, Sam began his last year as an associate at the firm. He was certain to be invited to join the partnership—he worked long hours, did excellent work, and was well liked by judges, clients, and everyone at the firm—but he took nothing for granted. That wasn't his way. He worried, and Evelyn worried about him.

One Friday night in July when he was late coming to bed, she found him in the den at 10:30 reading a deposition transcript. When he looked up, she gave him instructions. "I want you to call Jeff first thing in the morning. You're overdue for a campfire and some time in the woods."

He smiled. "Trying to get rid of me?"

She smiled back and held out her hand. He took it, and she led him to the bedroom. Half an hour later, she rolled onto her side and put her hand on his chest. "I'm not trying to get rid of you, as I believe I just demonstrated, and I'll demonstrate it repeatedly when you get home. But I want you to call Jeff in the morning. You've been burning the candle at both ends for way too long."

"Can't I just take a few days off and stay in bed with you?"

"No. I can't take the time off, and if you're in Jackson, you'll be working. We both know that. Call Jeff."

"Yes, ma'am. How could I disobey a woman who treats me so well?"

"Very wise."

As instructed, and with Evelyn sitting beside him, Sam made the call the next morning. Jeff was shocked. "Let me pinch myself. I need to make sure I'm not dreaming. Is this really Sam nose-to-the-grindstone Thompson? Sam all-work-and-no-play Thompson? I'm always the one asking you to go camping, and I usually get rejected. Are you really calling to ask me?"

"Evelyn made me."

"I approve of her, by the way."

"I know you do, and I knew you would. I said so, if you'll recall."

"So when can you squeeze me into your busy schedule for a few days, Counselor?"

"I'll be going full speed until the end of August—a trial and a bunch of briefs—but things should slow down after that. I just might—and get ready to pinch yourself again—be able to take off for a whole week."

"Wow. I'll believe it when I see it."

"Just watch me. You have any ideas for where we might go? I haven't thought about it. I just agreed to call you in a weak moment after Evelyn took advantage of me last night."

"I'm sure you played hard to get. Funny you should ask. I was just reading an article in the new issue of *Outside* about a canoe trip out west. I was figuring I might have to do it by myself. Or maybe take a date. A bed's better, but a tent's not bad. It's not whitewater, and it's not a clear mountain stream, but the article said it has gorgeous scenery, tons of wildlife, plenty of solitude, and terrific campsites."

"What river? Where?"

"The Upper Missouri in Montana. Big Sky country."

"We've never been to Montana."

"There's a section of the river that's a little over a hundred miles long. Six days on the water. It would be our longest canoe trip since the Allagash. We could fly out one weekend and fly home the next. Let's book it before you change your mind."

"Why not? You only go around once."

"I can't believe you're saying that. You don't have a fever, do you?"

"Evelyn has promised to shower me with affection upon my return."

"Please thank her for me. What week is best for you? I'll research flights and let you know."

"The second week of September looks best. Monday of that week is the ninth. Where would we fly into?"

"Great Falls. There's an art museum there I want to see."

"An art museum? Really? Have you suddenly become a man of culture and breeding?"

"Always have been; you just haven't noticed. It's the Charlie Russell Museum. Great western artist."

"As a man of culture and breeding, I'm familiar with his work."

"So who do you want to be?"

"Want to be? What are you talking about? I like being Dr. Thompson's boyfriend." He smiled at Evelyn and squeezed her thigh.

"We'll be paddling where Lewis and Clark paddled and camping where they camped. One of us should be Lewis, the other one Clark."

"You decide."

"Okay, I'll be Clark. He was the badass. Lewis was the science nerd. Plus I've seen portraits. Clark had better hair."

The flight west had three legs. They flew first to DFW, then Salt Lake City, then Great Falls. Sam was having a hard time disconnecting and still thinking about work on the last of the three. He marked his place in the book he was reading, John Irving's *A Prayer for Owen Meany*, and gazed out at the mountains.

"What are you thinking about now?"

"Just a couple of things I needed to get done at the office. I stayed late last night, but then Evelyn called and said I better come home if I wanted a proper sendoff. I should have finished them."

"You can't let it go, can you?"

"My clients are counting on me."

"I can picture you now. It's fifty years from today, September 7, 2041. You're on your deathbed. Time is short. You're thinking about all your regrets. Number one on the list: You never should have gone on that trip to Montana in 1991 with your best friend.

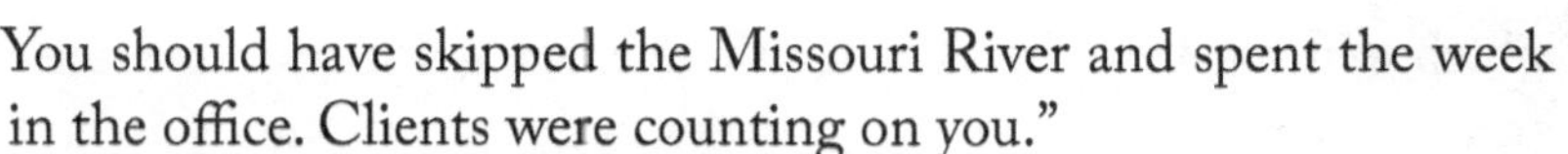

You should have skipped the Missouri River and spent the week in the office. Clients were counting on you."

"But they are counting on me."

"Imagine if Meriwether and Captain Clark had said, 'Sorry, Tom, no can do. Clients are counting on us.'"

"Tom?"

"Thomas Jefferson, the President of the United States, the man who sent them on the grand expedition across the Rockies to the Pacific. Let it go, Sam. There's nothing you can do about it now, and it'll still be there when you get home."

He looked over at Jeff and smiled. "I'll try."

They had a big breakfast Sunday morning, their last meal in civilization until Friday night, then went to the C. M. Russell Museum on 13th Street in Great Falls. The artist lived on the site with his wife Nancy until his death in 1926. Sam and Jeff decided their favorite of Russell's paintings was a huge landscape dominated by a bull elk standing on a rise. His harem was spread out behind him, and there were snow-capped peaks in the distance. It was magnificent. Jeff spotted the title of the painting and had a change of heart about his name for the trip. "Forget calling me Captain Clark," he said. "I'll be 'The Exalted Ruler.'"

On the forty-five-minute drive to the outfitter's headquarters in Fort Benton, they listened to a cassette Sam had bought just before the trip. It was *The Missing Years*, John Prine's new studio album, the tenth of his career. As always, it was unique and wonderful. Sam liked to invoke a Latin term used by lawyers to describe his favorite songwriter. Prine was *sui generis*, one of a kind.

In the title track, "Jesus: The Missing Years," John explores what Jesus did during the time of his life the Bible skips over and imagines that the years were eventful. Jesus moves to Rome, marries an Irish girl, and invents Santa Claus. He discovers the Beatles, records with the Stones, and even opens a show for old George Jones.

One of their favorite songs on the new album was "All the Best," which John wrote in the back of a Winnebago going fifty-five miles an hour while he was making tacos and going through a divorce. The message of the song is that it's best to take the high road and wish your ex a happy life, but it's sure not easy. He was in love, but now she's gone, and he's in pain. He wishes her all the best, at least he guesses he does. If she's lucky, she won't do what he did and fall in love with someone like her.

They also liked "The Sins of Memphisto," a quirky tune in which John pairs Adam and Eve with Lucy and Ricky and rhymes hula hoops with therapy groups and Quasimodo with exactly-odo. John invented a word from time to time. The song also features an old man who stands in his yard, stares at his rake, and wonders if his marriage was a terrible mistake. It was more classic Prine. In just one line, John revealed that a long marriage isn't necessarily a happy one. He made the same point in two of his classics, "Hello in There" and "Angel from Montgomery."

Their first afternoon on the river, Sam and Jeff saw bald eagles for the first time since paddling the Allagash more than a decade before. There were also golden eagles and bighorn sheep, and Jeff spotted a lone coyote. "Look," he said, "it's Wile E. He's looking for the Roadrunner. *Shh.* Stop talking."

"I'm not talking. You're talking. But why should either one of us stop?"

"So we can listen for the Roadrunner's *beep beep.*"

Beside the campfire that night, Sam returned to a familiar topic. Jeff was still single and showed no sign of taking the plunge. Whenever a woman started getting serious and hinting that it was time for a ring, Jeff called it quits. Sam asked him for the umpteenth time when he was ever going to settle down and get married.

"What's the hurry?"

"You're thirty-one years old. It's time."

"Why are you in a hurry for me when I'm not in a hurry for me?"

"Don't you want to have kids?"

"You don't have kids."

"We've started trying."

"Good for you. When you have kids, I'll be their Uncle Jeff."

"But they won't be your kids. You won't have any."

"And that's the way I want to keep it."

"Why?"

"Private school tuition. Dirty diapers. Uncle Jeff will love your kids, but he won't change their diapers."

"You don't know what you're missing. Asking Evelyn to marry me was the wisest thing I've ever done."

"But what if I'm not as lucky as you are? What if I wind up like one of those poor guys today?"

"What poor guys?"

"One of them fell in love, but the woman left him. The other one wished he'd never gotten married."

"Who are you talking about?"

"The men in the songs on the new Prine album. One was 'All the Best.' The other one was 'The Sins of Something or Other.'"

"'Memphisto.' How do you know that's what they're about?"

"Because I listened to the words. In the first one, the poor guy was in love, his woman left him, and now it's hard to want her to be happy. In the other one, Grandpa regrets spending his whole life with his wife. He feels just like you'll feel in fifty years for spending this week on the river and not in the office."

"I guess maybe that's what they're about."

"That's definitely what they're about. The old guy wouldn't wonder if his marriage was a terrible mistake if it wasn't. And I don't want to risk making a mistake. I could marry a woman who's right for me, but I might not be right for her. She might leave me and break my heart."

"No woman is ever going to leave you, Romeo."

"You don't know that. Or I could marry a woman who turns out to be wrong for me. And then where would I be? I'd be standing in the yard staring at a rake."

"You sure are pessimistic. It's not like you."

"It's not just that. I might hit the jackpot and be as happy as you are, but I'm happy already. I love being a bachelor. What is it they say is the spice of life?"

"I know what you say it is. Variety. But it's wonderful to have a life partner."

"Meriwether, my boy, you're all the life partner I need."

One of the beauties of a canoe trip is that you can leave civilization behind but take plenty of creature comforts with you. Sam and Jeff had camp chairs, charcoal and steaks, two coolers, and plenty of beer. The weather was perfect. No rain, highs near eighty and lows around fifty. They had a campfire every night but never put on long pants. Their fires and sleeping bags were all they needed to keep them warm.

It was late in the season, so there were few boats on the river. With one exception, they had the campsites all to themselves. The exception was a memorable night they spent with two beautiful girls in a cottonwood grove across the river from towering white cliffs.

Just before dusk, they heard high-pitched voices coming from the water. The girls landed their canoe, then began unloading. Sam and Jeff watched in silence. They were speechless. The girls were tall, blonde, tanned, and gorgeous. They were barefoot and wore but two garments apiece: a bikini bottom and a crop-top tee shirt.

"I believe we've been invaded by the Swedish bikini team," Jeff whispered. It was a reference to the popular but controversial Old Milwaukee commercial that ran for several months earlier in the year but was dropped after protests by the National Organization for Women and others. "Should we offer to help them unload and put up their tent? Perhaps massage their aching muscles?"

"Stay where you are, Exalted Ruler. No good can come from an offer to help."

"I beg to differ," said Jeff, but he stayed put.

But he didn't have to make the first move. After putting up their tent, the girls walked over to Sam and Jeff's campfire and introduced themselves. They were just nineteen, but they spoke with the confidence of beautiful women who've long understood the power they have over men. The trip, they said, was their last outing before beginning their sophomore year at the University of Montana in Missoula. Jeff offered them his chair, which forced Sam to follow suit. They declined because they'd been sitting in the canoe all day. Again without consulting Sam, Jeff offered them a beer and invited them to share the campfire for the night. They accepted this time and retrieved their camp chairs and food. The four cooked dinner and shared their food.

Two hours and three beers later, the more confident girl popped the question: "Are both of you guys married?"

Sam answered first and told them about his wonderful wife and the toast Jeff gave at their rehearsal dinner. He made a point of saying the wedding was more than six years earlier and was after he graduated from law school. He wanted the girls to appreciate their age difference. The same girl then turned to Jeff with a smile and asked, "What about you, Jeff?"

"I'm not married," he said. "I don't even have a girlfriend. I'm just a lonely bachelor." The girls looked at each other and smiled. Sam rolled his eyes.

After one more beer, the girls announced they were turning in. They thanked Sam and Jeff for a wonderful night and hugged them, Jeff longer and harder than Sam. Jeff gazed intently at the two beauties as they walked away, illuminated by the firelight. They were as gorgeous going as they were coming. When they reached their tent, they turned around and waved. One blew a kiss. Jeff waved back.

Sam shook his head. "Don't even think about it."

"How could I not think about it?"

"Fair enough, but you can't do what you're thinking about."

"Why not? C'mon, Meriwether, it was meant to be. It's manna from heaven, a gift from the gods. And it's rude to turn down a gift."

"They're just one year out of high school, Jeff."

"Jeff? Who's Jeff?"

"Okay, okay. They're teenagers, Exalted Ruler. They're barely out of high school."

"I bet there's room in that tent for me. If not, one of them could stay in our tent with you. I'll let you take your pick."

"Don't you dare."

"Why do you always have to be such a party pooper?"

"They're barely over half our age."

"Are not. Nineteen plus nineteen is thirty-eight. We're only thirty-one."

"Okay then, they're twelve years younger than we are. Less than two-thirds our age."

"But did you watch them walking to the tent?"

"Actually, I didn't. I watched you watching them. I'm surprised your tongue didn't fall out of your head."

"You're no fun."

"Don't do it. You can't do it."

"I know, but it sure would be fun."

Sam rose first thing the next morning and stoked the campfire back to life. When the girls were loaded and ready to launch, they walked over to say goodbye. The one who'd asked if they were married leaned over Jeff's camp chair, put her arms around him, and whispered something in his ear. Five minutes later, after their canoe was out of sight, Sam asked, "Okay, what?"

"She said they knew you weren't interested, but they thought I might pay them a visit. She said it was my loss. Damn, Sam. It was my loss, but it was your fault."

"It wasn't my fault. I'm not the boss of you. You're the Exalted Ruler, remember."

"I know, but it sure would have been fun."

They camped the next night between the river and a huge prairie dog town. Sam and Jeff walked quietly to the edge of the cottonwoods to investigate. Hundreds of the rodents were above ground socializing in small groups.

"What are they talking about?" whispered Sam.

"I don't know. Maybe how all people look alike."

"What are you talking about? They're the ones that all look alike."

"Not to them, they don't."

They watched for a few more minutes in silence, then Jeff yelled *boo*. Every prairie dog went racing to a burrow and disappeared. The prairie was empty in seconds.

"Just like the wood ducks," said Sam.

"What wood ducks?"

"The ones on the day we met. We sneaked up on them, you yelled boo, and they disappeared."

"I guess I did do that, didn't I? That was a long time ago."

"Twenty-three years and three months."

"You're such a nerd."

The outfitter had agreed to shuttle their rental to the take-out point. They were nervous as they rounded the last curve at noon on Friday, but there it was, just like on the Allagash. Per the plan, they found the keys on the ground inside the left front tire, drove back to Great Falls and, for the first time in six days, took showers, dined in a restaurant, and slept in beds. They boarded the plane to fly home the next morning.

After the last flight took off from DFW, Jeff declared that he had an announcement to make. Sam performed a drum roll with his fingers on the armrest between them. Jeff let the suspense build, then raised his hand for silence.

"The Exalted Ruler has made a decision."

"I thought you were the Exalted Ruler only when we were on the river."

"I'm the Ruler until our plane touches down in Jackson."

"Okay, Ruler, what's your decision?"

"The Exalted Ruler has decided, and now decrees, that from here on out, as long as we're able, we'll go on a camping trip every year that lasts at least a week."

"And by what authority have you issued this decree?"

"I'm the Exalted Ruler, as you just acknowledged."

"I see. What if I'm too busy and can't get away for a week?"

"Then I will bring in the big guns and enlist the real Exalted Ruler."

"And just who might that be?"

"Evelyn Drayton Thompson, M.D."

"You got that right."

# Chapter Twelve

March 11, 1999

Other Plans

"Jeff, this is Evelyn. I hate to call you at work, but I need a favor. A big one."

"Sure. Anything."

"Well, since I'm almost thirty-nine, my OBGYN says I have what he calls an at-risk pregnancy, so he ordered me to stay home until the baby comes. And I was standing at the kitchen sink just now rinsing the dishes and, lo and behold, my water broke."

"But you're only seven months pregnant."

"Seven and a half actually, but it doesn't really matter how pregnant I am now, does it? I need to get to the hospital, but I can't get anybody to answer the phone. I also need to find somebody to keep Sara." Sara, named for Sam's mother, had just turned three.

Evelyn continued. "Sam's in trial in Biloxi with his phone turned off. His parents are on a river cruise in Europe. It's spring break, and all my friends who were wise enough to have their children before they were my age are on vacation. I tried Olivia, but she didn't answer."

"She's at your clinic with Marsha."

"She's okay, I hope."

"Just a cold, we think. Making sure it's not strep. Don't worry about her. We need to take care of you. I'll be there in fifteen minutes."

"No need to rush. My contractions are still weak and far apart.

Uh-oh, wait a second. This is the strongest one yet. Maybe you shouldn't take your good, sweet time either."

"I'm on my way."

"Thank you, Jeff. I don't want to have this baby at home by myself. Sara's excited about having a baby brother, but she wouldn't be much help delivering him. I'll be packed and ready when you get here."

Olivia answered Jeff's call as she was leaving the clinic. Marsha was fine, nothing serious. He asked Olivia to meet him at the Thompsons'. They talked as they drove and decided on a plan. Like most mothers, Olivia was better at childcare than her husband, and she was almost six months pregnant herself. The last thing she wanted was to watch another woman go through labor just a few months before she would have to go through it herself. Olivia would take Sara and Marsha to the Freemans'. Jeff would drive Evelyn to the hospital and stay until Sam or one of Evelyn's girl-friends showed up.

Loading Evelyn took less than a minute. She hugged Olivia, kissed Sara, and told her to behave herself. Jeff helped her into the pas-senger seat, and they sped away. Evelyn's contractions were stronger and more frequent now. Jeff turned on his flashers, drove fast, and ran three red lights. He figured if he saw blue lights he would lead the police car on a chase to Baptist Hospital and try to talk his way out of the ticket after Evelyn went inside. But no blue lights appeared. When he let her out at the entrance before pulling into the parking lot, she said she would be in Labor and Delivery.

"Really?" he asked. "I thought I ran all those red lights so you could go to the gift shop."

"Don't make me laugh, Jeff Freeman, or you'll be delivering this baby."

The Thompsons and Freemans had a friend who famously gave birth to her third child in the entrance lobby of this very hospital. Her husband saw what was happening, caught his newborn son as he came into the world, and kept him from landing headfirst on the tile floor. The incident was preserved for posterity by the hospital's security cameras. Jeff had to circle the multilevel parking lot three times to find a space. Evelyn was already in bed in a hospital gown when he got to her room.

"I thought maybe you decided to drop me off and make a run for it."

"I considered walking across the street to Keifer's for a few beers to calm my nerves, but I decided you might not approve. Sam either. I didn't even have time for one. The parking lot was packed. It was that way when Marsha was born."

Evelyn had another contraction, the worst one yet, and she reached for Jeff's hand and squeezed. He reminded her to breathe. When the contraction ended, she let go of his hand and turned to face him.

"This is weird, isn't it?"

"You're telling me. I thought it was weird when it was my own wife having my own baby."

Evelyn and Jeff were ten days apart in age. They were both very attractive and had become close friends during their years together in Jackson, but there had never been even a hint of flirtation between them. Their mutual love for Sam made that unthinkable.

A young nurse came into the room. "Dr. Thompson, how are you feeling? You need anything?"

"I've felt better, but I know the drill: no pain, no baby. Maybe you could bring me some ice water."

"Sure thing."

"That would be wonderful. Thank you."

"What about you, Mr. Thompson? You need anything?"

"I don't need a thing, thank you, but I'm not Mr. Thompson. I'm Mr. Freeman, but please call me Jeff."

The nurse gave him a look, then checked Evelyn's chart. "I'm sorry, Dr. Thompson. It says here you're married, and I assumed your husband was Mr. Thompson. I shouldn't have."

"No need to apologize. You assumed correctly. My husband *is* Mr. Thompson, but he's not here."

"So who is this?"

"He's my husband's best friend. He was the best man in our

wedding. He brought me to the hospital. His wife is keeping our daughter."

"But where's your husband?" It was none of the nurse's business, but she couldn't help herself.

Jeff saw an opportunity for self-amusement and seized it. He answered the nurse before Evelyn could. "I'm afraid he had other plans."

"Other plans?"

"Yes. It seems he made another commitment. He's out of town."

The nurse was angry now. "What kind of commitment?"

"Some kind of work thing, I think."

"Does he even know she's in labor?"

"Not yet. He's indisposed."

"Indisposed?" Her face turned red.

"We tried to call him—both of us did—but he has his phone turned off. I guess he's doing something more important than the birth of his son."

"Well, that son of a—"

She stopped herself when Evelyn cleared her throat. Jeff was having fun, but it was time to put a stop to it.

"I apologize for my friend. Sometimes—most of the time, actually—his conduct is inappropriate. My wonderful husband, Sam, is not a son of a bitch, I assure you. He's a lawyer. He's in trial in federal court in Biloxi. The judge makes them turn off their phones in the courtroom."

"But why did he go to a trial in Biloxi when you were about to have a baby?"

"Well, I wasn't supposed to be having a baby just yet. I'm only seven and a half months pregnant. Dr. Robinson assured us I would be fine and Sam could go to the trial. And yet here I am."

Jeff interjected again. "Typical doctor. Often wrong but never in doubt."

The nurse had recovered and was smiling now. Evelyn continued. "He'll find out when they break for lunch, and I'm sure he'll get here as fast as he can. And if he's late and misses the birth of his son, well, he'll owe me big time. I'm thinking those diamond earrings at Juniker I've been wanting would be a suitable way for him to make amends."

After the nurse returned with ice water, Evelyn had another contraction, even worse than the previous one. Her face turned red, and she squeezed Jeff's hand until it hurt. He told her to breathe, but she didn't. When the contraction passed, Jeff offered advice.

"When it hurts real bad, make like Mr. Kelly."

"Mr. who?"

"Mr. Kelly. You know, the profane parrot Sam and I rescued from the Easter flood. When Olivia's contractions got bad, I told her to make like Mr. Kelly and cuss like a sailor at the top of her lungs. It seemed to help, but the nurse wearing a cross pendant didn't much like it."

"Thanks for the advice, but I'm on the staff here, and I treat a lot of the nurses' children. I'll try to watch my language."

"Mr. Kelly watched his language after we put him in the canoe."

Sam's trial was before federal district judge Walter Gex. When they broke for lunch, Sam turned on his phone and checked his messages. He called Evelyn's cell immediately.

"You already at the hospital? You okay?"

"Yes. I'm here. It hurts, as you'll recall from last time, but Dr. Robinson has been in to see me and says everything looks good. The baby looks fine. Your son just decided he wanted to come early. He's ready to get his show on the road."

"Who's with you? My parents are in Europe."

"I have surrogate father Jeff Freeman sitting right here beside me. He's reminded me to breathe and recommended that I cuss like Mr. Kelly when the contractions get bad. I haven't yet, but I might start."

"Please thank him for me. I'm so sorry, Sweetheart. I should be there. But Dr. Robinson told us there was no way you'd go into labor this week."

"I know what he told us, but he was wrong. Even those of us

who perform medical miracles are not infallible. And it's not your fault. When can you leave?"

"I'll need to find the plaintiff's lawyer and meet with Judge Gex and tell him what's going on. I'll get there as fast as I can. I'll call when I'm on the road."

"Be careful coming home. I'm fine, really I am. Wait a minute. Jeff has something he wants to tell you."

She handed Jeff the phone. "Sam, all good here. I'm a pro at this from when Marsha was born. Listen, I'm sure you're familiar with the longstanding tradition regarding fathers who are absent when their sons are born."

Sam knew some BS was coming, but he played along. "What tradition is that?"

"If you don't get here before the baby's born, you lose naming privileges. I've been thinking Horatio. Or maybe Bartholomew."

Evelyn took the phone back. "Don't drive too fast. I won't let your crazy friend name our son. I love you."

"I love you too."

Sam flagged down the plaintiff's lawyer in the parking lot as he was leaving for lunch. He then called Judge Gex's deputy clerk on his cell and said he had a family emergency and they needed to meet with the judge as soon as possible. She said he was eating a sandwich at his desk and could see them now.

"Gentlemen, please excuse me if I chew while you talk. I've got two calls before we start back this afternoon. What is it, Sam?"

"Your Honor, I'm very sorry about this, but I need to leave for Jackson right now. My wife's in labor."

"I'm relieved to hear it. Kathleen said you had a family emergency. I was afraid it was something bad. But why didn't you tell me before the trial started? I would have continued it."

"I'm sorry, Judge. She's only a little over seven months pregnant. She wasn't due until the end of April. Her doctor said there was no way she'd go into labor while I was down here."

"The doctor was wrong. Imagine that." Judge Gex turned to

plaintiff's counsel, a capable but difficult advocate whose name suited him to a tee. "What say you, Dick?"

"I understand Sam needs to get home, Judge, but the jury's here, and we're in the middle of trial. I don't see why his associate can't take over from here."

Judge Gex looked over the top of his reading glasses and smiled. "You'd like that, wouldn't you? Sam goes home, and a baby lawyer who looks like he's never even shaved handles the rest of the trial. Sam, when did your associate finish law school? Has he ever tried a case?"

"He just graduated from Ole Miss in December, Your Honor. He's never even taken a deposition."

"Okay, gentlemen, this is what we're going to do. It's Thursday, and we weren't going to finish by tomorrow anyway. When the jury comes back from lunch, I'll tell them what's happened and say we'll start back at nine o'clock on Monday. That should give Sam time to get his wife and his—is it a boy or a girl?"

"A boy."

"Congratulations. To get his wife and his son home from the hospital. As for me, I was invited to go on an overnight fishing trip to Chandeleur Island tomorrow. I love catching and eating redfish and speckled trout, but I had to turn it down because of this trial. As soon as I dismiss the jury, I'm going to call and see if they still have room for me."

"Thank you very much, Judge. I really appreciate it."

"You're welcome. I don't see that we have any choice." He cut his eyes at Dick. "Y'all don't need to stick around for me to dismiss the jury. Sam, you need to get on the road. I know you're a law-abiding man, but I suspect you might be tempted to exceed the speed limit on the way home. Here's one of my cards. It has my cell number on it. If a patrolman pulls you over, show him the card and ask him to call me."

"Thank you, Your Honor. I will speed, and I will ask him to call you."

"I knew you would. Now git." As Sam opened the door to leave, Judge Gex spoke again. "And one more thing—Walter is a great name for a boy."

Sam called Evelyn as soon as he was on I-10. She didn't pick up, so he called Jeff. When he answered, Sam needed reassurance. "Is Evelyn okay? She didn't answer."

"Her phone's dead, and we don't have a charger. She's fine except when she's having a contraction. I don't think she likes them at all. But your old pal Jeff has things under control. The doc was just in here. He said you better hurry if you want to get here for the main event. You don't want your son to imprint on me and think I'm his father. Evelyn wants to speak to you."

"You okay, Sweetheart?" she asked.

"Am I okay? I'm not the one having a baby. How are you?"

"I've felt better, and I wish you were here, but otherwise I'm fine. Dr. Robinson says things are still looking good. I'm glad you got away so soon."

"Judge Gex is a great guy. He gave me a card with his cell number on it. If I get pulled over, he told me to get the highway patrolman to call him."

"Sam Thompson, you listen to me. I know you're speeding right now." He looked down at the speedometer. He was going ninety. "Don't be going too fast. I don't want Jason's father to have a wreck on the day he's born. And Jeff really does have things under control. The nurses love him."

"I'm sure they do."

"Let me go now. I feel another contraction coming on. We'll call you when we know more. I love you."

"I love you too."

After the contraction ended and Evelyn let go of Jeff's hand, he said, "So Jason, huh?"

"He's my favorite uncle, Daddy's little brother. He'll be thrilled."

"I met him at the wedding. Good guy. But why not name him for your father?"

"Ambrose? Seriously? Daddy has forbidden it."

"What about the baby's middle name?"

"I don't know. I chose his first name, so Sam gets to choose his middle name. If he's decided, he hasn't told me. We didn't think he needed to come up with one for seven more weeks."

For the next hour, Sam looked down at his phone every five minutes, wanting to call. But this was about Evelyn, not him, and she said they would call when they knew more. He was making great time zooming up Highway 49. At this rate, he would break his personal record for fastest trip home from Biloxi by half an hour. So far, no highway patrolmen. When he was almost to Okatoma Creek, which he and Jeff had canoed a dozen times, his phone finally rang. It was Evelyn.

"Slow down, big guy, you're not gonna make it."

"Well, damn."

"Damn for you, but hooray for me. Dr. Robinson said it's time to start pushing. Your son is ready to make his appearance."

"How do you feel? Any problems?"

"No problems, and I feel fine since the epidural."

"Is Jeff still there?"

"By the hardest. When the doctor said it was time, Jeff said his work was done and he would wait outside. I said no way; we were in this together. I wasn't gonna let him leave me at the moment of truth. He agreed to stay if he could steer clear of the business end."

"May I speak to him?" Sam's mother had taught him the difference between may and can before he learned to read.

"Sure." She handed Jeff the phone.

"I owe you."

"Damn right you owe me. And not just for watching your wife suffer for the last five hours but also for the deal I made with her doc."

"Deal?"

"I talked him into letting us have you on the phone during the delivery. You won't see your son being born, but you'll hear it. Or at least you'll hear Evelyn."

"Thank you. I can't believe I'm not there."

"We'll call back when it's time. Maybe you should pull over then. You don't want to rear end an eighteen-wheeler while you're listening to the birth of your son. That would knock the bloom right off the rose."

When Evelyn started pushing, she held Jeff's hand with one hand and the bed rail with the other. She looked up at him between pushes, saw he was smiling, and asked why.

"This is beyond weird."

"The weirdest ever."

Jeff waited to call Sam again until Dr. Robinson gave him the go-ahead.

"Is it time? Should I pull over?"

"It's time. Where are you?"

"Just passed Piney Woods School. I'm pulling over now."

"You almost made it. Evelyn wants to speak to you."

"The doctor says Jason should be here in five minutes. Jeff will hold the phone to my ear. I love you."

"I love you too. I can't believe I'm not there."

"Not your fault. Let me get back to work."

Dr. Robinson came in and shook his head. "I've been delivering babies for thirty-five years, but I've never brought one into the world while the mother was on the phone."

It took only two minutes, not five. When Sam, Evelyn, and Jeff heard Jason's first cry, they all cried too. The doctor cleaned the baby's face, wrapped him in a blanket, and handed him to his mother. She let go of Jeff's hand and took the phone. "I'm fine, Sam, and he's beautiful. I need to rest now. Don't drive too fast. Jason and I will be waiting for you."

Jeff took the baby out to be evaluated while the nurses took care of Evelyn. Jason weighed six pounds, eight ounces, didn't look like a preemie, and had perfect Apgar scores. This nurse, like the first one, assumed Jeff was the father. "Congratulations, Mr. Thompson. Your son is as healthy as a horse."

"Thank you, and that's great news, but I'm not Mr. Thompson. I'm Mr. Freeman. Mr. Thompson's not here."

"I don't understand. Is the baby yours or his?"

"I'm pretty sure it's his. Let me take another look. Yeah, definitely his. Mr. Thompson is already losing his hair, and this baby has hardly any. I have many faults, but as you can see from this luxurious mane, lack of hair is not one of them."

"So where is Mr. Thompson?"

"At home, I guess. He stayed out partying until early this morning, I was told. I heard he really tied one on. He's bad to do that. And when his wife's water broke this morning and she woke him up, he told her to go away. Said he needed to sleep, so she called me."

The nurse's mouth hung open, but no words came out.

"Not really. I made all that up. The baby came nearly two months early, and Mr. Thompson was in federal court on the Coast. He's a lawyer. He should be here any minute."

When Jeff returned to the room with Jason, the nurses were gone, but Sam was there. In the space of two minutes, he'd apologized three times, told Evelyn he loved her five, and kissed her ten.

Jeff didn't want to interrupt the tender moment, but he was the one with the baby. He cleared his throat, and they turned to look at him. "Well, look who we have here. If it's not the prodigal father. You'll be pleased to know the nurse says your son, who she thought was my son, is in perfect health. Six and a half pounds. Perfect scores."

He continued. "What am I thinking? Where are my manners? I should be making introductions." He handed the baby to Sam. "Jason, I want you to meet your father, Sam. Don't hold his absence against him. He wanted to be here, really he did. He's a good guy. You'll see in time. And Sam, since I've known Jason all his life and you've never even met him, let me introduce him to you. Please meet your son, Jason Jeffery Thompson."

Sam had been looking down, smiling, staring at Jason's face. But now he looked up, startled. Jeff was about to say that Jeffery was better than Horatio or Bartholomew, but Sam spoke first.

"How did you know? How could you know?"

"Know what?"

"That his middle name was going to be Jeffery. I didn't tell you. I didn't even tell Evelyn. I didn't tell anybody. It was gonna be a surprise."

"I didn't know. It was a joke. You lost naming privileges, remember? So I named him for me."

Sam smiled. "No, you didn't. I named him for you."

Three months later, when Jeff and Olivia's first and only son was born, they christened him Eric Samuel Freeman.

# Chapter Thirteen

November 10, 2007

Beech Trees

"What are you doing calling me at ten o'clock on Saturday morning?" Sam asked. "You're supposed to be on the golf course."

"I've had a change of plans," Jeff replied. "I don't know if you have any plans, but if you do, you need to change 'em too."

"Let's hear it."

"It's a beautiful day. Jason and Eric are eight years old. How old would you say we were we when we discovered those beech trees at the river?"

"Eight years old."

"Bingo. Let's take the boys to the river and camp under the beech trees. It's a perfect day, and the leaves will be at their golden finest."

"I'd like to, but I really need to go to the office for two or three hours."

"*I really need to go to the office.* You're like a broken record, you know that? What do you have to do this weekend that can't wait till Monday?"

"I just have a busy week coming up. I want to get a head start. The law is a harsh mistress. What can I say?"

"It's like you're married to that place. You're pitiful. Disgusting."

"Jeff, in my twenty-two years of practicing law, I've found that insults are rarely an effective tool of persuasion."

"Then I'll go with shame. If you won't go, I'll take both the boys. Jason loves his Uncle Jeff. His Uncle Jeff will take him camping even if the poor boy's own father can't find the time."

"Okay, okay, I'll work till midnight on Monday. Let me check with Evelyn and make sure we don't have any plans tonight. Hold on a second."

"If you do, change 'em."

"She says I'm good to go. But I've got a question. How will we get all our gear out there? It's not like the boys can carry all that much."

"I thought of the solution before you thought of the problem. We'll make two trips. I'll come to your house with Eric at one o'clock. We'll leave the boys there, park at the end of Meadowbrook, and hike in with half our stuff. Then we'll go back and get the other half and the boys. I'll handle dinner and bring us a Cabernet for tonight and sandwiches for lunch tomorrow. You do breakfast."

"Sounds good. We'll be ready."

They played the quiet game on the hike in with the boys and saw half a dozen deer, including a buck with at least a ten-point rack. They put up their tents under the canopy of gold and had a campfire going by the time the sun went down. When the barred owls started calling, Jeff joined the chorus, but there were too many to know if they were calling to him or each other.

Sam offered an observation. "You've been talking to birds nearly all your life, haven't you?"

"Sure. Not all birds, but some."

"You know what that makes you, don't you?"

"I give up. What?"

"A birdbrain." The boys were used to hearing Jeff tease Sam, not the other way around.

"You're just envious because I'm the bird whisperer."

They had hot dogs roasted over the fire on coat hangers for dinner and s'mores for dessert. Then it was time for music. Sam and Jeff chose mostly songs by John Prine, but they sang others too. They loved to sing "Sweet Baby James" while sitting by their fire because it's about a cowboy who sings while sitting by his. When they sang Prine's "Please Don't Bury Me," the boys tried to sing along and asked some questions at the end. Sam, the expert on all things Prine, had all the answers.

"Why does he say Milwaukee should get his stomach if they run out of beer? What's Milwaukee?" asked Eric.

"It's a city in Wisconsin. Way up north. They brew a lot of beer there and drink a lot too. John Prine drinks beer. If Milwaukee runs out, they can get more from his stomach."

"That's weird," Jason opined. "Why does he say to put his socks in a cedar box?"

"Because his feet stink, so his socks stink too. A cedar box smells good, so put his socks in one and close the lid."

"What is Venus de Milo?" It was Eric again. "Is that another city? Why does it get his arms?"

"Not a city. It's a famous statue of a woman. The statue doesn't have any arms, so John says it can have his. Why not? He doesn't need them in heaven."

Jason had one more. "And it says deaf people can take his ears but only if they don't mind the size. I understand why a deaf person would need ears, but why does he say that about the size?"

"'Cause he has big ears."

"Does John Prine really have big ears?" asked Eric.

"Beats me. I've never noticed. Have you, Jeff?"

"Not me."

"John Prine's a funny man, isn't he?" asked Jason.

"Sure is," answered Sam.

"I sure like his songs," Eric added.

"And you'll like 'em even more when you're our age," Jeff said.

"He's the best," Sam concluded. "None better."

Jeff raised his tin cup chalice of Cabernet and offered a toast: "To John Prine, the best ever."

Sam and Jeff enjoyed reading to their children at bedtime. The girls had outgrown it, but the boys still loved it. The Thompsons and Freemans often read the same book at the same time so the boys wouldn't miss a night if one of them slept over at the other's house.

They were currently reading *Watership Down,* the magical novel about rabbits by Richard Adams, and were nearing the end. With the boys in their laps, they took turns reading until they finished. Then they led the boys to their tents, got them situated in their sleeping bags, and returned to their chairs. Sam added two sticks to the fire, then brought it back to life by poking it with a third. He looked up at Jeff. "Thank you for calling me this morning. This has been great."

"You're welcome."

"Litigation is just so consuming. At least once a week, I start thinking about one of my cases while I'm in the shower. When I'm ready to get out, I don't know if I've washed my hair, so I wash it again to make sure. Sometimes I wish I'd been a banker or a car salesman."

"Maybe it's litigation, Sam, but maybe it's you. You went to your eight o'clock class after we worked all night at the power plant. You were second in your class at Prep and the Founders' Medal winner at Millsaps. If you were selling cars, I bet you'd be up half the night memorizing the specs of the new models. It's the way you're wired."

"Maybe so. Who knows?"

"And you'd be even worse if not for me. I'm a good influence."

"You were today, but not always. Sometimes you're a terrible influence."

"Not true. I amn't a terrible influence."

"Amn't's not a word."

"Well, it should be. Isn't's a word. Aren't's a word. Amn't should be a word too. But it's not, so instead we have ain't. Sounds ugly and ignorant. Amn't should be a word. I protest."

"Protest all you want. Make your case to Merriam-Webster. Maybe you'll win them over and become famous. Jeff Freeman, the father of amn't."

After breakfast they followed a trail that led south along the river. Sam and Jeff didn't try to get the boys to play the quiet game this time, and any wildlife in their path took cover or scattered to the four winds. After a mile or so, they came to a large pond that owed its existence to an impressive beaver dam that kept it from emptying down a creek bed into the Pearl.

Sam pointed to the lodge in the middle of the pond. "That's where they live."

The boys stared at the lodge. There was no sign of movement. "Where are they? What are they doing?" Jason asked.

Jeff looked at his watch. "It's 9:30 on Sunday morning," he said. "They're probably lying in bed reading the *New York Times* or watching *Meet the Press.* Tim Russert is great." The boys continued to stare, but there was still no sign of life.

Sam and Jeff headed back to the car after lunch with the boys and half their gear and drove them home. Then they returned to the river for the other half. When they reached their campsite, Jeff proposed another change of plans. "You know what we should do? We should spend another night. We've got a tent and two sleeping bags. We can have another fire and sing some more. We sounded fabulous last night."

"But it's a school night. I need to get to the office at a decent hour."

"We'll break camp at dawn. You can be at your desk by 8:30."

"But we don't have anything to eat or drink."

"There you go, being a party pooper again. What do you think the pioneers and fur trappers did when they were in the wilderness with nothing to eat or drink? Did they just give up and walk out to their car and drive home? They did not. They found things they could eat and drink. They lived off the land. I'll go look."

Before Sam could object, Jeff headed down the trail. What had he dreamed up this time? Sam found out in five minutes.

"Look what I found! Nature provideth!" Jeff had a cooler in one hand and a bag of charcoal in the other.

"I don't think nature provided that," Sam responded. "And I don't think that qualifies as living off the land either."

"Does too. The cooler and charcoal were sitting right there on the land behind a tree. Let's see what's in the cooler. Whaddaya know?

We're in luck! Two filets, a Caesar salad, some Sister Schubert rolls, and a bottle of Glenfiddich. What are the odds?"

"How'd that cooler get out here. You didn't bring it yesterday."

"Did too."

"No, you didn't. I would have noticed."

"Did too. Scout's honor. Put on your thinking cap, Mr. Founders' Medal Dude. Show me what you got in that big brain of yours. If I brought it yesterday but you didn't notice, what does that mean?"

"I'd say it means I walked out here twice and you walked out here three times."

"Bingo. I came yesterday morning after we talked, then went home and got Eric and came to your house."

"I'll be damned. I hope I've got cell service so I can call Evelyn."

"No need."

"What are you talking about? She'll be worried sick if I don't show up."

"No, she won't."

"She already knows, doesn't she?"

"Bingo again."

# Chapter Fourteen

May 17, 2014

A Big Win and a Big Surprise

The first four and a half months of 2014 were all work and no play for Sam. He was completely consumed defending a securities-fraud class action in federal court in Jackson. His client was the regional wealth management firm where Jeff worked. Sam had able assistants working with him—a young partner, two associates, and his longtime paralegal—but the client was looking to him, not to them, and he always found it difficult to delegate. He wanted to go over every witness examination and edit every brief. It wasn't that he didn't trust his team; it was that there was always room for improvement. As a result, nobody on the team worked harder than its oldest member. Sam spent six days a week, twelve hours a day, getting ready for trial, then picked up the pace to seven days and fourteen hours when the trial began in early April.

But all the hard work paid off. The afternoon before, against all odds, the jury returned a unanimous verdict for Sam's client. The lawyers representing the class of plaintiffs kicked themselves for turning down a settlement offer in the high seven figures. Sam celebrated that night with his trial team and officials from Jeff's firm. Jeff was there to offer a toast. It was his victory too. He'd recommended hiring Sam to head the defense team when the suit was filed.

Now they were having a second, smaller celebration, for both Sam's victory and Jeff's birthday. He would turn fifty-four in two days. They were dining with Evelyn and Olivia at their favorite

Jackson restaurant, Walker's Drive In, a seventy-year-old institution on North State Street in the city's Fondren district. When the art deco restaurant opened in the 1940s, carhops served burgers, fries, and shakes. Now the restaurant offered some of the finest dining in the South.

The stifling heat of the Mississippi summer would come soon enough, but it was still pleasant in the evening in mid-May, and the couples chose one of the wrought-iron tables on the restaurant's patio. Friends saw them and came over to congratulate Sam on his victory. A young woman in the passenger seat of a convertible on State Street, an associate in Sam's firm, yelled "way to go, Sam" when the car passed by. Jeff ordered an expensive bottle of champagne for the occasion, and after the waitress filled their glasses, offered a toast.

"To my best friend Sam, the finest lawyer in town."

Olivia raised her glass, then raised her husband. "Just Jackson, Jeff? I don't think so. To Sam Thompson, the finest lawyer in Mississippi."

Now it was Evelyn's turn. "Y'all need to think bigger. To my wonderful husband, the best lawyer in the South and the best kisser too."

Sam was grinning from ear to ear. Jeff asked him, "So what do you think, Counselor? Best in Jackson, best in the state, or best in the South?"

"I was thinking best in the country, but I won't quibble."

Having been out-toasted, Jeff rose to his feet to make amends. He tapped a spoon on his champagne flute and lifted it high. The other diners on the patio turned to look at him and returned his smile. When he had everyone's attention, he offered a second toast, in a voice loud enough for all to hear. "To Sam Thompson, my best friend and the finest lawyer in America. Not only that, but his lovely wife Evelyn says he's a great kisser too. I'm proud to say I know nothing about that." Everyone on the patio applauded. Sam was too happy to be embarrassed.

The couples were creatures of habit, and all four ordered the same dish, Redfish Anna, a redfish filet sauteed in a charred lemon butter sauce, topped with lump crabmeat, and served over garlic mashed potatoes with thin green beans. Everything Walker's served was excellent, but nothing could beat Redfish Anna.

When their plates were clean, Jeff cleared his throat and said he had an announcement to make. Sam was reminded of the Exalted Ruler's announcement on the flight home from Montana more than twenty years before. Evelyn and Olivia were beaming. From their faces, Sam could tell this would be a surprise only to him.

"An announcement? Well, don't keep me in suspense. Let's hear it."

"You're going on a trip."

"Is that right? Am I going by myself? Or will someone accompany me?"

"No one who's going to kiss you, that's for sure. I'm going, and so are Eric and Jason. We'll spend most of the time outdoors."

Jason had just turned fifteen, and Eric soon would. They had both recently attained the rank of Eagle in Troop 1, the troop in which their fathers had become Eagle Scouts nearly four decades before. Like Sam and Jeff, the boys loved the outdoors.

"And just what will we do on this trip?"

"I don't know everything, but we'll definitely camp and hike. Probably do some rafting. Perhaps catch a few fish."

"Sounds like you've planned our entire trip without consulting me."

"Is that a problem?"

"I would never plan a trip for you without consulting you."

"Au contraire, Kemosabe. Not only would you do it, but you have most certainly done it. Surely you remember the time you planned a trip for me without bothering to tell me."

"I don't remember it, and I deny it."

"I bet you ten bucks you did it and another ten that you remember it. It was to Charleston nearly thirty years ago. You scheduled me to be there without even asking if I was available. You planned my entire itinerary, from morning to night."

"That was our wedding. That's different."

"And that was after you asked this woman to marry you without securing my approval and before I even met her."

"But you approve now, don't you?"

"Of Evelyn, most definitely, but you deprived me of the opportunity to warn her that she was about to marry a workaholic who would soon start losing his hair."

Evelyn and Olivia loved watching them when they carried on like this.

"So when is this trip you planned without consulting me?"

"We leave on Wednesday, four days from now. The boys have their last exams at Prep on Monday. They don't know about the trip yet. They'll have a day to get ready."

"I hate to rain on your trip parade, Jeff, but I can't go anywhere other than the Coast on Wednesday. I'm deposing the plaintiff in a breach-of-contract case in Gulfport on Thursday, and I've got a hearing in Oxford the following Tuesday."

"I hate to rain on your work parade, Counselor, but the deposition's been postponed, and the hearing's been continued."

"What? How did that happen?"

"I know people who get things done, Sam. Your calendar is clear for three weeks starting Wednesday."

"Three weeks? I can't take off three weeks. I didn't even do that for our twenty-fifth anniversary."

"Sam, let me ask you a question. How many hours have you billed so far this year?"

Sam smiled. "I don't know. I've been too busy to keep up."

"Well, I know. Lydia told me. She's one of the people I know."

"You asked my secretary about my billable hours?"

"I did, and she told me. Maybe it was none of my business, but too bad. She told me you could take off three months and would still be ahead of the game. I know you'd never do that, but you will take off three weeks. The trip is booked, and you're going."

"So tell me about this trip I may be going on."

"Are going on. We fly to Denver on Wednesday and rent a car. We have a guide lined up to fish for trout on the Blue River the next day, but first we're going to Red Rocks Amphitheatre Wednesday night."

"Cool. I've been wanting to see a show there forever. Who's playing?"

"Oh, what's that guy's name? Short guy. John something. You know him; he did that song about old people, Hello something."

"Don't tell me we're seeing Prine at Red Rocks."

"John Prine, that's the one."

"You're kidding."

"We have seats on the third row in the middle. Sorry, but first and second were sold out. The boys and I are going, but if you don't want to join us on this trip I planned without consulting you, I'm sure I can find someone else who would be grateful to have your seat."

"Hot damn."

"I thought for sure I'd get a scalding hot damn for that."

"You're right. Hot as the surface of the sun damn. Prine and trout fishing the next day. Then what?"

"I figure two or three days hiking and camping in Rocky Mountain National Park. After that we'll head northwest to the Tetons and Yellowstone, then up to Glacier. I'm thinking we'll have ten days for the three parks."

"Cool."

"The boys are gonna love it."

"I suspect my bride has been a co-conspirator in your shenanigans. True?"

"It was her idea. She's quite pleased with herself, as she should be. She figured you'd be desperate for a trip after you lost your big case, which everybody was sure you would. But it's too late to call it off now. I've spent too much time planning it. I bet I spent three weeks planning our three-week trip."

Sam reached over for Evelyn's hand. "So three or four days in Colorado, then ten or so in Wyoming and Montana. What do you have in store for us for the last week?"

"We head back south to a tiny town in Idaho called Stanley."

"Never heard of it."

"Fewer than a hundred people live there, but it's where our outfitter is."

"Outfitter for what?"

"For our six-day raft trip on the Middle Fork of the Salmon."

"Wow! That's supposed to be one of the best."

"Then the next day we drive to Boise, turn in our rental, and fly home to our wives and the heat."

"After three weeks, I'll take the heat to see my hot wife."

"You're a smart man to say that. And here's the best part. All of it—flights, rental car, beer, John Prine tickets, fishing guide, food, more beer, raft trip, the whole works—won't cost either of us a dime."

"What? Who's gonna pay for it?"

"Your grateful client. My firm is picking up the tab. It was our chairman's idea, and the board approved it unanimously this morning. Eric and I get our trip paid for too because I'm the brilliant guy who recommended we hire the best lawyer in America."

"That's very generous, but I can't take a gift from a client without the firm's blessing."

"Already blessed. Our chairman called your managing partner. You've made your firm a lot of money this year, and you saved my firm far more. It's gonna be great. The Middle Fork is filled with cutthroats."

"Sounds wonderful, but what about everybody else who worked on the case? I can't go on a fancy trip on the client's nickel if they get nothing."

"I told my boss you'd say that. I know you pretty well, you know. Not to worry. We're making generous gifts to all of them."

"Including my paralegal?"

"And Lydia and the other members of your staff who went the extra mile."

"You know you're my hero, don't you?"

"Hey, wait a minute," said Evelyn, "I thought I was your hero."

"Jeff's my hero; you're my heroine."

"You're a smart man to say that," Jeff said again.

The waitress arrived with a single serving of bread pudding and four spoons. It was topped with one candle. Jeff blew it out, Sam sang the first line of "Happy Birthday to You," then all the other diners on the patio joined in.

# Chapter Fifteen

June 11, 2014

## Serenading a Grizzly

Sam and Jeff ordered Bloody Marys and settled into their seats for the first of their three flights home. The boys were in the row behind them. When the jury returns a defense verdict in a case your client offered $8 million to settle, you and your companions get to fly first class.

It had been a magnificent trip that rivaled the one to the other side of the country in the summer of 1978, but Sam couldn't wait to get home to Evelyn. This was the longest they'd been apart since their first date nearly thirty years before.

Sam and Jeff both loved to read. They'd finished the four books they bought to bring on the trip from Lemuria, the finest bookstore in Jackson, so they bought paperbacks in the Boise airport for the trip home. Before opening them, they decided to review the trip from beginning to end.

They agreed that the John Prine show on their first night was the best concert by any artist they'd ever seen, bar none. Both had seen Prine multiple times—Jeff three or four and Sam seven or eight—but never this close to the stage and never in a venue as magnificent as Red Rocks.

That John was still touring was a miracle. He had throat cancer in the late 1990s. The extensive surgery to remove the tumor damaged his vocal cords and gave his head a permanent tilt. His magnificent career as a singer-songwriter appeared to be over. But after a year of voice therapy, he was able to perform again. He was better than ever, and so was his voice.

But his health problems weren't over. More than a decade later, John was again diagnosed with cancer, and part of his left lung had to be removed. Once again, he bounced back. His training regimen was to run up and down the stairs of the home in Nashville he shared with his wife, Fiona, and their sons, then sing two songs. He was now pushing seventy but still touring, and he celebrated beating cancer for the second time by performing with the energy and enthusiasm of a man half his age. His relationship with his fans was a love affair. He loved them as much as they loved him.

On the brisk, clear night in Colorado, John played all his old standards, including "Sam Stone," "Angel from Montgomery," "Hello in There," "Far from Me," and "Illegal Smile." All the songs were written at least four decades earlier, when John was much too young to be so wise. And yet he was.

John rarely played other artists' songs. He said he had a hard enough time remembering how to play his own. In his set at Red Rocks, which lasted more than two hours, he played only one cover, but it was a special one. "Clay Pigeons," written by the late Blaze Foley, is a beautiful ballad about a man who takes a trip on a Greyhound bus to change the shape that he's in, get back in the game, and start playing again. When John introduced the song, he said he should have written it.

Sam, Jeff, and the boys sang along to nearly all the songs at Red Rocks, including "Clay Pigeons," which John recorded for his album *Fair & Square* nearly a decade earlier. Sam and Jeff had made certain all four of their children would know and love the music of John Prine. When the boys were younger, their favorites were the funny ones: "Please Don't Bury Me" as well as "Dear Abby" and "That's the Way the World Goes Round," which features a verse about a man who gets stuck in the ice while taking a bath when the radiator breaks and the water freezes. He starts crying ice cubes and hoping he'll die, but then the sun comes out, the ice melts, and he stands up and laughs at the absurdity of it all. From hoping to croak to laughing at the joke, the verse concludes, is the way that the world goes round.

After Prine performed "Lake Marie," with the line about the

couple hoping to save their marriage and perhaps catch a few fish, Jeff turned to Sam and the boys. He and Olivia were struggling to save their marriage, but he was in a fine mood and focused instead on the couple's second goal. When the song ended, he promised they would catch more fish than they could count on the Blue River the next day.

Another gifted songwriter, Josh Ritter, opened the show and, in keeping with tradition, returned to the stage to help John close it. They first performed a beautiful version of "Mexican Home," John's haunting ballad about the death of his father when he was only fifty-seven. In the last verse, after his father dies on an August afternoon, John sips bourbon with a friend and cries by the light of the moon.

They ended the show with "Paradise," the song on John's first album named for the tiny town in western Kentucky where his parents grew up. When John's parents took him and his brothers home to Paradise to visit relatives, he said his four grandparents treated him like something they found under a Christmas tree. While John was in the Army in Europe, his father sent him a letter telling him Paradise had been wiped off the map. The TVA had bought the land to make way for the Peabody Coal Company to build the world's largest coal-fired power plant.

The town was gone, but John kept the memory alive in what became his signature song. Sam and Jeff and the boys sang along to the third verse, in which the coal company tortures the timber and strips all the land, and to the chorus, in which John wants to go back to Paradise, but his daddy says it's too late—Mr. Peabody's coal train has hauled it away.

John's father died before John's first album was released but not before hearing his recording of "Paradise." John brought it home and played it on a reel-to-reel tape player. His dad sat in the dark in another room so he could pretend he was listening to it on a jukebox.

After a long standing ovation when they came to the end of "Paradise," the crowd filed out into the night in silence. It wasn't like other great concerts. Sam and the boys remained quiet on the

Day two of the trip was almost as special as day one. Jeff knew it would be hard to rouse the boys after they got up before dawn to head to the Jackson airport the day before and stayed up until midnight after the Prine concert, so he arranged to meet the fishing guide at two o'clock. They slept late, showered for what would be the last time for several days, then headed to the nearest Waffle House. Sam was at the wheel, as always. He liked to drive, and Jeff liked to navigate, choose the music, and provide running commentary. They no longer debated the issue. Unless they were in Jeff's BMW, Sam kept the car keys from the beginning of every trip to the end.

After ordering but before the food arrived, Jeff told them his oft-repeated Waffle House story. Sam and Eric had heard it many times, but this was the first time for Jason. Years earlier, a group of Jeff's colleagues had gone to a Waffle House on the Gulf Coast. They slid into a booth and ran their mouths instead of looking at the menu. When the busy waitress arrived and demanded orders, there was no time for deliberation. The first one to order said he would have the pancakes.

To finish the story with a bang, Jeff stood up beside the booth and impersonated the waitress. He thrust out one hip and put a hand on it, stuck a straw in the corner of his mouth, and said it was a Marlboro Light. He squinted his right eye because of the imaginary cigarette smoke, then declared in a disgusted tone, "Mister, this here's the Waffle House. We ain't got no pancakes." The customers in the adjoining booths stopped chewing and stared.

All four ordered All-Star Specials: bacon, eggs over easy, waffles, toast, and hashbrowns. Jason and Eric ate every bite of theirs, then polished off what their dads couldn't finish. Sam said there was a time when he and Jeff could wolf it down like that. Loaded with carbs, they headed into the mountains to fish.

It was a bluebird day on the Blue River. As they walked quietly toward the bank, their guide, Robbie, spoke in a hushed tone. "Looks like we'll have some competition from the real thing." A hatch was rising from the bottom of the stream. Trout feeding on the tiny flies before they could rise into the air dimpled the surface. Robbie caught one in mid-air and selected four artificial ones to match.

After tying on the flies, Sam, Jeff, and the boys waded into the stream. They were twenty yards apart, far enough to give them room to fish but not so far that they couldn't see when one of the others hooked one. The boys had never fished with dry flies in moving water, but they caught on fast, and the browns and rainbows were hungry and indiscriminate. The rule was catch and release with barbless hooks, which was fine by Sam and Jeff. They loved catching and eating trout, but the two steps in the middle—cleaning and cooking—not so much. Other than moving the quartet of fishermen upstream every so often so they could fish new water, Robbie had nothing to do. He lay back in the grass and enjoyed the warm spring day. It was rarely this easy.

After two hours, Jeff and the boys showed no sign of stopping, but Sam had caught enough. He sat down in the grass beside Robbie with the sun on his back, watched the others fish, and enjoyed the sights and sounds of the mountain stream. The river made beautiful music as it descended over the rocks, and the surface sparkled like diamonds in the sunlight. Sam told the guide there was nothing in all the world that could look and sound better. Robbie begged to differ. His girlfriend, he said, was gorgeous and sang like an angel.

Robbie had brought a small soft-side cooler to the river and pulled out two beer bottles, one from inside, one from a pocket on the outside. Condensation ran down the side of the ice-cold one, a Moose Drool. The other was a Founders Breakfast Stout, best served at fifty degrees. He told Sam to pick one; he would drink the other.

"Robbie, my man! I usually say Jeff's my hero, but you're my hero today. Let's see what we have here. I love a Moose Drool, but I don't know the other one." He took the Breakfast Stout and studied the label. "I'm guessing this isn't what Kris had for breakfast. Craft beers weren't a thing back then." Robbie looked to be around thirty. Sam figured he would have to explain the allusion to Kristofferson's "Sunday Morning Coming Down"—the song was older than the guide—but he was wrong.

"Kris didn't have one more of these for dessert either, and that's a good thing," Robbie said. "It's more than eight percent alcohol. If he'd had two of these, he would have stumbled back to bed instead of down the stairs. He wouldn't have put on his cleanest dirty shirt, smelled the chicken frying, or heard the Sunday school singing. And that, my friend, would have been a tragedy. This stout is not for the faint of heart, but it's delicious."

"Then I'll try it. Says here it's flavored with roasted coffee. Got to be better than that weak stuff we had at Waffle House this morning."

Sam took a sip, then heard Jason yell. The three fishermen still in the river had all hooked trout at the same time. Sam and Robbie walked to the bank to watch the action. Jeff and Jason soon reeled in their fish and released them, then all eyes turned to Eric. His rod was bent into the shape of a fishhook. He'd hooked the fish of the day.

Robbie called out advice. "Keep the line tight, but don't force him. He'll break off. Let him tire himself out."

The magnificent rainbow jumped three times, then made three runs, one upstream, one down, and one to the opposite bank. But the hook held, and the leader didn't snap. Eric was breathing hard when he slid the fish into shallow water and picked it up for the others to admire. Robbie produced a tape measure. Twenty-two inches, which he declared was the biggest rainbow of the year so far. Sam pulled out his iPhone and took a photo of Eric and one of Robbie and Eric, then asked Robbie to take one of the four of them. The handsome trout was the centerpiece in all three. Eric then kissed the fish on the head and lowered it into the water. The trout hesitated briefly, then swished its tail and was gone.

They hiked the next two days in Rocky Mountain National Park.

The first night was perfect for a campfire, and they told stories for three hours. The boys said little but listened intently. They were learning from two accomplished practitioners of the art. The next day dawned clear and cold. They weren't yet acclimated to the elevation, so they chose two relatively easy trails, five miles out and back in the morning to Ouzel Falls, named for John Muir's favorite bird, and the six-mile Bear Lake Area Loop in the afternoon. They saw herds of elk in the meadows below the trails and mule deer in the woods alongside them. Marmots peered at them from the rocks.

They were looking forward to another night by the fire when they made it back to camp, but clouds came rolling in just before dark and it started to rain. They managed to boil water for their dehydrated meals, which they ate while sitting in their tents. There was nothing to do after that but crawl into their sleeping bags and read.

In addition to the books from Lemuria, Jeff ordered a copy of *Night of the Grizzlies* to bring on the trip. The book by Jack Olsen was about one night in the summer of 1967 when two grizzly bears killed two nineteen-year-old girls in Glacier National Park. They were the first two fatal maulings since the park was founded nearly half a century earlier. Jeff thought it would be fun to give Sam the book so he would have something to think about while they were camping in Glacier.

The sky was clear by morning, and they caucused and decided to break camp. They would take one more hike, spend some time in the town of Estes Park, then drive up to Wyoming and find a hotel in Cheyenne. After the unpleasant night in the rain, Sam and Jeff were ready for a hot shower. After two nights of dehydrated meals, Jason and Eric wanted pizza or a cheeseburger.

They chose a longer, harder hike than the two the previous day. They would climb five miles up to Sky Pond via Glacier Gorge Trail with nearly 1,800 feet of elevation gain, then descend to the trailhead. Sam and Jeff were in decent shape, but nothing they did at home three hundred feet above sea level could prepare two men in their mid-fifties for a steep climb at high elevation. They stopped often, took their time, and cursed the boys under their breath. For the teenagers, it was a piece of cake.

The hike featured a beautiful mountain stream, multiple lakes and waterfalls, and magnificent views. When they stopped to take a breather and gaze at the snow-covered peaks, Sam switched to a Brooklyn accent and said, "This looks nothin' like Mississippi." It was a reference to another of his stories. Many years before, when the Bar Convention was still held at the Broadwater Beach Hotel on the Mississippi Coast, Sam saw an older couple at a marina leaning on the rail, staring at the murky water. When he walked past them, the man complained to his wife in the accent Sam imitated, "This looks nothin' like the brochure," which he pronounced "broshooa."

Sam and Jeff got even with the boys as they hiked through snowfields near the top of the trail. The men had trekking poles, but Jason and Eric had turned down Jeff's offer to buy them some. They slipped and fell multiple times while their dads marched past with the aid of their poles. The foursome reached glorious Sky Pond at nearly 11,000 feet, opened their day packs, and ate beef jerky, apples, and Raisinettes. After wandering around the lake, they hiked back down to the trailhead in half the time it had taken to hike up. They spent only an hour in Estes Park, which was too touristy for their tastes. The boys got ice cream cones, their dads a beer apiece. As the sun began to set, they climbed back into the rental for the drive east through Loveland, then up to Cheyenne on I-25.

As part of Jeff's extensive preparation for the trip, he burned half a dozen CDs while Sam was in trial. The trip was in the works long before Jeff's firm decided to foot the bill. The generous gift was the cherry on top.

The CDs included nearly a hundred songs, with a limit of two per artist. It was the music of their lives, from the late 1960s to the present. Jeff included famous artists, but he also included songs by contemporary Americana singer-songwriters, including a young genius named John Fullbright, Kevin Welch, Houston Marchman, Hayes Carll, Walt Wilkins, and James McMurtry. McMurtry came by his writing chops naturally. His father Larry wrote *Lonesome Dove*.

It was dark by the time they reached the interstate, and they spotted city lights in the distance when they topped a rise near the Wyoming border. Headlights climbed toward them in the southbound lanes. Jeff had been waiting for this. He punched the eject button, put in a new CD, and forwarded it to the fourth track. When Sam heard the first notes, he didn't take his eyes off the road, but he reached over and patted Jeff's arm. It was "Lights of Cheyenne," one of McMurtry's finest. Sam and Jeff sang along.

When the song ended, Sam repeated his favorite line. The diesels grinding up from the plain, McMurtry wrote, were all bunched up like pearls on a string. Jeff looked into the back seat. The boys were fast asleep. He wished they were awake to see the lights of Cheyenne while they listened to "Lights of Cheyenne."

More than a hundred mountains in Colorado are taller than the Tetons of northwest Wyoming, but none is more dramatic. Most mountains in Colorado ascend gradually from a high base elevation, but there is nothing gradual about the Tetons. They rise straight up from Jackson Hole, the valley that lies east of the range. The Grand Teton, the tallest of the Tetons, is 13,770 feet tall, nearly a mile and a quarter higher than the valley below.

Sam and Jeff had camped and hiked in the Tetons but never approached them by car from the east. The boys had never seen them at all. At three o'clock, when they reached Togwotee Pass at nearly 10,000 feet, the snow-capped mountains thirty-five miles across Jackson Hole came into view. Sam pulled over, and the boys took photos to send home to their friends. Then they descended for the drive across the valley. Along the way, they spotted a dozen antelopes and a herd of elk.

As they approached the mountains, Jeff asked a question: "Boys, you know how the Tetons got their name?"

"Seriously?" asked Sam. "You're going to tell them that?"

"Come on, Sam. Jason's fifteen; he's already shaving. If he takes after you, his hairline will soon be receding. Eric'll be fifteen in two weeks. Remember when we were their age? Boys, raise your hand if you've noticed that girls and women have breasts." Two hands shot up. "I thought so. Now raise your hand if you like them." Two hands again. "Good answer."

Sam capitulated. "And you claim you're a good influence. Okay, go ahead."

Jeff smiled and began. "French-Canadian fur trappers were out here in the mountains, far from home, trapping for beaver. They had no female companions. Not one. They were lonely."

"How lonely?" Jason asked. He liked to give Jeff the opportunity to embellish.

"They were forlorn. So lonesome they could cry. As lonely as a man can be. And, like you and Eric and your father and me, the trappers liked breasts. They missed them. They hadn't snuggled up against a plump pair in what seemed like forever. And when one of them gazed up and stared at the top of these magnificent mountains, guess what that poor, lonesome man imagined they looked like."

Eric leaned over so he could see the tops of the peaks through the gap between the front seats. "They don't look like boobs to me. I mean breasts."

"Ah," his dad said, "but you're not lonely like the lonely trappers were. Tetons is a French word. What do you think it means in English? Any ideas?"

Eric hazarded a guess. "Tits?"

"Bingo," Jeff confirmed.

He turned in his seat and held up his right hand. Both boys high-fived him. Sam shook his head. It was always three against one.

They crossed the Snake River and parked in a lot near the base of the mountains. Sam checked his watch. "If we hustle, we can hike the Jenny Lake Loop before we make camp. It's seven miles but flat."

Jeff agreed. "Let's do it. We'll sleep when we're dead."

"Sleep when we're dead?" asked Jason.

Eric provided the two-word explanation: "Warren Zevon."

It was Sunday, the day before Memorial Day. The trail was crowded, and not just with people. Jason and Eric, who were out in front, came upon a trio of mule deer under a stand of firs on the edge of the trail. The boys approached within ten feet, but the deer stood their ground. When Sam and Jeff caught up, the deer were still there. "What's wrong with them?" Jason asked. "Why don't they run away?"

"I'm afraid they've been afflicted with something your dad and I call National Park Disorder," Jeff explained.

"What?"

"National Park Disorder. Animals are smarter than we give them credit for. There's no hunting in national parks, and the animals have figured it out. People aren't a threat, so they're not afraid of us. Sam and I have seen it in parks all over the country, and we've seen just the opposite in national forests. Hunting is legal there, and the wild animals really are wild. The deer don't pose for pictures like the ones here. If these deer had opposable thumbs instead of cloven hooves, they might be sitting at a table signing autographs."

They walked across the bridge spanning the steep creek connecting Jenny and String Lakes and returned to the car, then drove to Jenny Lake Campground and set up their tents. They had nothing for dinner, so they drove into the town of Jackson. The boys had gotten their pizza fix in Cheyenne, so they went with burgers, but they chose options they couldn't get back home. Jason picked elk; Eric chose bison. Sam and Jeff ordered ribeyes. The boys vetoed dehydrated meals in favor of real food for the next two nights, so they went grocery shopping after dinner.

Their hikes the next three days featured magnificent views, beautiful wildflowers, massive evergreens, cascading waterfalls, and creeks running loud and swift with snowmelt. They saw an abundance of wildlife, including deer, elk, moose, pikas, marmots, and one memorable bear.

On the first day, they hiked to Phelps Lake, then climbed along Death Creek between the sheer granite cliffs that marked the entrance to Death Canyon. After the trail levelled, they came upon an obstacle, a huge bull moose standing astride the trail. They shouted and waved their arms. Annoyed, the moose finally ambled to one side and let them pass. When they came to a meadow strewn with enormous boulders, they climbed to the top of one to have lunch. Jeff winked at the boys, then spoke to Sam.

"Sam, did you recognize that moose?"

"Recognize him?"

"Yeah, that was the same bull moose we saw in that creek on the Allagash."

"You're crazy. That wasn't the same moose."

"Was too. Looked exactly the same, only bigger. And he stared at us exactly the same way. Like he didn't have a care in the world. It was the same moose alright."

"When was that, 1978? That was thirty-six years ago. No way the Allagash moose could still be alive."

"So you're now an expert on the life expectancy of moose in the wild, are you?"

"No, but I don't need to be."

"Don't claim you know what you don't know, Sam. It's the same moose, I'm telling you."

"No, it's not. Even if that moose were still alive, what would it be doing in the Tetons? Maine must be 2,500 miles from here."

"Did you see the legs on that moose? Long and strong, wouldn't you say?"

"Sure, but so what?"

"Here's so what. That moose could walk here from Maine in two months, three if he stopped to see the sights. And as you just conceded, he's had thirty-six years to make the trip. I don't have a calculator, but that's less than a hundred miles a year."

"But why on earth would a moose leave his home in the North Woods of Maine to come to Wyoming? He looked pretty content there, as I recall."

"To see the world, that's why. We paddled the Allagash, and now we're exploring Wyoming. So is the moose."

Sam turned to Eric. "I hate to break it to you, but your father is crazy."

"No doubt about it," said Eric, "but I've been wondering who's crazier, my father or the man who's arguing with him."

"Touché," said Jason, and high-fived Eric. It was three against one again. They finished their lunch and retraced their steps to the trailhead.

They had a great time around the campfire that night. The boys were now in the swing of things and told their share of stories. Inspired by the story of the naming of the Tetons, Eric told Sam and Jeff about Emily Latham. She was the first girl in their class to have big boobs. She grew them in the sixth grade. The boobs made Emily a sensation, and she knew it. Eric said all the boys in the class were mesmerized. Jason corrected him. "Hypnotized, more like it."

Sam knew he wasn't supposed to laugh, but he did. Jeff not only laughed, but he offered a toast with his Moose Drool to big boobs. Jason and Eric raised their soft drinks in agreement. Sam surrendered and clinked the other bottles with his beer. The trip was a rite of passage for the boys. Their relationships with their fathers were changing.

The hike the next day was the longest and hardest of the trip, more than fifteen miles round trip up Cascade Canyon to Solitude Lake and back, with an elevation gain of 2,500 feet. They again had grand views and the sights and sounds of a mountain stream to keep them company, this time Cascade Creek. They saw another bull moose in a meadow beside the trail. As they walked past, Jeff noted that this was a different moose.

By the time they reached the lake, Sam and Jeff were exhausted. They took a nap after lunch while their tireless sons explored the picturesque cirque. Then they headed back down to the trailhead, where they caught the ferry across Jenny Lake to keep from having to walk around it again. They made it back to camp at 6:30 and put filets on the grill. Because of the long, hard day, the campfire was much quieter than usual. All but Sam turned in by nine o'clock. He loved to sit alone by a dying fire, but he soon dozed off. When the chill awakened him at midnight, he joined Jason in their tent.

For their last day in the Tetons, they picked a trail that wasn't much shorter than the one the day before, but they could hike it much faster by riding to the top, then walking down. After breaking camp, they drove to Teton Village, the ski resort just south of the park. After a big breakfast, they hitched a ride on the ski tram to the top of Rendezvous Mountain, where the temperature was much lower than at the bottom. They felt cold and foolish in their shorts and tee shirts.

The hike began above the tree line and offered magnificent views of the tallest of the Tetons to the north. As they descended, they saw more waterfalls and wildlife. They walked past several more deer that were afflicted with National Park Disorder and more moose, which were no longer a novelty. Jeff declared that the plural of moose was meese—goose/geese, why not moose/meese?—but for once the boys sided with Sam. Meese was voted down three to one.

As they rounded a curve in the trail with Eric in the lead, they came upon an animal with its head down and its large, dark-brown rump aimed their way. It appeared to be another moose. Eric approached cautiously. The other three arrived and bunched up like McMurtry's pearls. Then they heard a huff, and the animal stood up on its hind legs and turned around. It was a huge black bear, and it was much too close for comfort. The four pearls shifted into reverse and slowly backed away. The bear lost interest, ambled down the ridge below the trail, and the hikers' heart rates returned to normal.

They descended the length of Granite Canyon, accompanied for the third day in a row by a mountain stream, then turned back south and returned to Teton Village. Going downhill all the way, they covered nearly thirteen miles in less than five hours. They weren't exhausted like the day before, but the descent of 4,000 vertical feet had taken a toll. Sam and Jeff were sore—their backs, knees, and feet. The boys, as always, were unaffected. They grabbed a late lunch in the same place they'd had breakfast, then headed north to Yellowstone.

The two national parks in the northwest corner of Wyoming are less than ten miles apart, but Yellowstone is nothing like the Tetons, or anywhere else for that matter. Yellowstone doesn't have mountains as grand as the Tetons, but its geothermal features—geysers, hot springs, fumaroles, and mudpots—are unique and amazing. The Grand Canyon of the Yellowstone is magnificent, and wildlife is everywhere. The elk in the park are also afflicted with National Park Disorder and lounge like oversize dogs in populated areas. Herds of bison have the disorder too and often cause traffic jams. Gray wolves don't have it and are rarely seen, but they keep the park's elk and deer populations in check. Bears, both black and grizzly, are plentiful.

Jeff had decided they would be tourists rather than campers during their short time in Yellowstone. They would spend the first night in the southwest corner of the park in the historic Old Faithful Inn, which opened its doors more than a century earlier. The next night they would stay in the Mammoth Hot Springs Hotel near Roosevelt Arch and the park's northern boundary. In between they would see all the sights they could pack into a single day. Jeff's plan for the morning after they stayed in Mammoth would be easy to sell to Sam, but the teenagers might balk.

They arrived at Old Faithful a little before seven p.m. A sign posted outside the inn said the geyser was due to erupt in eight minutes. They walked out to the crowded boardwalk and waited. Right on time, water at just below the boiling point started spitting from the surface. The fountain gradually grew to a height of more than 150 feet, then lost strength and began dropping. The eruption was all over in a few minutes. Pressure then began to build for the next one, which would take place in ninety minutes or so. As they left the boardwalk, Sam used the geyser to teach the boys a lesson. "Gentlemen," he said, "as you go through life, strive to be as faithful as Old Faithful."

They returned to the car for their bags and walked into the magnificent lobby of the inn, which was dominated by an enormous stone fireplace stretching eighty-five feet to the roof. After showering for the first time in nearly four days, they dined on fresh rainbow trout, then turned in.

To beat the crowd, they rose early and hiked the easy five miles through Upper Geyser Basin before breakfast. The scene was otherworldly. Sam and Jeff had been here once before, but the boys had not, and they were astonished by the odd shapes and magnificent colors of the hot springs and the burbling sounds the water made when it rose to the surface.

After eating, they headed north to Biscuit Basin, which was also strewn with geysers and springs, then climbed a short trail for an elevated view of Grand Prismatic Spring, the largest hot spring in America and the third largest in the world. The water in the spring was deep blue in the middle and light green in the shallows. The spring was surrounded by a layer of yellow on the inside and orange on the outside made of something called microbial mats. The massive spring didn't look real. They came down the trail to see it up close. On the downhill side, the 160-degree water overflowed into the Firehole River at a rate of more than five hundred gallons a minute, warming the river dramatically.

They continued north on the road along the Firehole, then turned northeast and headed for the Grand Canyon of the Yellowstone. Along the way they stopped to see Gibbon Falls, Virginia Cascades, and Artists Paintpots, where a sign warned tourists to watch for flying mud. They ate lunch at Canyon Village, then set out to explore the canyon.

The Yellowstone River rises in the Absaroka Mountains south of the park at almost 13,000 feet, then drops precipitously to Yellowstone Lake. From there it winds its way to the nearly twenty-five-mile-long canyon, then continues north to Montana. The highlights of the canyon are the multi-colored walls and two waterfalls that drop a combined four hundred feet. Many short hikes lead to magnificent views of the canyon. The foursome decided to take as many of the hikes as they could before heading northwest to Mammoth for the night.

Over the next three hours, they saw the canyon from half a dozen overlooks on the North and South Rims. They climbed to Inspiration Point on the North and walked to Artist Point on the South. The volcanic rock of the walls featured nearly every color of the rainbow—from off-white to yellow, orange, red, and deep purple. They saw the waterfalls up close and from a distance. Their last stop was the brink of Lower Falls, where they leaned out over the rail to see the water drop more than three hundred feet before continuing on its way to the sea.

The trail to the falls wasn't long, but it was steep—six hundred feet straight down, then back up. After they finished the climb and were walking back to the car, Jeff checked his watch, saw it was six o'clock, and declared he'd had enough. "I don't know about you boys, but I'm ready for happy hour. I can't wait for that first sip of Moose Drool."

Jason protested. "No fair. I can't drink beer. I wish I could."

Jeff stopped and turned to him. "You can't drink beer? Why on earth not?"

"Daddy won't let me."

"But you're fifteen years old. Surely you're old enough to drink beer. Your dad was sure old enough when he was fifteen." Sam shrugged.

Eric seized the opportunity. "Sweet. I'll be fifteen next week. That means I can start."

Jeff backtracked. "We're not talking about you. We're talking about Jason."

Wildlife was active in the early evening. On the drive north, they came to gatherings of bison and solitary bulls on both sides of the road. One stood motionless in the northbound lane. Jeff leaned over to the driver's side and honked the horn; he was thirsty. There were elk on the treeless hills leading into Mammoth Hot Springs. The bulls' antlers were still covered in velvet, which provides the nutrients that make antlers the fastest-growing bones in the world.

Once they were seated in the hotel dining room, Jeff secured Sam's blessing and a promise from the waiter to look the other way, then ordered a round of Moose Drool for the table. Eric was the first to take a sip. "This is great. Try it, Jason. It's way better than . . . ." His voice trailed off. Jason shook his head.

"My, oh my," Sam exclaimed, "it appears this is not our sons' first beers."

"Knock me over with a feather," Jeff added. "We'll have a serious talk about the importance of moderation and responsibility soon, but we're in Yellowstone National Park now, and this is not the time. Let me instead tell you the plan for tomorrow. We will schedule wake-up calls for five o'clock."

"Five o'clock? Come on, Daddy," Eric protested.

"Don't be a wimp. When did Zevon say we could sleep?"

"But y'all made us get up at 6:30 today. We're growing boys. We need our beauty rest."

"Then sleep in if you want to, gorgeous, but here's what you'll miss. We'll drive east to Lamar Valley, climb to the top of a short hill, and pull out our binoculars. Our goal is to see wolves in the wild. Sam and I have lived more than a century between us, and we've never seen a wolf."

"Sure we have."

"When? Where?"

"In that exhibit in West Yellowstone."

"I mean in the wild. Come on, we're supposed to be on the same team here."

When Sam and Jeff met in the lobby at ten after five, they were alone, and the boys were still asleep when Sam and Jeff returned at 8:30. After they ordered breakfast, Jason asked, "So go ahead and tell us. What did we miss?"

Sam said, "You tell 'em, Jeff." Jeff was better at keeping a straight face.

"It was the most unbelievable thing I've ever seen. You agree, Sam?"

"No doubt about it."

Jeff began. "It was just getting light enough to see. Sam spotted them, three wolves sneaking up on an elk cow. They were spread out and loping along, keeping low and quiet. The elk was standing there, grazing. She didn't suspect a thing. Suddenly, as if on cue, the wolves broke into a sprint. The elk saw them and turned to run. Just when they were about to catch up, a huge bull elk came over the hill and stopped in his tracks. The wolves stopped too, but the cow kept running."

"Wow. What happened then?" Jason was leaning forward.

"It was cold; the elk was breathing smoke. He pawed the ground, daring the wolves to charge. And they did. The first one came straight at him, and the elk rared back on his hind legs and kicked the wolf in the head. The wolf whimpered and retreated. The second one came from the side, and the elk lowered his head and gored him. But the third one jumped on his back and went for his throat. The other two came back in to finish the kill."

"Did they? Did they take him down?"

"They did not. Just when it looked like it was all over, a huge grizzly came rumbling over the ridge. He wanted that elk. The wolves scattered. They wanted no part of the bear. They probably figured they could eat whatever he didn't. The elk was in shock and just stood there as the bear approached."

"Did the grizzly finish him off?"

"He did not. Just as he was about to reach the elk, a bald eagle came swooping low up the valley, not ten feet off the ground. He screeched when he was right over the elk and the bear. They both looked up, and that's when it happened."

"When what happened?"

"The elk trotted off in the same direction as the cow, but here's the crazy part. That grizzly sauntered up to the parking lot, just as pretty as you please, and climbed into a white BMW SUV. I don't know how he squeezed into the driver's seat, but he did. As he drove off, we could hear Steely Dan's 'My Old School' on the stereo. The grizzly's left arm was hanging out the window, and he was keeping time by tapping on the door and singing along. Like I said, the most unbelievable thing I've ever seen."

Eric had been suspicious from the beginning and now spoke for the first time. "Y'all didn't see a thing, did you?"

"Not a thing," Sam confessed.

"Not true," Jeff protested. "We saw a bunch of elk and bison, and a red fox ran across the road."

"But you didn't see any wolves, did you?" Eric was considering law school.

"Well, no."

"No grizzly bear either, am I right?"

"But there are lots of grizzlies in the park."

"But y'all didn't see one."

"Not yet."

"And there was no bald eagle, was there?"

"A man can dream, can't he?"

After breakfast they hiked to the massive Mammoth Hot Spring and the many springs on the limestone hills around it, then returned and checked out. With Sam at the wheel, they drove across the state line into Montana, passed under Roosevelt Arch, and left the park. Their goal for the day was to make it to Missoula, then drive on to Glacier the next morning.

As they headed north along the Yellowstone River in Paradise Valley, Sam pointed at the river beside them. "Gentlemen," he said, "let me tell you something fascinating about this river and the water in it."

"Just a second, Sam." Jeff threw his left arm over the edge of his seat, smiled at Jason and Eric, then turned to Sam. "I can't wait to hear about the river and the water—I'm on pins and needles, really I am—but let me provide a little background for the boys first." Jason and Eric glanced at each other and smiled. This was going to be good. Sam smiled too. He'd been the straight man for forty years.

"Sam and I are nearly four decades older than y'all are," Jeff began. "You're fortunate we were still able to father children at such an advanced age. Life was very different when we were growing up than it is now. We walked three miles to school. Uphill both ways in the snow. There was an Ice Age in Jackson then, wasn't there, Sam?"

"Absolutely."

"And there was no Internet. Have y'all ever heard of something called the *Encyclopedia Britannica?*"

Eric shrugged. Jason said Sam had mentioned it a time or two, but he didn't really know what it was.

"Well then, let me tell you. The *Encyclopedia Britannica* was a series of maybe twenty books. They were in alphabetical order and had hard covers, words, pictures, everything. You could look up almost anything in the *Encyclopedia Britannica*. Think of it as an Internet on paper. Sam's parents had a set, you won't be surprised to hear. And Jason, you won't be surprised to hear this either, but your dad spent every waking hour reading them. He was a total nerd before I came along and saved his life. Not partial, total.

"It's true; I was."

"See. I wouldn't lie to you. Well, maybe about three wolves, two elk, a grizzly bear, and a bald eagle, but not about my best friend Sam. Anyway, our houses were close to the Pearl River. There were woods and creeks to explore, wild animals and fish to catch. There was a whole wide world out there just waiting for us. But what did Sam do? He spent his days inside, sitting in a chair, reading the *Encyclopedia Britannica*. He was a total nerd, a pale one too, and he was kind of chubby to boot.

"How bad was it? Well, it got so bad his parents moved the set of books into his room. He just came out for meals and to use the bathroom. It got so bad I started calling him Britannica to embarrass him and try to break him of the habit. He knows more stuff about more stuff than anybody I know—I'll grant him that —but back then he was a pale, pudgy nerd. If I hadn't come along, there's no way a girl would have ever given him the time of day.

"Come to think of it, Jason, you owe your life to me. But for my profound and positive influence on your dad, no way your beautiful, accomplished mom would have gone out with him, much less married him. What woman would want a pale, pudgy nerd? And I won't even mention the fact that I had to pinch hit when you were born because your dad was in Toledo trying out for the professional bowling tour."

Sam laughed so hard he spit out his gum. In the fifteen years since Jason was born, Jeff had invented a dozen different stories to explain why Sam missed his son's birth—he was pheasant hunting in Argentina, marlin fishing in Cabo San Lucas, auditioning for a Broadway musical—but vying for a spot on the PBA tour was a new one.

"Okay, Sam, back to you. Tell us about this fascinating river and the water in it. I just wanted to put things in context so the youngsters would understand why you know millions of things normal people don't."

Sam mounted a counterattack as soon as he caught his breath. "Thank you for that kind introduction, Jeff. Now boys, let me set the record straight before I tell you about this amazing river. It's true I read a lot when I was young. I still do. But Jeff? He was eight years old when we met, and he didn't even know the alphabet. I had to teach him. If I hadn't come along and saved his life, he would have flunked out by the fifth grade and moved to a tar paper shack in the woods. He'd still be there today, living off crawdads, fish, and fried mud. But then I came along and taught him to read and write, he graduated from high school and college, and, amazingly enough, has even been able to hold down a job ever since. All thanks to me.

"Come to think of it, Eric, you owe your life to me. If I hadn't come along, no way your mom would have gone out with your dad, much less married him. And though it's true that Jeff was at the hospital when Jason was born, that's only because he could never break a hundred bowling. He was the king of the gutter ball."

Sam continued. "Now, about this river and the water in it, how far do y'all think it will travel from where it started to where it will empty into the sea? You don't know, do you? Of course not. Only the nerd knows."

"Please, please tell us," said Jeff. "If I can only know how far the water will travel, my life will be complete."

"First you must apologize for your cruel and unjust comments."

"Alright, I apologize. I apologize unreservedly. I offer a complete and utter retraction. And I deeply regret any distress my comments may have caused you and your son."

Jason chimed in from the back seat. "Hold him out the window by his feet, Daddy." On a recent Friday night, they had watched John Cleese apologize unreservedly while Kevin Kline held him out the window by his feet in *A Fish Called Wanda*.

"Thank you. Your apology, though utterly lacking in sincerity, is accepted."

"So how far?"

"Nearly 3,500 miles. As far as from New York City to London. Amazing, isn't it? This river, the Yellowstone, flows nearly seven hundred miles from its headwaters in the mountains south of the park until it joins the Missouri River in North Dakota. From there the Missouri travels nearly 1,600 miles until it merges with the Mississippi just north of St. Louis. The Mississippi then goes another 1,150 miles before it empties into the Gulf of Mexico. Hard to imagine, but in a few months the water beside us right now will flow through New Orleans and into the gulf."

Jeff looked back at the boys and winked. "How many states?"

"How many states? What do you mean, how many states?" Sam asked.

"How many states will it go through? It started in Wyoming. Now it's in Montana, but it still has a long way to go."

"Well, it forms the boundary between some."

"Count 'em both."

"Okay, I'll name 'em, you count 'em."

"Hold on a second. I never learned to count real good while I was living off fried mud. Is it more than ten? If so, I'll need to take off my shoes."

"Don't know yet. Here goes. There's Wyoming, Montana, North Dakota, South Dakota, Nebraska, Iowa, and Missouri. Then there's Illinois, Arkansas, Tennessee, Mississippi, and Louisiana. I think that's all. Let me close my eyes and picture the map to make sure."

"Don't close your eyes, Daddy. You're driving."

"Good point. I think I got all of them. Ever how many states that is, that's my final answer."

"That's twelve. I used my ears to count the last two. Let me look it up on this new-fangled Internet and see if you're right. Uh-oh, you missed two."

"Really? What?"

"Kansas and Kentucky."

"I knew I should have closed my eyes."

"Don't beat yourself up, Sam. Just think what a nerd you'd be if you named all fourteen. You boys want to hear something that's even cooler than Sam's 3,500 miles?" Jeff was no Britannica, but he'd done a lot of research to plan the trip.

Sam objected. "What could possibly be cooler than my 3,500 miles?"

"This could. There's a mountain in Glacier National Park called Triple Divide Peak," he continued. "You can climb to the top, pee in a circle, and feed three different bodies of water. Pee to the west, it goes to the Pacific. To the southeast, it goes to the Missouri, meets up in North Dakota with this water beside us, and heads to the Gulf of Mexico. And when you pee facing northeast, it winds up in Hudson Bay. If you add up the distance your pee travels in the three directions, it's way more than 3,500 miles. Pretty cool, huh?"

"Way cool," Jason responded, "but I think Daddy's rubbing off on you."

When they walked into the Montana Club in Missoula, Sam asked for a table for four. Jeff interrupted and said he had a reservation for six in the name of Freeman. Sam looked at him, his eyebrows raised. "Better not be those girls from the river."

"What girls? What river?"

"The gorgeous girls on the Missouri. They were in school here."

"That was more than twenty years ago. Thanks for the reminder, but not them."

"Then who?"

"You'll find out soon enough," Jeff said.

Roger Wentz was in Sam and Jeff's class at Spann and was a fellow Eagle Scout in Troop 1. After the spring semester of their sophomore year of college, the three friends drove to New Mexico and spent a week backpacking in the Sangre de Cristo Mountains. Roger was so taken by the experience that he vowed to return to the mountains of the West after college and spend his life there. Unlike most flatlanders who make the same vow, Roger kept his.

Sam and Jeff saw Roger when he came home to Jackson, but his parents soon moved away, and he stopped coming. The three promised to stay in touch, but they all had busy lives, and the calls became less frequent, then stopped altogether.

But as Jeff was planning the trip to the West, he thought of Roger. He did a Google search, and there he was—Roger L. Wentz, Ph.D., Senior Professor in the School of Parks, Tourism & Recreation Management at the University of Montana in Missoula. *The perfect job for him,* thought Jeff, and the photo in the university directory confirmed it. Roger was gray at the temples, but he looked young, fit, and happy. Jeff found his contact info and called. Roger answered after the first ring.

"Guess who this is."

"I don't know, but I'll hazard a guess. I'll say Jeff Freeman."

"Wow. That's impressive. How'd you know?"

"Two clues. 601 area code on caller ID, and I know only one person who sounds just like Jeff Freeman."

"How in the world are you, Roger? How long has it been? Your picture in the school directory looks great. Photoshopped?"

"No photoshopping until the next edition. I'll be teaching here until they roll me out on a gurney. I'm wonderful. You?"

After they spent some time catching up, Jeff told Roger about the trip he was planning to take with Sam and the boys. They were going to spend a night in Missoula on the drive up to Glacier, and he asked if Roger could join them for dinner. Roger said he would be delighted and recommended they meet at the Montana Club. He would bring his son to meet their sons. Everybody loved John, he said. Jeff ended the call with a request. "There's no reason for you to be talking to Sam between now and then, but don't get a wild hair and call him. Let's make it a surprise."

Jeff chose a seat facing the entrance. He spotted Roger when he came in, and they made eye contact. He assumed Roger's son would be older than Eric and Jason, but John looked to be no more than five feet tall. As they approached the table, Jeff saw why. John had Down syndrome.

Roger walked up behind Sam, grabbed his shoulders, and kissed him on the ear. Sam looked over his shoulder and yelled, startling the patrons at the surrounding tables. While Sam, Jeff, and Roger were hugging each other—Sam even hugged Jeff to thank him for setting it up—Eric didn't hesitate. He stood, approached John with his right arm extended, and introduced himself. John smiled, said his name, and shook Eric's hand. After Jason shook John's hand, Eric said, "John, come sit down on this end of the table with us. We're tired of talking to those old men."

As Sam watched Eric take charge and welcome John to the

fold, he was reminded of something. He couldn't place it at first, but then it came to him. It was the time Jeff marched right up to Freddie, the huge black inmate overseeing work during the Easter flood of 1979. No hesitation, no fear. Never met a stranger. Like father, like son.

Sam remembered when the three friends last saw each other. It was Christmas of 1986, more than half their lives ago. There was a lot of catching up to do. Roger had met his wife, Sandra, on a hiking trip not long after his last trip to Jackson. They had three children, John and two girls. John was the oldest. Occasionally Sam would sneak a peek at the other end of the table to make sure all was well. Roger noticed. "You don't need to check on them, Sam. As I told Jeff, everybody loves John."

Sam looked down at the other end of the table again. "He sure looks happy, but it must be hard."

"I appreciate your concern, but let me tell you the same thing I've told more people than I can count in the last two decades. Don't ever feel sorry for me or Sandra because of John. He has brought us more joy than I could have ever imagined. He brings out the best in people." He smiled and nodded toward the end of the table. "He's doing it now.

"And don't feel sorry for John either. He will never have the mind of an adult, but he knows he's loved, and he's better at loving others than anyone I've ever known. Everyone who knows him feels it. All of us who know him have better lives because of him.

"Let me send you something while I'm thinking about it. A few years ago, a friend sent me a song about a special-needs child who was also named John. He lived in New Orleans down the street from Andrew Duhon, who wrote the song. The title is "Till I Met John." I'm going to send you a link to it right now before I forget. There, you should have it.

"The song has a line that explains better than I ever could why it's so wonderful to be John's father. While the rest of us are dealing with the fear of growing older, the John in the song runs out into the rain to feel the raindrops on his shoulders."

Jeff smiled. "To feel the raindrops on his shoulders. That's beautiful. I got the link. Thank you. We'll play it for the boys. I assume John lives with you and Sandra. Will he ever be able to live on his own?"

"No. He's always helping around the house. He loves doing the laundry and can do lots of other things, but he could never live by himself."

"This is none of my business, and feel free to say so, but what will y'all do when you can't take care of him anymore? We're the same age. Eric often reminds me I'm no longer a spring chicken. He says I'm not even a summer chicken."

"I'm happy to tell you about the plan for John. People with Down syndrome have a shorter life expectancy than the rest of us, so he may not outlive us. But if he does, it will be a serious problem. You wanna know why?"

"Sure."

Roger, the proud father, grinned from ear to ear as he looked at his son smiling and laughing with the sons of his two old friends. "Because his little sisters will fight over him, that's why. The older one, Janie, just got engaged. Before she would say yes, her boyfriend had to promise that John could live with them if Sandra and I get to where we can no longer take care of him. He didn't hesitate. He loves John too. And our youngest, Jessie, has a stubborn streak a mile wide. If she doesn't get John half the time, she'll take her sister to court."

Jeff raised his mug of Moose Drool. "That's even more beautiful."

On the drive to the hotel, Sam looked at the boys in the rearview mirror. "I'm proud of y'all. I know Jeff is too."

"For what?" Jason asked.

"For being so kind to John."

"It was easy. He's a great guy. He invited us to come back to see him."

"Yeah, but you wouldn't know he's a great guy if you hadn't been kind to him."

"Eric gets the credit for that," Jason said. "You know how he is."

"Mr. Congeniality," said Sam, "just like his dad."

Jeff interjected. "Roger sent me a link to a song. It's about another special-needs child named John. Let's listen to it."

When "Till I Met John" came to an end, Eric asked Jeff to play it again. When it finished for a second time, Jeff started it again without being asked.

Sam pulled into a parking space at the hotel when the song was halfway through for the third time. They sat with the car running until it ended. When Sam turned off the ignition, Eric said, "Till we met John."

On the drive up from Missoula the next morning, Jeff read excerpts aloud from *Night of the Grizzlies*. Sam hoped he wouldn't have nightmares or, worse still, come face to face with the real thing. The black bear in the Tetons was enough. But the boys were young and immortal. They weren't scared of any grizzly bear.

Glacier was magnificent. On the first day, they did two mostly flat, easy hikes, one at low elevation on the east side of the park, the other 3,000 feet higher on the Continental Divide. The first was along beautiful Avalanche Creek to a spectacular lake of the same name. The sheer cliffs surrounding the lake on three sides are the site of many waterfalls and the avalanche chutes that gave the lake and creek their names.

They retraced their steps to the car, then wound up the aptly-named Going to the Sun Road, one of the most magnificent drives in all the world. When they stopped at Logan Pass on the Continental Divide for their second hike, they saw more victims of National Park Disorder. A handful of Rocky Mountain goats lounged in the parking lot. Jeff wondered aloud if the Park Service had hired them to serve as guards. The views as they began their walk along the Garden Wall just west of the Great Divide stretched for miles.

They stopped to rest after an hour, and Jeff offered a thoughtful reminder. The campsite below Granite Park chalet, the site of one of the fatal bear attacks in *Night of the Grizzlies*, was on this very trail. They continued, with Eric in the lead, but he soon came to a sudden stop. A large, buff-colored animal was just off the trail, its head behind a boulder. It had to be a grizzly. The others bunched up behind him just as they had in the Tetons, but Eric was wrong again. What he thought was a moose in the Tetons was a bear; what he thought was a bear in Glacier was a bighorn sheep. A ram with huge, curling horns stepped out from behind the boulder and proved to be as tame as the goats in the parking lot. Eric photographed him from thirty feet away, then twenty, then ten. The ram stood, waiting patiently, as the four hikers filed past. After another half hour, they turned around and headed back to the trailhead. The guard goats were still on duty in the parking lot. Sam, Jeff, and the boys climbed into their accustomed seats in the rental and descended to Rising Sun Campground, where they would spend the next three nights.

Their hikes the next two days were more strenuous but less crowded than the two on the first day. They drove north to Many Glacier the next morning, then began the five-mile climb to Ptarmigan Tunnel, which was blasted through the rock of Ptarmigan Wall in 1931. Along the way they heard a howl from the direction they were headed. It could have been a coyote, but after their failure in Yellowstone, Jeff declared it to be a wolf. There was no question about it, he said.

Ninety minutes later, he was vindicated. After sweating up a series of switchbacks, they walked through the tunnel. When they emerged on the north side, they were greeted by a winter wonderland. The north slope, in the shade of the mountain, was still covered with snow from the winter. As they descended on the trail, Jeff spotted a canine pawprint that was much too large for a coyote. A track wasn't as good as seeing the real thing, but it would have to do.

The wolf had been looking in the direction of the valley half a mile below, with lakes to the south and north. Like the two in Prine's "Lake Marie," they were named for women. The larger lakes in both song and valley were named Elizabeth. The smaller lake in the song was Marie; the smaller one here was Helen. The Belly River connecting Helen and Elizabeth carried snowmelt bound for Hudson Bay. Sam pointed to the north and told the boys to take a good look. "There's Canada," he said. "Jeff and I got closer

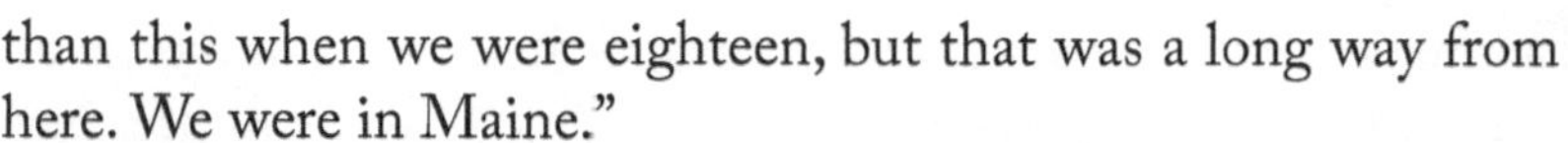

than this when we were eighteen, but that was a long way from here. We were in Maine."

"Hanging out with that moose we saw in Tetons," added Eric.

On the return hike, they took a side trip to magnificent Iceberg Lake, which had steep cliffs rising from the surface and was filled with the bergs for which the lake was named. Jason spotted mountain goats on one of the steep cliffs and wondered if they were wilder than the guard goats at Logan Pass. On the descent to the trailhead, they stopped to soak their sore feet in ice-cold Ptarmigan Creek. They had climbed more than half a vertical mile, hiked twelve miles, and still had two to go. They descended to the trailhead and, after arranging for a shuttle the next afternoon, returned to Rising Sun, grilled steaks, and had another perfect night around the fire.

The hike on their last day began at Siyeh Bend on Going to the Sun Road and ascended for nearly five miles to Piegan Pass. Like the day before, they found snow when they crossed the pass and reached the north slope, and they again spotted tracks. They assumed they were following another hiker, but when they descended to where the snow was only a few inches deep, they realized they were tailing a grizzly.

To keep the bear at bay, the foursome took turns singing John Prine songs. All had good voices other than Eric, who couldn't carry a tune in a bucket. But he was a good sport and took his turn. After his ghastly version of "Please Don't Bury Me," Jeff made up a new version of the chorus.

> *Please don't sing to me atop this cold, cold ground*
> *I'd rather a bear slice me up and pass me all around*
> *Throw my brain in a hurricane cause I won't need a thing*
> *And please get rid of both of my ears so I can't hear you sing.*

The scenery along the east side of the Garden Wall, which divided the continent, was magnificent. Waterfalls dropped from the cliffs, and streams crossed the path. When they came to Morning Eagle Falls, the boys stopped to investigate. Jeff followed them while Sam continued down the trail.

After Jeff and the boys resumed their descent, they saw Sam

standing with his arms raised. He heard their voices and ordered them to stay back. A female grizzly was on all fours on the trail facing him. Two cubs were behind her. She was pawing at the ground, threatening to charge. Jeff whispered to the boys to back away slowly. All three parents, the bear and the men, were protecting their young. Jeff caught up with Sam, stopped beside him, and raised his arms. He had a canister of bear spray in his right hand. Without taking his eyes off the bear, Sam said, "I told you to stay back."

"And who has the bear spray, Sammie? That mama's just doing what she should. Before she charges and I have to blast her, let's try something else."

"Like what?"

"Let's get Eric to sing."

Sam grinned. "Couldn't hurt."

Jeff looked over his shoulder and called out, "Eric, sing "Please Don't Bury Me" again. Louder this time."

Eric did as he was told. He started the song by waking up and putting on his slippers, then he walked in the kitchen and died. He was just as awful as before but at higher volume. The bear cocked her head to one side, then ambled away, her cubs in tow. Unlike in the song, nobody died. When they were a safe distance away, Jeff called for the boys to join them. He high-fived Eric and said, "No grizzly bear is a match for my son, at least not when he sings."

They broke camp the next morning, drove back across the park, and headed south. Jason asked if they were going back through Missoula. When Sam said they were, Jason suggested they meet John and Mr. Wentz for lunch. Jeff called Roger. He had a meeting and couldn't make it but said John would love to, that he'd talked about nothing other than Jason and Eric since their dinner at the Montana Club. He said John would be waiting and gave Sam their address.

John was sitting on the front porch when they arrived. They got out, and he hugged all four of them. Sam and Jeff were not at the other end of the table this time, and they saw during lunch why their sons had taken such a liking to John. He was kind and joyful and loved being with them. Jeff told him about Eric's awful singing that chased the bears away, and he almost fell out of his chair. When they took him back home and got out to walk him to the door, he hugged all four of them again. He was about to go inside but then thought of something. "Eric," he said, "please sing the song that scared the bears away."

Eric sang it again while the other four howled with laughter. Jeff asked John if he'd ever heard anything so awful. John said, "No, Mr. Jeff, it was beautiful. It saved your life. Mr. Sam's too."

Before backing out of the driveway, Sam sent Roger a one-sentence text message: "I don't feel sorry for you."

Their six days and five nights on the Middle Fork of the Salmon exceeded all expectations. The scenery and river were beautiful. They rode the rapids in rafts and inflatable kayaks and caught cutthroat trout on dry flies in the crystal-clear water. One afternoon they hiked up a creek to a hot tub Chinese miners had created by damming a hot spring with huge timbers more than a century earlier.

The trip was the first time Sam and Jeff had ever gone camping and done none of the work. The guides did it all on the Middle Fork. They captained the rafts, put up and took down the tents, and cooked all the meals. Jeff called it candy-ass camping. Sam felt guilty and gathered firewood for their campfire the first night. Jeff and the boys helped him the rest of the trip.

The others on the trip came from all over the country, and there were also couples from England and Australia. Jason and Eric were the two youngest, their dads among the oldest. They all played well together and became friends. When they parted ways at the end, one of the guides promised to distribute a list with contact information so they could stay in touch.

Sam and Jeff were still talking about the trip when the flight attendant came on the speaker to announce they were beginning their descent into Minneapolis. After she finished, Jeff asked a question. "You think all those people on the Middle Fork are really as nice as they seem?"

"Sure. Why wouldn't they be?" It was Sam's nature to think the best of people.

"I was just thinking, who wouldn't be nice on the Middle Fork of the Salmon River—catching fish, soaking in a hot tub, guides waiting on you hand and foot?"

"There's no reason not to be on your best behavior, that's for sure."

"I was wondering about Frank, the lawyer from Boston. Is he really a good guy? He sure seemed like it, but he might be like one of those insufferable lawyers you have to deal with. He might be a Masshole."

"I guess he might, but I doubt it. He didn't seem the type."

"Maybe he's on a plane right now wondering if you're like one of those insufferable lawyers he has to deal with."

"Me? Surely you jest."

"This is definitely one of the two best trips we've ever taken," Jeff declared.

"Definitely."

"I've been thinking about the other one. Thirty-six years ago. We were three years older than the boys are now."

"A magnificent trip."

"So which one was better?"

"Wow. That's hard to say," Sam responded. "Different parts of the country. Different ages. Having the boys with us. I don't know."

"I don't either, but I know one thing that would have made this one better."

"What's that?"

"Finding an envelope in the glove compartment filled with cash and a note telling us to stay as long as it lasts."

"Daddy did many great things for us, but that was the best."

"He was the best."

Dr. Thompson died two years before.

"Here's an idea. On the flight to Memphis, let's talk about our trip in 1978."

"Deal. And let's plan our next one."

# Part III

## Doing The Right Thing

# Chapter Sixteen

July 13, 2023

## Wisdom From a Wise Man

Sam had another hard time sleeping the second night after the accident but not as hard as the night before. He called David when he woke up the next morning and arranged to meet with him at ten o'clock at Chapel of the Cross. Before heading to the church, he took Buddy for a walk.

David's office wasn't in the chapel itself but in a newer building nearly a hundred yards away. When the chapel was built before the Civil War, churches in the rural South had no full-time employees and no need for offices. Pastors worked in the fields during the week, prepared their sermons at night, and preached on Sunday. That was it.

In their wisdom, church leaders had chosen to site the new building at a respectful remove from the chapel. A garden and grove of hardwoods separated the old from the new. The beautiful chapel, its cemetery filled with gravestones marking the passing of church members over the course of three centuries, stood alone. Now, as when the chapel was new, members of the congregation dug the graves.

The land on which the chapel stood was filled with oaks, magnolias, and cedars. Every autumn, on the first Saturday in October, the congregation hosted a festival called Day in the Country, a fundraiser attended by more than 10,000 patrons when the weather was clear. Members of the congregation grilled burgers and hot dogs, directed traffic, and painted children's faces. Bands played, and vendors hawked their wares. The proceeds were initially devoted to restoring the chapel but in recent years were used to maintain the property and fund servant ministries. When the festival began in 1979, the title was fitting because the chapel really was in the country. Now the festival was more of a day in the suburbs.

David's office could have passed for a John Prine museum. On one wall were a dozen album covers John had signed and David had framed. Behind the desk was a photo of the two of them, their arms around each other, grinning from ear to ear. On the desk was a birthday card John had sent David when he turned eighty. The note on the inside included allusions to "Hello in There" and "All the Best": "I could have passed by the birthday cards as if I didn't care, but I do. And it's easy to wish you all the best. Happy 80th, John."

David rose from behind his desk to greet Sam. Sam stuck out his hand, but David wrapped his arms around him. "I'm so sorry about Jeff. I just heard this morning. I know he's been your best friend forever. What a tragedy."

"Thank you. That's what I came to talk to you about."

"Then let's talk."

David gestured for Sam to sit down in one of the two chairs facing each other in front of the desk and turned to take the other. David raised his eyebrows when Sam closed the door.

"David, I assume you're familiar with the priest-penitent privilege."

David raised his eyebrows again. "I am. I'm not a lawyer, and I don't know all the ins and outs, but I know what it means to me. Anything said to me in confidence remains in confidence."

"No matter what?"

"No matter what. Let me tell you a story that won't violate any confidence. I counseled a woman, a member of our congregation who was going through a messy divorce. Her husband found out she was meeting with me, and his lawyer served me with a subpoena to give a deposition. I called the lawyer and told him he was wasting his time, that I had nothing to say. But he didn't let it go. He was a bully; you know the type."

"I'm afraid I do."

"He said if I didn't come to the deposition, he would get the judge to hold me in contempt. I asked if he was familiar with the priest-penitent privilege. He said he was, but he mumbled some legalese and claimed it didn't apply. Told me if I didn't show up, he would get a court order requiring me to testify and pay his fees."

"I bet I know who it was."

"I told him it wouldn't do any good, that I wasn't going to testify even if a judge ordered me to. He got mad and said he would ask the judge to hold me in contempt and jail me if I still refused. Then I got mad. I said he obviously didn't know me if he thought I would compromise my principles because some two-bit lawyer threatened me."

"You called him a two-bit lawyer? That's great."

"I did, and he was. I said a subpoena wouldn't make me testify, a court order wouldn't, and a jail cell wouldn't. But if he thought trying to get a priest thrown in jail would help his client's case, he should have at it. He said I was making a big mistake and would be hearing from him. I told him to kiss my ass and hung up. I never heard from him again."

Sam smiled for the first time in thirty-six hours. "That doesn't sound very Christian, David."

"I wasn't feeling very Christian. Anyway, that's how I feel about maintaining the confidences of those who confide in me. Why do you ask?"

Sam's smile disappeared. He took a deep breath. "Because I did it."

"Did what?"

"Killed Jeff. I'm the one who hit him."

"What? You hit Jeff? That can't be. I don't believe it."

"It's true. I'm the one who hit him."

"But I heard it was a hit and run. It couldn't have been you."

"It was me, and what you heard is right. I killed him, and I left him on the side of the road."

Sam's shoulders shook, and the sobs came again. When David recovered from the initial shock, he stood and wrapped his right arm around Sam's shoulders. "Take all the time you need. Then I want you to tell me what happened. You're a good man. I know there's a good reason."

"But I'm not a good man. I killed my best friend." He reached up with his left hand and rested it on David's right. The sobs subsided, and David returned to his chair.

"Start whenever you're ready."

Sam stared down at the floor. He took another deep breath and began. "Evelyn and I were at the Bar Convention banquet at the Westin downtown. It got moved here from Sandestin because of the hurricane." He looked up at David. "Turned out they could have kept the convention at the beach. If they had, Jeff would still be alive, and I wouldn't be here. I'm the new Bar president. I gave a speech and announced my retirement. People were shocked."

"I'm surprised too."

"I was ready to quit, tired of the stress. Tired of dealing with lawyers like the one who threatened you. It was a fun night. I was drinking but not too much. Two cocktails, maybe three glasses of champagne, but we were there for more than three hours. When we left, I wasn't even feeling tipsy."

"You can hold your liquor better than I can, that's for sure."

"I was driving home on the Trace and glanced over at Evelyn for a split second. That's when I hit him. I never even saw him. Thought he was a deer. You know how dark it is."

"You just kept going?"

"No. I slammed on the brakes and pulled over. Evelyn had seen him and said it was a man. I started to get out, but she told me to stay. She's the doctor. I tried to watch her in the rearview mirror, but it was too dark to see much of anything. She came back and told me he was dead. I asked if she recognized him. She said it was too dark, and he was lying face down."

"So how'd you find out it was Jeff?"

"His daughter called me yesterday afternoon. Marsha. She lives in Oxford. She and her husband named their son for Jeff. When she told me, I was driving on the Trace again, believe it or not. I pulled over, opened the door, and got sick."

"I'm so sorry, Sam."

"After Evelyn told me the man was dead, I started to call 911, but she stopped me. She asked if I was sure I could pass a breathalyzer test. How would I know? But I knew I wasn't drunk, and I knew it wasn't my fault. I wasn't going too fast, and I was in my lane. He must have fallen off his bike right in front of me. Evelyn found it on the edge of the road. I wish I knew how it happened. Maybe he pulled off the pavement when he heard a car coming and lost his balance when he hit the edge. But why was he out there on his bike at that hour? Why?

"Evelyn said he was dead, we couldn't help him, and we should leave. She was trying to protect me, I know that. I would have done the same thing if she'd been driving. I argued a little but didn't put up much of a fight. What she said made sense, but it was wrong. I should have stuck to my guns and called 911, but I drove home instead. Until I found out it was Jeff, I suffered more from leaving the man than from hitting him. But then Marsha called."

"I'm terribly sorry."

"She asked me to pick up Jeff's son at the airport last night. Eric's in law school at UVA and working for a firm in D.C. for the summer. Fine young man. On the ride into town, Eric said something I'll never forget. He said, 'I can't believe the bastard just drove off and left him. What kind of person would do that?'"

Sam started to cry again. "What kind of person would do that, David? What kind of person? Marsha and Eric asked me to meet them at the funeral home today, but I don't think I can do it. Marsha asked me to call Jeff's friends and tell them, and I couldn't do that either. I got Evelyn to do it. I hate myself, David. I've been thinking I want to walk out to the Trace tonight and throw myself in front of a car. How can anyone forgive me? How can you forgive me? He was your friend too."

"First of all, you have no need to seek forgiveness from me. You didn't hurt me. You didn't do anything to me. Second, forgiveness from God is far more important than forgiveness from any mortal, and I assure you of this: God has already forgiven you. He knows you're suffering. He knows you're sorry for what you did and that you're hating yourself now. You wouldn't be you if you weren't. You're a good man, and good men feel remorse. Often too much remorse.

"How long have we known each other, Sam? Fifteen years?

Twenty? I feel like I know you pretty well, and I know the hardest thing for you will be forgiving yourself. It will take time, and it will take work. I want to tell you some things I hope will help.

"First of all, never forget that it was an accident. It wasn't your fault you hit the man, and it wasn't your fault the man was your best friend. You were just in the wrong place at the wrong time. Jeff's death and your role in it have made your pain unbearable, but it was still an accident. It was not your fault."

"I know it wasn't my fault, David. I keep telling myself that. But then I left him lying there on the side of the road, drove home, and went to bed. Hitting him was an accident, but leaving him wasn't."

"Let's talk about that. I know you believe it was wrong, that the honorable thing, the right thing, would have been to call 911, take a breathalyzer test, and face the consequences. And I understand why you feel that way. But sometimes there are no good options. Sometimes we're faced with nothing but terrible choices and  choose the lesser evil. The better choice for you, because you're a man of honor, may well have been to call 911 and face the music.

"But I want you to think about what that choice would have meant for the people you love the most—for Evelyn and your children. Sara and Jason have looked up to you their whole lives, and for good reason. Their father could have been faced criminal charges for killing a man. They would have been devastated."

"But I did kill a man."

"It was an accident. Repeat after me: It was an accident."

"It was an accident. But I left him on purpose."

"This may sound strange, Sam, but sometimes doing the honorable thing can be selfish. Think about the young man who volunteers for the army and goes off to war, leaving his wife and children behind. He didn't have to go. He could have stayed home and supported his family and helped his wife raise their children. But he would have felt ashamed that other young men fought while he stayed behind. People might have looked down on him and talked about him behind his back. He preferred risking death on the battlefield to the shame he would have felt. And that may have been the better choice for him.

"But what about his family? What would dying on the battlefield to preserve his honor do for them? What would it do *to* them? Because you're an honorable man and you try to do the right thing, calling 911 may have been the better choice for you. But what about your family? Would that have been the better choice for them?"

"I don't know. Maybe not. But maybe it would have been better for them to know their husband and father did the right thing."

"Not if you got prosecuted for an accident that wasn't your fault."

"Maybe you're right."

"I'm not saying you have to agree with me, but I want you to go home and think about it."

"I will. I know we couldn't do anything for him, but it was Jeff. I killed my best friend."

"I understand, and I can only imagine the pain you're in. But you already have God's grace, and you will need to learn to give yourself grace. Grieve the loss of your best friend, but don't hate yourself."

"I'll try. Thank you for meeting with me. I knew you would have words of wisdom and wouldn't burn me at the stake."

"If you ever need me, if you just want to talk, I want you to call me whenever it is. Or come back to see me. Forgiving yourself won't be easy, and it's going to take time, but I hope you'll be able to do it. You're a good man, and it wasn't your fault."

"Thank you. I feel better."

"Here's one more piece of advice. You've listened to this guy sitting here. Now spend some time listening to that one." He gestured toward John Prine in the photo behind his desk. "He wrote some of the wisest words of all."

Sam smiled. "That's always good advice. You know, Jeff may not have loved John as much as we do, but he loved him. Jeff taught me to love the outdoors, and I taught him to love John Prine. When we were planning our first camping trip after he and Olivia divorced, he said, 'I guess it's too late to save my marriage, but perhaps we can still catch a few fish.'"

"Ah, 'Lake Marie.' Standing by peaceful waters. You're a good man, Sam. Many people love and admire you. Never forget that."

"Thank you, David. I'm glad you're my friend."
"And I'm glad you're mine."

# Chapter Seventeen

July 13, 2023

Making Arrangements

Sam felt better after his meeting with David. He wasn't persuaded that he'd done the right thing, but he now realized how painful doing the right thing would have been for his family. And it was too late to do it now. Confessing at this point would be even worse, both for him and for them. Evelyn would insist on taking responsibility for making him leave the scene. What would that mean for her?

But other than keeping the secret he could never reveal, he promised himself he would do the right thing from here on out. He had lunch with Evelyn, told her about his talk with David, then drove to the funeral home to meet with Marsha and Eric. Sam dreaded it, but it was the right thing.

They were waiting for him in the lobby. Marsha was a beautiful young woman who was always smiling. She smiled when she saw Sam but not for long. He hugged her, then shook hands with Eric. They'd hugged the night before but now returned to their customary method of greeting.

Marsha was the first to speak. "The man asked if we wanted to see Daddy. What do you think, Sam?" When Marsha graduated from high school, Sam made her stop calling him Mr. Thompson. He did the same when Eric graduated three years later. It took a while, but they were used to it now.

"We should do what y'all want."

Eric offered his opinion. "I think I want to see him. When I brought his suit this morning, the man said his face looked okay."

"Marsha, if you don't want to see him, I'll go in with Eric."

"No, I think I want to see him too."

Sam knocked on the glass office door and introduced himself after the funeral director motioned for him to come in. He said he was Jeff's best friend and explained what they wanted. The man led them to the room where Jeff was lying in his suit in a temporary casket. Marsha and Eric had not yet chosen the one he would be buried in. The man told them to take all the time they needed, then left and closed the door behind him.

When they walked over to the casket, they could see makeup covering a gash on one cheek. It was the only sign that Jeff had died a violent death. They stood alongside the casket, Sam in the middle with an arm around each of Jeff's children. The two men cried; the woman did not. Sam muttered, "I'm so sorry." Eric and Marsha would never know how sorry. Sam decided he would stand there all day if they wanted, but after ten minutes Marsha said she was ready. Eric nodded. Marsha leaned over, kissed Jeff on the forehead, and said she loved him.

Sam returned to the funeral director's office, and he directed them to the casket display room, where he again left the three of them alone. Their time walking up and down these aisles gave them a short break from their sadness. Some of the caskets were ridiculously ornate and ostentatious, others unimaginably tacky. You could be buried in an Ole Miss casket decorated with Colonel Rebel or a Mississippi State casket featuring a bulldog. Though they were in central Mississippi, there were also an LSU casket featuring a tiger and one with Roll Tide in script across the top. Millsaps, whose alums were not as rabid about football as those who attended SEC schools, was unrepresented.

Another casket, presumably intended for a woman who excelled at feeding her family, was adorned with depictions of pots and pans. Marsha wondered what the deceased cook would do with them. There were also medallions, including one of a quilting kit and another of a cocker spaniel, that could be purchased a la carte and affixed to the inside of a coffin lid. Marsha and Eric were amused at the absurdity and preferred something simple and modest. Sam agreed, but the options that fit the bill still varied widely in price. He decided to tell them a story from a few years before.

"Y'all get whichever one you want," he said, "but first let me tell you something about your daddy. He and I went to a funeral four or five years ago for a man named George Kaufman. A successful businessman. I represented him, and Jeff managed his money. We both liked him. Great guy.

"When we got to the church, there was this beautiful, ornate casket down front. It was finer than any piece of furniture in the sanctuary. Hand-carved cherry, gold trim. Magnificent.

"After the funeral, we stopped for a drink on the way home, and Jeff said, 'George hasn't been in the ground half an hour, but he's already spinning in his grave.' I asked why, and he said, 'That ridiculous casket. I bet it cost fifteen grand, they just covered it up with dirt, and nobody will ever see it again. If George could see it, he would blow a gasket. He was a generous man, but he never wasted a cent.'

"So let me tell you what I think Jeff would want. I think he'd want you to buy the cheapest casket they've got and spend the money you save to go on a trip to someplace he loved, a river or someplace in the mountains. Y'all know some of them. I can make you a list of others."

"You're right," Marsha said. "He loved his family and friends and doing things with us and with y'all, but other than his precious BMWs, he didn't care at all about fancy things. He wore clothes till he wore them out. I had to take him shopping to make him buy new ones."

Eric agreed. "Yep. That was Daddy. If it wasn't illegal, he'd want us to roll him into the grave without a casket."

Sam volunteered to tell the funeral director. "If he tries to talk us into buying a more expensive one, I'll tell him about Jeff and George Kaufman. I'll make Jeff the bad cop."

When Sam broke the news, the man was taken aback. "But he was such a fine man. A pillar of the community. Do you believe your selection is appropriate to honor him?"

Sam took a deep breath. He didn't want to be in the room with this man long enough to tell him the story about George Kaufman's funeral, so instead he said this: "Jeff was my best friend for fifty-five years. I knew him better than anyone did. And I know for a fact that he would not want his children spending any of their inheritance on a fancy box to be lowered into the ground day after tomorrow never to be seen again." That ended the casket discussion.

The director tallied up the bill. There was a separate charge for every little thing, and even with the cheap casket, the total came to nearly $8,000. How on earth, Sam wondered, could the poor afford to bury their dead? He was reminded of "Mr. Banker," the old song by Lynyrd Skynyrd in which a man offers his 1950 Les Paul guitar as collateral for a loan to bury his papa.

"Payment is due now," the director said. Sam had seen returned checks tacked to the bulletin board behind the director's desk for all the world to see. *Classy.*

"I don't think there's any way we can get any money from one of Daddy's accounts today," Marsha said, "and Bob and I don't have that much cash in our account. I'm sure Eric doesn't either. Will you take a credit card?"

"Certainly, though there will be a four percent transaction fee if you pay that way."

Sam felt his face flush. "A transaction fee? Really? What's your mark-up on those caskets?" It felt good to be mad at someone other than himself for a change. "Put your credit card back in your purse, Marsha. I'll write a check."

"But it's not your responsibility, Sam."

"Maybe not, but it will be my honor to pay it."

"We'll pay you back."

"No, you won't. I won't allow it, and I won't hear another word about it." He wrote the check and slid it across the table. He then stood up, said "Good day, sir," and walked out into the heat.

When Marsha and Eric caught up with him, she said they needed to talk to him about one more thing. "Not here," Sam said. He was still fuming. They agreed to meet in the bar at Bravo, a popular

Italian restaurant. It was 3:30. The lunch crowd would be gone, the dinner crowd not yet there. It would be nearly empty.

After two sips of his Tito's and tonic, Sam had cooled off. "I apologize for acting like that, but damn. Y'all didn't see this, but there were returned checks on the bulletin board behind his desk. Some poor guy just lost one of his parents, but let's rub salt in his wound and shame him too."

Marsha put her hand on his shoulder. "Don't apologize. That was perfect."

Eric quoted him. "*Good day, sir.* Marsha's right. Perfect."

"He deserved it, that's for sure," Sam said. "*Do you believe your selection is appropriate to honor him?* I wonder if anybody's ever punched the guy."

"I doubt it," said Marsha. "He would have learned not to act that way. Sam, we have one more favor to ask, and it's a big one."

"Sure. Anything."

"Daddy loved to watch you give closing arguments. He would come home and tell us all about them. When you won that case for his firm, that's all he talked about. And as you told that awful man, you knew him better than anybody. We want you to deliver his eulogy on Saturday. Will you do it? Please?"

Sam had wondered if this might be coming. He was a trial lawyer and Jeff's best friend. He was the obvious choice. Before he met with David, he was planning to make up some excuse and decline. He would say he was suffering too much. But that wouldn't be the right thing. "Of course I will," he said. "It will be the greatest honor of my life. Thank you for asking me."

# Chapter Eighteen

July 14, 2023

Remembering the Stories

Being asked by Jeff's children to give the eulogy was the best thing that could have happened to Sam. Deciding what to say about his best friend gave him a task, and thinking about all their good times together was a welcome distraction from the grief and the guilt.

Sam had prepared and given many opening statements and closing arguments, but he'd never delivered a eulogy. First thing Friday morning, he decided to ask someone who would know what he should say. David answered on the first ring.

"Sam, good to hear from you. You doing okay?"

"You didn't convince me I did the right thing, but I'm better."

"Good. It will take time."

"If you have a few minutes, I need some advice about a matter on which you have a great deal of experience and I have none."

"Sure. What is it?"

"Jeff's son and daughter asked me to give the eulogy tomorrow."

"Good. You're gonna do it, I hope."

"I am, thanks to you. I was afraid they might ask, and I was planning to beg off. But after you and I talked, I decided I wanted to get back into the habit of doing the right thing. I knew Jeff better than anybody did. I should be the one to deliver his eulogy."

"You're right, and good for you. And let me guess: You want my advice about what to say."

"Exactly."

"You have a pen and paper handy?"

"I do."

"Okay, here's my advice: Tell stories."

Sam wrote down the two words and waited, but the line was silent.

"That's it?"

"That's it."

"That I should tell stories? You've preached at hundreds of funerals, and that's all you have to say?"

"You're a good storyteller, Sam, and you have a million stories about Jeff. You've told me half a million. Tell the best ones. Choose stories that will make people smile and laugh and show what kind of man he was, what kind of friend and father he was."

"That should be easy enough. I do have a million stories."

"And I'm sure you'll do a wonderful job. I'll look forward to hearing it."

"You're coming?"

"Of course. As you reminded me, he was my friend too. And so are you."

Sam sat down at the desk in his study, pulled out a legal pad, and wrote "Jeff Stories" across the top of the first page. Nearly four decades of litigation had taught him the benefit of being organized. He thought back through all the times they'd spent together and made the list in chronological order. He skipped a line after each entry in case he remembered another story later. The first entry was for the day Jeff rang the doorbell in June 1968—he wrote one word, *doorbell*. The final entry was for their last trip together fifty-five years later. Two months before Jeff's death, they went fly fishing on the Norfork and Little Red Rivers in the Ozarks, took Buddy and Josey with them, and caught more than a few fish.

By the time Sam finished his list, it was three pages long. The challenge would be cutting it down to size. He was reminded of that old song by Bob Seger with the line about deadlines and commitments and what to leave in and what to leave out. Sam's commitment was to prepare the eulogy. His deadline was eleven o'clock the next day, when the funeral would begin. He would have to decide what to leave in and what to leave out by then. He'd given an emotional talk Tuesday night at the Westin, and he would give an even more emotional one less than four days later. It would again be in downtown Jackson, this time in the sanctuary of Galloway United Methodist Church.

Sam was deep in thought when Evelyn got home from the clinic. He didn't notice her until she cleared her throat when she was three feet away.

"Sorry, Sweetheart. I was in hyperfocus mode."

"I could tell." She'd seen it many times.

She walked over, leaned down, and kissed him. She was pleased both that Marsha and Eric had asked him to deliver the eulogy and that he had agreed to do it. He needed something to do to keep from spiraling deeper into depression; she knew that. Sam loved a project, whether it was preparing for trial or building a deck in a friend's backyard. And if any project was ever a labor of love, it was his best friend's eulogy.

"How's it coming?"

"Good, I think. I asked David what I should say, and his advice was to tell stories about Jeff. I could do that all day long, as you know. Deciding which ones not to tell is the hard part." He smiled. Remembering all the good times with Jeff had lifted his spirits. "What time do the kids get in?"

"Jason's flying through Atlanta. They managed to book the same flight from there. It lands at 7:30."

Sara was an architect in Atlanta; Jason worked for an investment firm in Manhattan. Neither son had followed in his father's footsteps but instead had chosen the career of his father's best friend.

"I figure we'll grab a quick bite, then stop by Olivia's so they can see Marsha and Eric. You going to able to go with me to get them?"

"Sure. It's not like I need a lot of notes. One word per story is all it will take."

"You do know the stories." She'd heard them all, many of them multiple times. Sam loved telling stories about Jeff and their good times together.

"Sam, you realize Sara and Jason can't know, don't you? The two of us and David, that's all who can ever know."

"I understand." What's done was done. There was no going back, and there was no point in telling anybody else, even his own children. He'd shared his burden with David, but he would never share it with anyone else.

The flight from Atlanta was on time. Before stopping by Olivia's to see Marsha and Eric, Evelyn suggested they go to Keifer's, the Greek restaurant where Jeff wanted to have a few beers before coaching Evelyn through labor a quarter century before.

Keifer's opened in early 1980, when Sam was nineteen and a sophomore at Millsaps. More than thirty years later, the growing Baptist healthcare complex purchased the original Keifer's on the south side of Poplar Boulevard in Belhaven, razed it to the ground, and erected a medical office building in its place. The owners of Keifer's were undaunted. They built a new restaurant across the street on the north side of Poplar and didn't miss a beat. The menu, other than the prices, had hardly changed in forty years, and the service was fast. The Thompsons ordered gyros all around, two orders of cottage fries to share, and a pitcher of Amber Bock.

They avoided talking about the accident on the drive from the airport, but Jason brought it up after Sam poured the beer. "Was he at least killed instantly?"

"I believe so," said Evelyn. "A park ranger told Olivia there was very little blood. From his injuries, there should have been much more if his heart was still beating."

"I can't believe the driver just drove off and left him."

Sam winced. "It's hard to imagine," Evelyn agreed. "Maybe the driver just panicked or thought it was a deer. Listen to me for a second. For Eric and Marsha's sake, don't bring up the accident or mention that it was a hit and run. I'm sure they're suffering enough as it is without being consumed by anger."

Evelyn told them not to mention it for Eric and Marsha, but Sam knew it was really for him. Talking to David and preparing the eulogy had been good for him, but one comment from his son was like a dagger through his heart. He decided the best therapy would be working on the eulogy for another hour or two after they got home. Then maybe he could sleep.

The Thompsons had been married nearly a decade before the Freemans tied the knot, but their daughters were born in the same year, as were their sons. Evelyn didn't want to start a family during her pediatric residency, and when she and Sam began trying, she had difficulty conceiving. Sara wasn't born until Evelyn and Sam were thirty-five.

Jeff was a confirmed bachelor until Olivia, ten years his junior and the most recent in a series of gorgeous girlfriends, broke some startling news on Christmas Eve in 1994. After they exchanged presents, Olivia said she had a surprise. She pulled an ultrasound image from her purse and announced she was going to have a baby, *his* baby. They married two weeks later in Sam and Evelyn's living room. There were no rehearsal dinner and no toasts this time, but Sam served as Jeff's best man, just as Jeff had served as Sam's in Charleston. Marsha was born in July.

When Marsha was little, Jeff would read the same book to her every December, *The Best Christmas Pageant Ever*, a delightful story about a family of hooligans named the Herdmans. The six Herdman children, who've never attended church, take over the primary roles in the annual Christmas pageant at a church in their hometown. They teach the congregation the true meaning of Christmas by learning it themselves. When Marsha was old enough for Jeff to tell her how and when he learned he would be a father, he said she was the best Christmas present ever.

The Thompson and Freeman children were more like siblings than friends. They did everything together and spent countless nights in each other's homes. The boys often stayed at one on Friday nights while the girls stayed at the other. There was only one serious bump along the way. When Sara and Marsha were juniors at Jackson Prep, both had a crush on the same boy, a handsome senior and the star quarterback on Prep's football team. But the falling out was brief. After one date with each of them, the young man rejected both in favor of a girl who was eager to climb into the back seat of his SUV.

There were hugs and tears when the four friends reunited at Olivia's, but there was also laughter when they began swapping stories. One was about Jeff's favorite Halloween trick. He would dress up as a ghost, get down on his knees before ringing neighborhood doorbells, and say "trick or treat" in a squeaky falsetto. The truth was revealed only when he stuck out his grown-up arm to collect the treats. He howled with laughter when the victims of his trick realized they'd been had.

The Thompsons didn't stay long at Olivia's. Sam needed to get home and put the finishing touches on the eulogy. There would be more time to visit after the funeral.

# Chapter Nineteen


July 15, 2023

Telling the Stories


Marsha and Eric asked all four of the Thompsons to sit with them on the front pew. Olivia would also join them there. When it was time for the service to begin, Reverend Stockett led them into the sanctuary from the side entrance. Sam nodded to friends in the congregation.

Sam took his seat and looked down at the printed order of worship for the service. Marsha and Eric, likely with Olivia's input, had chosen just the right hymns. Like Sam, Jeff was not especially devout. After he and Olivia divorced and the children left for college, his attendance at Sunday services was sporadic at best. He often skipped church to play what he called heathen golf.

But he loved his friends at Galloway, and he really loved old, traditional hymns, which he sang with gusto. His funeral would begin with "Rock of Ages" and end with "Amazing Grace." "Old Rugged Cross" would be in the middle, after Reverend Stockett delivered his message but before Sam gave the eulogy.

When the congregation sang the last line of "Old Rugged Cross," Sam walked to the lectern. He knew the stories by heart and had only a single page of notes. He smiled at the congregation and began.

"Welcome to this celebration of the life of my best friend. Having the opportunity to speak to Jeff Freeman's family and friends about him is the highest honor of my life. Marsha and Eric, thank you for asking me.

"This is my first time to deliver a eulogy, so I asked for advice.

My friend David Eldridge, who was Jeff's friend too, is with us here today." Sam nodded to David, who smiled in return. "David has been an Episcopal priest since Moses parted the Red Sea, so I figured he would know what I should say. He had a grand total of two words of advice. He told me to tell stories. That's all he said. Alright, I thought, easy enough, but how will I decide which stories not to tell? I have hundreds of stories about Jeff Freeman, and I love telling them all. If I did, we'd be here till Tuesday.

"I have been the beneficiary of countless blessings in my sixty-three years. One of the very best walked into my life fifty-five years ago, in June 1968. Jeff and his wonderful mother had just moved to Jackson, into the house two doors down from ours. He came to our house the day after they moved in, marched up the sidewalk, and rang the doorbell. He was eight years old but fearless even then. He told my mama his mama had kicked him out of the house with orders to find somebody to play with. Mama came upstairs and got me, and Jeff and I headed for the creek down the hill. By the time we went to bed that night, we were best friends. And we were best friends from that day until his life ended this week. No one—and I mean no one—could be a better friend than Jeff Freeman. Our son's middle name is Jeffery.

"Even those who didn't know Jeff all that well know he was the life of every party. He was always smiling and had a wonderful sense of humor. Everybody wanted to be like him, and everybody wanted to be with him. When that TV show with Ray Romano came out, I started calling him Raymond. Everybody loved Jeff.

"I could tell funny stories about Jeff all day long, but instead I'm going to tell a few that reveal some things about him you may not know. He was far more than the life of the party. He and my father were the two finest men I've ever known. They shared the job of best man when I married my wonderful wife Evelyn. At our rehearsal dinner, Jeff gave the best toast I've ever heard.

"Jeff was also the bravest man I've ever known. I'll tell you two stories that happened thirty-five years apart. The first, when we were eighteen, was in 1979, the year of the Easter Flood. Jeff and I worked from dawn till dusk on Easter Sunday, ate dinner, then drove downtown and worked from dusk till dawn. We rescued people and pets that day and helped save the power station over here at the east end of Tombigbee Street that night. I've never been so tired in my life, before or since. But he wouldn't quit, so I couldn't quit.

"When we got to the power plant, we saw that all the men were black prison inmates, hauled down from Parchman in their prison stripes and put to work. The one in charge, a huge black man named Freddie, spotted us and said, *Looks like we us got some fresh meat, some fresh white meat.* Fresh white meat is what he called us. I was scared to death, but not Jeff. He marched right up to Freddie, said we weren't very fresh because we'd been rescuing people and pets all day, including a parrot that cussed like a sailor. Freddie laughed and gave us a job. After we got started, I told Jeff he was my hero.

"Many years later, we went on a wonderful trip to the West with our sons. Jeff planned it all while I was in trial. I was in front of Jeff and the boys on a hike in Glacier National Park and came upon a mother grizzly bear and her cubs. She pawed at the ground and threatened to charge. I yelled at the others to stay back, but Jeff walked up and stood right beside me. I was shaking like a leaf, but he was as cool as a cucumber. Said he didn't want to have to shoot the mama bear with pepper spray—she was just doing her job—so he had another idea. As some of you know, Jeff loved to sing and had an excellent voice, but his son Eric didn't inherit it. He's a fine young man and like a second son to me, but he'll be the first to tell you he can't sing a lick. So what was Jeff's idea? He told Eric to sing. And it worked! The mama bear and her cubs ran away. Jeff never broke a sweat.

"Jeff had a deep and abiding love for his friends and family. He would have done anything for Marsha and Eric, he would have done anything for Evelyn and me, and he would have done anything for many of you. Sometimes he was loyal to a fault, like the time he lied to Mrs. Cheney, our fourth-grade teacher at Spann. He caught a king snake at recess, and we decided to put it in a classmate's desk. We thought it was a good idea at the time, but we were wrong. The snake got loose, the class went crazy, and Mrs.

Cheney stood on her desk chair and screamed like a banshee. Jeff sprang into action, caught the snake, ran outside, and released it. When he came back in, he confessed immediately. Mrs. Cheney asked if he had an accomplice, and he denied it. I couldn't let him take the fall alone, but when we got to the principal's office, he said it was all his fault, not mine. That was Jeff. He gave the credit to others when things went right and took the blame when they went wrong.

"Jeff also had an abiding love for the outdoors. By the time we met, he was already an expert. He taught me all there was to know about trees and birds and snakes. He knew that king snake was harmless. When we were in the woods on that very first day in 1968, we heard an owl call just before sunset. Jeff told me it was a barred owl, did a perfect imitation, and the owl called back. He was eight years old and talking to a bird.

"Jeff taught me to love the outdoors, and he and I taught our children to love it too. When I was thinking about all our good times together to decide what to tell you about him, I started counting up all the nights he and I sat together beside a campfire. I stopped when I reached two hundred. Two hundred nights beside a campfire with Jeff Freeman makes me a rich man indeed.

"You might think Jeff always entertained me by our campfires with jokes and stories. He did plenty of that, but we had our most serious talks when it was just the two of us and a fire. Jeff was a kind and generous soul and a deep thinker. On our last trip—and it hurts me to say it was our last—we camped beside a trout stream in the Ozarks and talked about how lucky we were and how wonderful our lives had been. Better even than George Bailey's in *It's a Wonderful Life*, Jeff said. And we talked about religion, about God and heaven and what comes next. Jeff was much more than the life of the party.

"How much Jeff loved the outdoors is obvious from how he spent his time and money. He donated to worthy causes dedicated to preserving the natural world, and he worked tirelessly to preserve an unspoiled part of Jackson. When we were Boy Scouts in Troop 1, his Eagle project was to clean and clear the trails along the Pearl

River. Few people know this because he never talked about it, but maintaining those trails became Jeff's lifelong Eagle project. Every year, from the time he graduated from Ole Miss until this past winter, he went into the woods and worked on the trails to make sure they were as pristine as they were when we were boys.

"Jeff's generosity wasn't limited to the outdoors. When he first started making a little money, he used some of it to buy his mother a new car. She'd never had a new car. It was a Chevrolet Caprice, not as cool as Jeff's BMWs, but that's what she wanted. He wrapped it in red and green ribbons and surprised her on Christmas morning. Giving his mama that car made Jeff happier than any gift he ever got. Nothing made Jeff happier than making the people he loved happy.

"Jeff's father was a helicopter pilot in the Marines. He was killed in action in Vietnam the year after Jeff and I met. The night he and his mother found out, he and I were sitting in the treehouse his dad built for us. Jeff looked over at me, smiled, and said his dad was a hero. He got shot but saved the lives of the wounded men in the helicopter by flying them to safety before he died. That was just like Jeff. Finding a silver lining in even the darkest cloud. You could never stay down and out for long when you were with Jeff. I wish he was here now to cheer us up. He would have made me tell the funny stories and skip this one.

"Jeff loved music. So do I, and we liked the same singers and the same songs. When he heard a new song or artist, he would call me immediately, excited to share the news. I thought about one of those songs last night while deciding how to tell you just how special Jeff was. The song is "Dead Drunk and Naked" by the Drive By Truckers. No comma between Dead and Drunk. The man in the song says his daddy used to tell him everything comes down to what they say about you when you're not around.

"There's a great deal of truth to that. The last time I heard somebody say something bad about Jeff was when Mrs. Cheney said some bad things about both of us when he caught that snake. But Jeff was right there when she said them. I never heard anybody say anything bad about Jeff when he was not around. Not once.

"I could go on till Tuesday, but I won't. Thank you for coming today to celebrate Jeff's life. I will always be grateful to Jeff's mother for choosing the house two doors down from ours and to Jeff for choosing to ring our doorbell. If she'd picked a different house or he'd rung a different doorbell, my life wouldn't be the same. It wouldn't even be close. I will miss him every day for the rest of my life.

"I've now shared some of my memories of Jeff and would like to hear some of yours. Evelyn and I cordially invite you to join us at our home in Madison after the graveside service. Our address is at the bottom of the order of worship. If you get there before we do, make yourself at home. We will break bread, give toasts, and honor the life of Jeff Freeman."

Sam returned to the front pew, and the congregation stood and sang all four verses of "Amazing Grace." After Reverend Stockett closed the service with the benediction, the Freemans, Thompsons, and many others lined up to thank Sam and hug him. In the parking lot, Sam checked his iPhone and saw a one-line text from David: "Best eulogy since Moses split the sea in two. I'm proud of you."

# Chapter Twenty

July 15, 2023

## Catch Him and Fry Him

Sam waited until the others had left the cemetery, then tossed a handful of dirt onto the top of the casket, apologized to Jeff, and said goodbye. The caterer had everything ready when he and Evelyn got home. A bartender stood behind the bar. Jeff's friends and family had already begun arriving. The eulogy had lifted their spirits, and the gathering was more celebration than wake. Wine and stories flowed.

Jeff was only sixty-three years old and died a violent, tragic death, but one thing was certain: Before he died, he lived. He was loved by many, and they all had stories to tell. Marsha, Eric, and Olivia even told some. Evelyn came into the living room and put her hand on Sam's arm. "This is what he would have wanted."

Sam's suffering was far from over, but he'd done the right thing since his meeting with David. He'd gone to the funeral home with Marsha and Eric, prepared a eulogy that was worthy of his best friend, and kept his composure while delivering it. He was feeling better about himself.

One of Jeff's golf buddies, Phil Hardin, walked over to speak. "Great job on the eulogy, Sam. Outstanding. Truly outstanding."

"Thank you. I had good material to work with, as you know. I'm sure you have lots of stories I could have added."

"No doubt about it. Listen, I was just wondering. Do they have any suspects? Any leads?"

"Not that I know of."

"Just seems like somebody would have seen something. I heard it happened between nine and eleven. It's not like it was three in the morning."

"If there were any witnesses, I haven't heard about it."

"I wonder if there were any security cameras anywhere."

Sam hadn't thought of cameras and felt his face flush. "On the Trace? I doubt it. I don't know where they would be."

"You're probably right. What about tire tracks? Did they find any tire tracks?"

"No idea."

"I figured you'd be checking every hour. I keep thinking of that scene in *My Cousin Vinny* when Joe Pesci and Marisa Tomei prove the 'two yutes' were innocent from the tire tracks left by the real killers."

"Great movie." Sam wanted to change the subject.

"Fabulous. Marisa Tomei, man oh man. You ever have a witness like her?"

"Not even close."

"You know who's handling the investigation? Is it the feds because it was on the Trace? I sure hope somebody's turning over every stone."

"Not sure. I haven't heard a word."

"I thought you'd know."

"If there's anything, I'm sure they'll tell Marsha or Eric, and I'm sure they'll tell me. But I haven't asked them. It's bad enough they lost their father. I don't want to make it any worse."

"You and Evelyn were at the Bar banquet that night, weren't you? I heard you announced you were retiring. Congratulations. Y'all come home on the Trace?"

Sam had figured somebody might ask this at some point, but he felt his face flush again. It was doubtful that anyone could prove they came home on the Trace, but why take the chance by lying about it?

"We did. I don't know if it happened before we got home or after."

"I don't guess y'all saw anything suspicious."

"Not a thing."

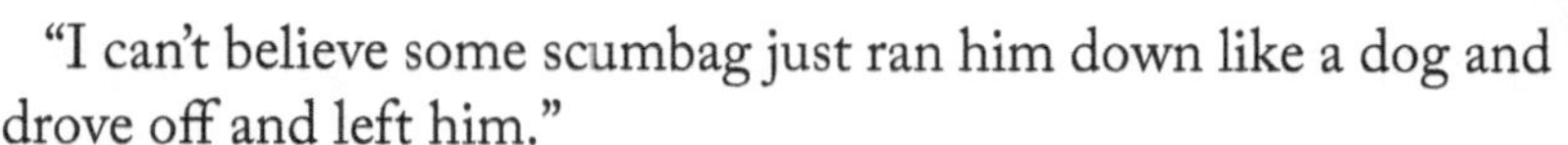

"I can't believe some scumbag just ran him down like a dog and drove off and left him."

Sam didn't disagree. "It's terrible."

"I mean, what kind of person would do that, Sam? What kind of person would plow into somebody who was riding a bicycle and just keep on going without a care in the world?"

"Looks like we may never know who did it."

"He might have still been alive. It's possible he could have been saved. But the guy just kept driving."

Sam decided to protest this one. "A park ranger told Olivia there was almost no blood. Evelyn thinks that means he was killed instantly. Maybe the driver stopped and saw he was dead and left."

"I sure hope they find him."

"Or her."

"Or her. Whoever did it deserves to fry. I hope they find him and fry him."

"Maybe they will."

"Let me know if you hear anything, okay?"

"Sure."

"And here's another thing that's been bothering me. What on earth was he doing out there on his bike on the Natchez Trace at that hour? He lived here all his life. He knew there weren't any lights."

"That bothers me too. Jeff took risks, but it was always when he thought the reward was worth it. This one doesn't make any sense. He liked to ride his bike on the Trace, but he never mentioned riding on it at night. But maybe this wasn't the first time. He wouldn't have told me because I would have given him an earful."

"I don't know if you know this, but he hadn't played golf with us since April. Said he was having back trouble. And yet he was out there riding his bike on the Natchez Trace at night."

"He told me about his back when we went fishing in May. I have no idea what he was doing on the Trace. I guess he thought there wouldn't be much traffic, and he could pull off the road if he heard a car coming."

"I guess so, but it was dumb, and Jeff was no dummy."

"You're right about that. I used to get him to help me with my opening statements and closing arguments. He would have been a great trial lawyer."

"Especially with a jury full of women."

"You're right about that too. I'm glad I met Evelyn before he did. I wouldn't have stood a chance."

"He was a great guy, that's for sure."

"The best."

"Our golf group won't be the same without him."

"I won't be the same either."

When Sam came to bed, Evelyn rolled over to face him and put her arm across his chest. "I can't tell you how proud I am. I know it's been hard. You were wonderful today. I love you."

Sam wrapped his arm around her shoulders and pulled her close. "Thank you. I love you too. You think we could have left tire tracks? Think they could trace them to the Explorer?"

"I doubt it. It hasn't rained in weeks. What made you think of that?"

"Phil Hardin mentioned it. He asked me if they had any leads. I'm about due for a new set of tires. I may get some Monday."

"If it'll keep you from worrying, do it."

"Phil said he hopes they catch the guy and fry him. Those were his exact words."

"That's because he doesn't know what happened. You know Phil. He would have left for sure. He probably wouldn't even have stopped."

"But I'm the one who did leave."

"*We're* the ones. It wasn't just you. And it was my idea. I know it's hard, but I hope you'll stop blaming yourself. You left because I made you."

"I'm okay."

"You sure? I worry about you."

"I'm okay. I've made my peace with it. David made me realize that staying may have been better for me, but it would have been worse for you and Sara and Jason."

"You don't think I told you to leave because of me, I hope."

"Of course not. Your first thought was to protect me. If you'd been driving, I would have wanted to protect you."

"Thank you. I wouldn't wish this on my worst enemy. I want to help you get over it. Listen to me. We were driving home on the Trace at night. A man on a bike lost his balance and fell in front of us. There was no way you could have avoided him. You didn't even see him. We couldn't possibly know it was Jeff. I made you leave. None of it—not one bit—was your fault. I just want you to be okay."

"I'm okay. Because I have the world's best wife, I'm doing pretty well for a man who killed his best friend and gave his eulogy four days later."

# Part IV

## Finding Out Why

# Chapter Twenty-One

May 13, 2023

The Head Dude

It was mid-May, too warm for a campfire in Jackson but still cool enough in the Ozarks. Sam poked the fire with a stick—he never could seem to leave a fire alone—and said, "This'll probably be our last campfire for a while."

Jeff stared at the flames. After a few seconds, he looked up and smiled. "Probably so," he said.

It was the last night of a last-minute trip. Jeff called on Tuesday with a proposal. They would drive up to Arkansas on Thursday afternoon, camp beside Greers Ferry Lake, and fish the Little Red River on Friday. They would camp the next two nights beside the Norfork River, fish the river on the day in between, then head home on Sunday. The forecast was perfect, and they would miss only a day and a half of work. Jeff said he needed to talk to Sam about something important.

Until recent years, Sam would have cited work demands and begged off, saying he couldn't go on such short notice. His law practice always came first, and there was always something that needed doing. But after he turned sixty and a law partner and another good friend died at their desks, Sam vowed to work less and play more. As Jeff often reminded him, life was no dress rehearsal. He accepted the proposal immediately and said he had something important to say too. Jeff picked him up in his newest BMW after lunch on Thursday. Their sons were now grown, so they took their dogs instead. Buddy rode with Josey in the back seat. They headed northwest on Highway 49 and crossed the Mississippi at Greenville.

Trout cannot abide muddy water or flatland lakes and rivers. They live in beautiful places, in clear mountain lakes and streams. The two Arkansas rivers Sam and Jeff fished were no exception, but neither would have been cold enough for trout if left to their own devices. Trout could live in the rivers only because man had interfered with nature by damming both. The Little Red was fed by cold water released from the depths of Greers Ferry Lake, the Norfork from Norfork Lake. Both had great trout fishing in the cold tailwaters below the dams. A world-record brown trout of nearly forty pounds was caught in the five-mile-long stretch below Norfork Dam.

Both the fish and the weather cooperated. Sam and Jeff caught rainbows, browns, cutthroats, and brookies, and Jeff caught the biggest trout of his life, a twenty-four-inch brown in the Norfork. The dogs sat beside each other on the bank and watched. When Sam or Jeff hooked a fish, they ran up and down the shoreline barking.

The men and dogs were now enjoying a campfire for the third night in a row. The stars were out, the temperature in the fifties. Sam and Jeff were sipping a fine single malt. All was right with the world, or so it seemed. They often sat in silence for long stretches, hypnotized by the flames, but Jeff had something on his mind. "You believe in God?" he asked.

The question came as a surprise. The two had talked about nearly everything over the course of their long friendship, but they'd never talked about this. Sam thought for a few seconds, then answered. "I do," he said. "But am I sure of it? I can't say that. Maybe it's because I'm a lawyer, but I need evidence beyond a reasonable doubt to be sure of anything."

"I hear you. I'm the same way."

"But when I look around, I see lots of things that make me think there's a god."

"Like that river and this campfire," Jeff said. "And these dogs."

"Dogs are some of the best evidence," Sam added. He reached down and scratched Buddy behind the ears. "The world seems to me to be just too complicated and too magnificent to be the result of pure, dumb luck. I think there must have been a creator, someone who designed the whole thing."

"The head engineer," Jeff declared.

"Not just the head engineer," Sam pointed out. "The head botanist and zoologist and landscape architect. And the head imaginator. Imagine imagining the whole world and everything in it and then creating it all.  All the plants and animals and mountains and rivers."

"And the people; don't forget us. If God's in charge of everything, that makes him the head dude. He should have a hard hat with 'Head Dude' on the front." They smiled at the thought.

"A tool belt too, and a clipboard," Sam added. "God might be taking it easy now, but just imagine how long his to-do list would have been when he first got started." Sam looked up from the fire. "Let me ask you something. Why are you asking me about God? What's on your mind?"

"I don't know. It's the last campfire of the trip. When we get all serious because we have to return to work and deadlines and commitments. What about heaven and hell? You believe in them?"

"I'm less confident of that," Sam conceded.

"Less evidence."

"Exactly. I know what the Bible says, and maybe it's all true. I'm sure not saying it's not."

"Me neither," Jeff said. "What do I know? So far as I know, I've never been dead before."

"But I also know it's human nature to believe we're not gone for good, that somehow we live forever."

"I was listening the other day to that terrific song by Greg Brown. You know it. 'Let the Mystery Be.'"

"Great song," Sam agreed.

"He's married to Iris DeMent, you know."

"Not only are they married, but she wrote the song."

"Man, I would sure hate to be their dog."

Sam looked up again and smiled. "And just why would you hate to be their dog?"

"Cause Greg's got like the lowest voice in the history of the world, and Iris has the highest," Jeff explained. "Must drive their poor dog crazy."

"You're the crazy one. Still crazy after all these years."

"I amn't either."

"Amn't's not a word. I told you that a long time ago."

"You just said it, didn't you? The person in the song says people are always worried about where they're gonna go when they die."

"But he thinks he'll just let the mystery be."

"I'm thinking that's what I'll do too."

"I think that's what we all do," Sam said. "What else can we do?"

"I guess we'll find out when we find out. Or maybe we'll be gone for good and won't find out. What did John Prine say his dad said in 'When I Get to Heaven'?"

"That when you're dead, you're a dead peckerhead."

"That's it."

"How about let's talk about before we're dead? I told you I had something I needed to tell you. Evelyn is the only person I've told so far. You're the second. I haven't even told Sara and Jason. Evelyn wasn't surprised. You won't be either, but everybody else'll be shocked."

"Enough with the drum roll. Spit it out."

"I'm retiring. Announcing it in July when I become the Bar president. Effective immediately. I've figured out what to do with my cases. I'm telling everybody at the firm and my clients next week, but I won't tell anybody else until the Bar Convention."

"Good for you. I wondered if you'd ever really do it. You deserve it. You've worked more in forty years than most people do in a hundred, though I guess nobody's ever worked for a hundred years. But who knows? Maybe Methusaleh did."

"I'm excited. Think of all the trips we can take. Remember when we promised to hike the AT from Georgia to Maine? I bet we could still do it. I decided to take the plunge first so I could start badgering you. My harassment campaign starts now. How much longer do you plan to work? You need to retire too. Let's set a date. Pull up your calendar."

Jeff looked up at Sam, then back down at the flames. "That's something I need to figure out. It won't be too long, I'm sure. Who knows? Maybe I'll stop working when you stop working."

"That would be great. We could go on a trip to celebrate."

A few seconds passed. "Do you know the date you'll announce your retirement?"

"July the 11th. That's the night of the big banquet at the Bar Convention. You said you had something you needed to tell me too. What is it?"

Jeff hesitated, looking at the fire, then spoke. "Nothing. It was something at the office I wanted you to help me deal with, but it worked itself out."

"You sure?"

"Positive. All resolved."

"I was wondering something else. You feeling okay?"

"Sure. Why do you ask?"

"You seemed to be having a hard time tying flies on your leader. And you looked like you were struggling to keep your balance in the river. You've never done that before."

"Oh, that. I can't see up close as well as I used to—I guess I need to get me some of those readers—and I did something to my back. Picked up something heavy I shouldn't have. Sometimes I forget I'm not still the kid stacking sandbags at the power plant."

"I hear you," Sam said. "That's one more reason you need to hurry up and retire. We need to do more things like this while we still can."

"We've already done a lot of things like this. George Bailey may have had a wonderful life, but he never caught a twenty-four-inch brown trout, at least not in the movie. And Donna Reed may have been gorgeous, but dealing with Mr. Potter was a huge pain. I'd say our lives have been much better than his. In fact, I'd say we're the luckiest men on the face of the earth."

"That's what Lou Gehrig said, isn't it?"

"He said he was the luckiest *man*. We're the luckiest *men*."

"We're a whole lot luckier than he was, that's for sure. And we're about to get even luckier." Sam looked down at the dogs. "And so are Buddy and Josey. I think they love campfires almost as much as we do."

Jeff put another stick on the fire, then looked up. "I love you, Sam."

Sam leaned back. "Wow. I love you too. Of course. But you've never told me that. I've never told you either. Where did that come from?"

"I don't know. I just wanted to say it."

A few minutes later, Jeff's breathing changed. He was asleep. Sam reached over and squeezed his arm. "You better turn in before you do a face plant in the fire."

A decade earlier, after Sam and Jeff both began snoring, they started sleeping in separate tents, preferably at least thirty feet apart. Jeff smiled, stood up, and headed for his. Josey followed. Half an hour later, when Sam could no longer keep his eyes open, he and Buddy went to theirs. The snoring didn't seem to bother the dogs.

# Chapter Twenty-Two

July 5, 2023

Facing the End

Jeff had planned to tell Sam when they were in Arkansas but decided against it on the last night. He didn't want to ruin the last campfire of their last trip or the drive home the next day. And he hadn't yet made his scheduled trip to Mayo, so he didn't have the second opinion his neurologist had recommended. And what was the point of telling Sam anyway? To have a shoulder to cry on? Perhaps misery really does love company, but why make his best friend miserable too? Jeff decided to spare him. He would go it alone.

He first noticed something wrong shortly after the first of the year. The muscles in his arms began twitching. He felt weak and had trouble keeping his balance. He slurred words. He waited for it to pass, but his symptoms got worse instead of better.

He tried to self-diagnose by searching the Internet. He found nothing definitive but one possibility that was alarming. He made an appointment with his personal physician. When he described his symptoms, the doctor immediately referred him to a neurologist. The appointment was scheduled for the first week of May.

The neurologist, an impressive woman with impeccable credentials, conducted several tests and confirmed Jeff's worst fear. She believed he had Amyotrophic Lateral Sclerosis, also known as Lou Gehrig's disease. But an ALS diagnosis is tricky, she said, and she couldn't be certain. She strongly recommended that he obtain a second opinion at one of the three Mayo campuses, all of which had multidisciplinary ALS clinics. She knew members of the ALS team in Jacksonville, Jeff agreed to go, and she arranged for him to have a complete assessment in the second week of June. Jeff decided he would try not to think about his future before the trip to Mayo. After seeing the neurologist in Jackson, he called Sam and invited him to go fishing in the Ozarks.

After their trip, Jeff went to Mayo and now had the second opinion. The team at the clinic performed a battery of tests. There were an MRI, muscle and nerve biopsies, and a nerve conduction velocity study. They performed a spinal tap to analyze his spinal fluid, blood and urine tests, electromyography (EMG) to measure the electrical activity of his muscles and the health of the nerves controlling them. There were more tests than he could count.

At the end of the second day, he met with the head of the team, who had finished at the top of her med school class at Johns Hopkins and was, according to Jeff's neurologist in Jackson, one of the world's foremost authorities on one of the world's cruelest diseases. She gave him the bad news: There was no single test or series of tests that could establish with certainty that someone had ALS, especially in the early stages of the disease, but Jeff had all the classic symptoms, and she'd ruled out the most likely alternatives. She'd seen thousands of cases and was as certain as she could possibly be that he had ALS.

Jeff asked her what to expect and requested that she not sugarcoat it. After describing the normal progress of the disease, she said the symptoms were relatively predictable, but the pace was not. She told him about two famous cases that were very different. Astrophysicist Stephen Hawking lived with ALS for fifty-five years until his death at seventy-eight. But in most cases, death comes much faster. Lou Gehrig took himself out of the Yankees' lineup in April 1939 because he was struggling at the plate and felt weak. He'd played in 2,130 consecutive games, a record that lasted for more than half a century, but he never played again. Only two months later, he returned to Yankee Stadium and told the crowd of 60,000 that he considered himself the luckiest man on the face of the earth. Less than two years after that, before his thirty-eighth birthday, he was dead.

Most ALS patients, the neurologist at Mayo said, die twenty to forty-eight months after the onset of symptoms, which in Jeff's case began five months earlier. Some drugs might slow the disease, but nothing could stop it. "So having ALS is a death sentence," Jeff observed.

She put her hand on his arm. "I'm afraid so," she said, "but so is being born."

After returning to Jackson, Jeff opened his laptop to read more about the disease. He trusted the doctors, but he wanted to see it for himself in black and white and let it sink in. The more he read, the more he agreed that Lou Gehrig really was lucky, at least compared to Stephen Hawking. ALS is an unspeakably cruel disease, to its victims as well as their loved ones and caretakers. A fast death is surely preferable to a slow one.

ALS is a neurological disorder that affects motor neurons, the nerve cells in the brain and spinal cord that control voluntary movement of the muscles, including those needed to breathe. The motor neurons slowly deteriorate as the disease progresses. They ultimately die and stop sending signals to the muscles. When the signals stop, the muscles stop working. Death is inevitable; the only question is when. The ultimate cause is usually suffocation. When the muscles required to breathe no longer work, the patient dies. It's a horrifying way to go.

The more Jeff learned about what lay before him, the more certain he became that he wanted no part of it. His symptoms had progressed just since the trip to Arkansas, though he did his best to hide them. During the pandemic, he often worked from home with a phone and a laptop. After the trip to Mayo, he stayed home nearly every day. And he invented excuses to turn down Sam and Evelyn's dinner invitations. Sam could see that something was wrong when they were in Arkansas. Jeff told him it was just a sore back and problems with his vision, but his symptoms had gotten worse, and Evelyn was a doctor. There was no way he could fool them now.

Jeff would soon need full-time assistance, but who would provide it? Marsha was a young mother with a husband, a baby, and a career.

She had no time to care for her dying father. Eric was in law school and would be launching his career in a year. Jeff wouldn't allow him to put it on hold. Sam and Evelyn would volunteer, but Sam was about to retire, and they wanted to travel. Jeff wasn't going to be the reason they couldn't.

Jeff had always been active and independent. He was happiest when he was outdoors, but he needed his health to enjoy it. Being unable to do the things he loved would be painful. Being a witness to his own decline, as his body wound down like a clock until the day he suffocated, would be excruciating.

But perhaps even worse would be the pain his family and friends would endure, especially those faced with the burden of taking care of him. They would do it and do it gladly, and they would never let him live out his days in an institution, but he couldn't bear to put them through it. The commitment of their time and disruption of their lives would be bad enough, but the horror of watching him waste away until the muscles he used to breathe stopped working would be far worse. He couldn't bear to put them through it. He wouldn't put them through it.

He began putting his affairs in order. He prepared an updated financial statement of his assets and liabilities, dated it the previous October, and put copies in drawers in his desks at his office and at home. There was no need to update his will. He had changed it after the divorce so his estate would be split equally between Marsha and Eric.

Though Jeff earned a good living, his estate would be relatively modest. He and Olivia had lived well and spent generously on their children. They sent Marsha to a wilderness program in the mountains of the West called Wilderness Ventures for several summers, then Eric went for several more to Keewaydin Temagami, a camp in northern Ontario that served as a base for wilderness canoe trips. Both cost many times what he and Sam spent on their road trip to New England in 1978.

Then came the divorce six years ago. Jeff and Olivia split the savings he had accumulated during their marriage, and his monthly alimony obligation made it impossible to recoup what the divorce cost him. He was also spending $100,000 a year on tuition and living expenses for Eric to go to UVA so he wouldn't be saddled with student loans when he graduated.

The divorce decree required Jeff to maintain a million-dollar life insurance policy with Olivia as the beneficiary. The policy was to protect her if he died and could no longer make alimony payments. Jeff approved of the provision. Olivia gave up her career in pharmaceutical sales when Marsha was born and was now in her fifties and had limited earning potential. Jeff was no longer married to her, but she was the mother of his children. He didn't want her to struggle, and he didn't want her to be a financial burden to Marsha and Eric.

The previous fall, before the onset of his symptoms, Jeff had replaced the life insurance policy he obtained when the divorce was finalized with a new one with lower premiums. He read the new policy at the time and now had a nagging feeling about one of the terms. He went to the bank, retrieved the policy from his safe deposit box, and brought it home. He found the provision in the fine print.

SUICIDE: No proceeds shall be payable if the insured dies by suicide or assisted suicide within two years after the effective date of the policy.

The effective date was October 26, 2022. The exclusion would remain in effect for nearly sixteen more months. The policy would be worthless if he died by his own hand before then.

Jeff weighed his options. One was to deal with his decline as best he could. If he was still alive when the two-year suicide exclusion ended, he could put an end to his misery then if he was not too debilitated to do so. If he was, his life would continue until ALS ended it. Choosing that option would also mean his friends and family would have to witness his deterioration. Some of them—most likely Sam and Evelyn—would have to upend their lives to take care of him. Everyone would suffer, not just Jeff. There would be plenty of company for his misery.

The other option—the preferred one based on all he'd heard and read—was to end his life now. But if he did that, Olivia would get nothing, neither the proceeds of the policy nor any further alimony. Nor could Jeff fix the problem by making her the sole beneficiary of his will. Not only would his estate be much less than a million dollars, but leaving it all to Olivia would mean his children would get nothing.

Both options were unacceptable. *Surely,* Jeff thought, *there must be a better one.*

# Chapter Twenty-Three

July 11, 2023

The End

Jeff's ALS diagnosis combined with the suicide exclusion left him in a state of despair. Not only was he dying, but others would suffer no matter how he chose to die. If he did nothing and let the disease take its course, his loved ones would have to witness the horror of his deterioration and death. If he ended his life now, his ex-wife would be left without the financial support he'd promised her.

Jeff considered a third option. It would leave Olivia financially secure and spare his friends and family from having to watch as ALS slowly killed him, but there would be other consequences. The effect on the insurance company didn't trouble him—if he did nothing and died of natural causes, the benefit the company paid would be exactly the same—but the impact on a person Jeff almost certainly didn't know would be far worse. The stranger, his unwitting accomplice, would suffer, and Jeff grieved over it. But in the end, he decided the third option was a lesser evil than either of the first two. He'd told Sam when they were in Arkansas that he might stop working when Sam did. Now he would do exactly that.

Jeff never learned to type, at least not the way typists type. He'd been hunting and pecking with two fingers for more than forty years. Sam badgered him to bite the bullet and take a typing class, but he never did. He got by.

And now he was glad he never learned. If he spread his fingers across a keyboard and tried to type now, the result would be nothing but gibberish. But by hunting and pecking and going slow, he was still able to get by. He made final revisions to the letter, addressed the envelope, then got behind the wheel of his BMW with Josey on the passenger side. He headed to the FedEx office on Main Street in Madison, taking his time so nobody would get hurt if he lost control. He sent the letter to Marsha and returned home.

Early that evening, before Jeffery's bedtime, Jeff placed a Zoom call to Marsha. She held the baby in her lap so Jeff could see them both.

"Look at you, Jeff. You've grown."

"It's only been a week since our last Zoom call, Daddy, and his name is Jeffery."

"Call him what you want. I call him Jeff. Isn't that right, Jeff?"

"But having two Jeffs will be confusing."

"No, it won't. I'm much older than he is. Bigger too. It's easy to tell us apart. Jeff, can you say Papa?"

"He can't talk yet, Daddy. You know that."

"But it's never too early to start training him. If I don't, he might wind up calling me Gramps or Pawpaw. I'm nipping that possibility in the bud."

"So you get to decide his name and yours too."

"Absolutely. I am the paterfamilias. Your Papa loves you, Jeff. He loves your mother too. When you learn to talk, call her Meemaw."

"I love you too, Daddy. You're crazy, but I love you. Jeffery doesn't love you yet, but he will. And we'll teach him to call you Papa."

Jeff reached Eric on his cell. He was having dinner with lawyers at the firm and couldn't talk long. Before they ended the call, Jeff told Eric he loved him. Eric smiled. That Jeff loved his son went without saying, so Jeff never said it. It was about time, Eric thought. He told Jeff he loved him too, then they hung up.

For his last supper, Jeff ordered a meat lovers' pizza from Soulshine. Pizza had become a staple of his diet because he didn't have to hold utensils to eat it. It wasn't healthy, but what did it matter? Soulshine didn't deliver, but their pizza was better than the places that did, and the restaurant was nearby. When he picked it up, he visited with William, the big black man with the big laugh who ran the place. Jeff could have eaten at the bar, but he took the pizza home so no one would see if he struggled with it.

It was just pizza, but it was his last one, so he decided to have one of his favorite wines, a full-bodied red blend by Bogle called Phantom. Using the corkscrew wasn't easy, but he had the will and found a way. He would limit himself to two glasses, three at the most, because there was still work to be done.

He ate all the pizza he could, but there were still two pieces in the box. He was about to toss them into the garbage, but then he stopped himself. He was thinking about the future. He slid the extra slices into a baggie and put them on the top shelf in the refrigerator. If suspicious investigators came snooping, they would have to ask themselves why on earth he saved the pizza.

Jeff filled Josey's food and water bowls, went out to the garage, folded down the back seat of his BMW, and managed to load his bicycle. He came back inside, invited Josey to join him on the couch, and loved on the dog with his right hand while he finished his third glass of wine with his left. Then he decided to finish the bottle. One more glass wouldn't matter, and it would give him liquid courage for the task that lay ahead.

When Jeff again walked out to the garage, Josey tried to follow. Jeff told him to stay, and he stopped and sat down. They gazed at each other. Only the man knew it was for the last time. Jeff stepped back inside, hugged his dog, then headed out into the night.

He parked in the lot behind the Parkway Information Cabin alongside the Trace. At this hour, there were no other cars. He made sure no one was watching, then unloaded his bike and put on his camping headlamp. He walked up to the Trace with the bike and pushed it along the shoulder, heading west. Just before the bridge passing over Highway 51, he came to a stand of trees and underbrush only a few feet from the road. He laid his bike down facing east, the wheels in the grass and the seat and handlebars on the edge of the pavement. He took cover behind the underbrush and turned off his headlamp so he couldn't be seen.

While he waited, he thought of Marsha and Jeffery. He would have lost the debate over what to call his grandson, but he wouldn't have given up without a fight. He thought of Eric, who was being courted by the finest law firms in America. He was a far better student than Jeff ever was. And he thought of Sam and all their glorious times together.

Headlights approached from the west. Jeff could tell it was either a full-size SUV or a pickup. He mouthed a silent apology to the driver, then took three quick steps and dove headfirst. His timing was perfect.

# Chapter Twenty-Four

July 18, 2023

Jeff's Last Letter

"Marsha, thanks for calling. It's good to hear your voice. I was going to call you tonight. You doing okay?"

"I'm not sure, Sam. Eric's on the phone."

"Eric, you okay?"

"I'm not sure either. Marsha said she had something important to tell me, but she needed to get you on the call first."

"What is it, Marsha?"

"After we made it home this afternoon, a FedEx truck stopped in front of the house. The driver had a delivery for me. I had to sign for it. It was a letter from Daddy dated the eleventh."

"The day he died."

"Let me read it to you.

*Dear Marsha, Eric, and Sam,*

*I was thinking about the three of you today—my beautiful daughter, the best Christmas present ever, my wonderful son, and the best friend a man could ever have. Marsha, I'm just sending it to you, but please call Eric and Sam and read it to them.*

*Marsha, you can tell Bob what it says, and Sam, you can tell Evelyn. And Sam, there's one other person I want you to tell. I don't know the person's name or even if it's a man or a woman, but you'll probably know by the time Marsha reads this to you.*

*I was thinking today what a wonderful life I've had. With two wonderful children and Sam as my best friend, how could I not?*

*The three of you, more than anyone else in the world other than my parents, have given me a wonderful life. Today I consider myself the luckiest man on the face of the earth.*

*I love all three of you to the moon and back.*

*Daddy/Jeff*

*P.S. Sam, Josey sure loved being with Buddy in Arkansas."*

Five seconds passed in silence, then Sam asked Marsha to read the letter again. He wanted to make sure he understood it all, not just what Jeff left in but what he left out. After she finished, Sam spoke. "Well, that sure explains a lot. Why he was on the Trace at night on his bike, for sure, but more than that.

"And I know why he wrote it and wanted me to be on the phone when you read it. He knew I would understand what he was saying, and he wanted to make sure y'all understood too.

"On our last night in the Ozarks in May, he told me we were the luckiest men on the face of the earth. I said I thought that's what Lou Gehrig said, and Jeff confirmed it. Now he's sent us this letter saying he considered himself the luckiest man on the face of the earth.

"Lou Gehrig used those exact words when he returned to Yankee Stadium after being diagnosed with ALS. The letter is Jeff's way of telling us he had ALS. He wanted me to be on the phone because he wanted all of us to know."

"You sure?" asked Marsha. "Why would he want us to know he had ALS?"

"I'm positive. I knew him better than anybody. And he wanted us to know so we wouldn't think of his death as such a tragedy. I've been thinking how horrible it was that he died just as he was about to enjoy a long, healthy retirement. But not with ALS, he wouldn't."

Sam continued. "This makes sense of a lot of things. When we were in Arkansas, I could tell something was wrong with him. He had trouble tying on flies and keeping his balance when we were fishing. He blamed it on his vision and a backache. And before the trip, he said he had something important to tell me, but when I asked about it, he told me it was something at the office that had worked itself out. But I got the sense there was something he wasn't telling me. Then, on our last night by the campfire, after he said we were the luckiest men on the face of the earth, he said he loved me."

Eric interrupted. "Really? He said he loved me when he called me the night of the accident."

Sam corrected him. "The night of what we thought was an accident. I knew he loved me, but he never told me. And of course he loved both of you. To the moon and back, like he said. He would beam with joy when he talked about y'all."

"I knew he loved me," Eric said, "but he never told me either. It was just understood. But I was glad he told me. I told him too."

"He called Jeffery and me on Zoom that night and told us too," said Marsha. "Sam, why do you think he didn't tell us before?"

"I suspect he didn't want us to suffer, so he decided to bear it alone. And he wouldn't have wanted us trying to take care of him. He would have despised being a burden. People with ALS get to where they can't even feed themselves. Can you imagine spoon-feeding a man like your father? Can you imagine him letting someone spoon-feed him?"

Marsha agreed. "That makes sense. He asked you to tell somebody else, but he didn't even know the person's name. Any idea what that's about?"

"I think I know that too. I think it's the driver who hit him. He had no idea who it would be, but he figured I would know by now."

"But why tell the driver?"

"So he wouldn't suffer either. Jeff wanted the driver to know he had a terminal disease so he wouldn't feel so bad about hitting him."

"And now it looks like the driver will never know," Eric chimed in. "Serves him right."

Sam let it pass. "What do y'all think? I'm trying to decide if I feel better or worse."

"I think I feel better," said Marsha. "I know a little about ALS. It's horrible. And for Daddy, it would have been unbearable."

Eric agreed. "He would have hated having somebody taking take care of him. He didn't even like for somebody to carry his luggage."

"And he would have hated for us to remember him that way,"

Sam added. "I had no idea he had ALS, but I'm not surprised he didn't tell us."

"I'm thinking of when he walked up beside you in Glacier with that mama grizzly threatening to charge," Eric said. "He didn't hesitate a second."

"He was fearless, that's for sure. He was what a man should be."

"*What a man should be*," Eric repeated. "I like that. And how could a man like that stand to be spoon-fed?"

"He couldn't," agreed Marsha. "Sam, please let us know if you have any luck finding the driver. It's been a week. I don't know how you could, but let us know if you do."

"Of course."

"And don't tell anybody else if you find him. Definitely not the police. Daddy sure wouldn't want that."

Sam greeted Evelyn at the door. "Come sit with me in the den. I have something important to tell you." Sam didn't start with a drum roll this time. "This is just between us, but it was suicide."

"Suicide? Who?"

"Jeff. He killed himself."

"How? He was riding his bike."

"We assumed he lost his balance and fell off in front of us. I found out today he did it on purpose."

"How? How'd you find out?"

"He had ALS. He sent Marsha the sweetest letter. He wanted me to tell the driver he had ALS. He didn't want the driver to suffer."

"He said that? That he had ALS?"

"Not in so many words, but that's what he meant. I knew him."

"You sure?"

"He sent her the letter the day I hit him. I'm positive."

"The day *we* hit him."

"It was addressed to Marsha and Eric and me, but he just sent it to Marsha and asked her to read it to us. He said he'd had a wonderful life and loved us to the moon and back."

"Wow. How do you feel?"

"I'm trying to decide. I wish he'd told me so I could have tried to help him, but I think I know why he didn't. He didn't want anybody trying to help him. He didn't want to be a burden, and he didn't want us to have to see what ALS would do to him."

"That's so sad. That terrible disease, and he kept it to himself."

"I hate he went through it without me, but I feel better about his being gone."

"He'd be glad we left him, you know."

"You think so?"

"Sure. You were the unlucky man who happened to come along at just the right time to give him the end he chose. He sure wouldn't want you to get arrested. Anybody else either."

"I guess you're right. Marsha told me not to tell the police if I find the driver."

"Sound advice. Women know best. She's right, and I was right to make you leave. Just imagine if you'd stayed and gotten arrested, then a week later the letter showed up. What then?"

"We'll never know, will we? Oh, one more thing: Jeff wanted us to keep Josey."

"He said that?"

"No. He said Josey had a great time with Buddy in the Ozarks, but that's what he meant. I knew him."

"Excellent. Buddy will be delighted."

# Chapter Twenty-Five


July 19, 2023

A Perfect Occasion


Sam was about to knock on David's door but stopped himself when he heard a familiar voice coming from inside. It was John Prine singing "She Is My Everything" from *Fair & Square*. Sam smiled to himself. Only John would rhyme Jackson Square and long black hair with everywhere or karate and Maserati with everybody. Sam waited until the song ended to knock. David turned off the stereo and came to the door.

"Don't ever turn off John Prine on my account. You know better than that."

"Sam, what a surprise. I wouldn't have turned it off if I'd known it was you. Come in. Have a seat. I've been meaning to call. You did a wonderful job on the eulogy. It was just right."

"Thank you. You were right that I had plenty of stories."

"And you picked the best ones. You hit all the right notes."

"Thank you, but I'm not here fishing for compliments. I have something to tell you. Jeff only gave me permission to tell Evelyn and the driver, but I'm sure he wouldn't mind, especially since our conversation is privileged."

"Jeff gave you permission? How could he do that? Permission to tell what?"

"That it was suicide."

"What? How do you know?"

"He sent Marsha a letter the day I hit him."

"And said he was going to kill himself?"

"No, but that's what he meant."

"How could you tell?"

"It was addressed to Marsha, Eric, and me. He told us he'd lived a wonderful life and how much he loved us. And he said something that made me realize he had ALS."

"ALS—that's horrible. Two members of the congregation died from it last year. You didn't know he had it?"

"He and I went fishing in Arkansas in May. I could tell something was wrong with him, but he made excuses. And he told me before the trip he had something important to tell me. When I asked, he said it had been resolved, but I could tell something was on his mind. That had to be it."

"Any idea why he didn't tell you?"

"I think he didn't want anybody trying to take care of him. You knew him. He couldn't have stood being waited on hand and foot."

"That poor man. Such a terrible disease, and nobody knew."

"I wish he'd told me. But he never would have wanted us trying to keep him alive, and he knew we would."

"Did he say how he was going to do it?"

"He didn't even say he was going to do it, but it was clear he was telling us goodbye."

"But why do it the way he did it?"

"No idea."

"You said you were only supposed to tell Evelyn and the driver."

"He didn't say the driver. He asked me to tell one other person. He didn't know who it was, but he figured I would know by the time Marsha read the letter to me. It had to be the driver. He wanted the driver to know he had ALS. He was always thinking of others, and he was thinking of the driver."

"And now the driver knows."

"And now the driver knows."

"Do you still feel guilty about hitting him?"

"Jeff's death has nearly been the death of me, but I've never really felt guilty about it. It wasn't my fault, as you kept reminding me. But I sure felt guilty about leaving."

"So do you still feel guilty about that?"

"I still know it was wrong. I always will. But Evelyn said Jeff would have wanted us to leave, and I'm sure she's right. He didn't want the unlucky driver to feel guilty, and he sure wouldn't have wanted the unlucky driver to wind up in prison."

"I'm sure you're right."

"I was thinking something this morning. If he'd known it was Evelyn and me, he would have let us drive on past. The unlucky driver would have been the poor man or woman in the next vehicle to come along."

"Friendships like the one you and Jeff had are very rare, you know."

"I do, and I'll always be grateful. We were best friends every single day for fifty-five years, from the day we met until last Tuesday night."

"Y'all were very fortunate."

"Since last week I've wanted to ask him something or tell him something several times, and it took me a few seconds to realize I couldn't. I even wanted to ask him about an idea I had for his eulogy. I couldn't very well do that now, could I?"

"But you didn't need his help. It was perfect."

"Thank you. I don't know how good it was, and I know pride is a sin, but I was proud of myself for being able to get through it."

"Here's a thought: How about I pick us up a couple of filets and potatoes and come to your house at seven o'clock. You can be in charge of salad and whisky. Call me if I need to get a steak and potato for Evelyn too. We'll share a single malt, listen to John Prine, and talk about our friend Jeff."

"You're on. I've got a bottle of twenty-year-old Mortlach a client gave me for Christmas. I've been saving it for a special occasion. A night of John Prine songs and Jeff Freeman stories is a perfect occasion."

# Epilogue

In mid-November, four months after Jeff's death, Sam decided to make a solitary pilgrimage to a place they both loved. He checked the forecast and chose three clear days with cool nights. He would drive north to Tennessee, camp alone, spend a day in Shiloh National Military Park, then come home to Evelyn.

Shiloh was the first major battle of the Civil War. In two days of fighting in April 1862, more soldiers were killed than in all previous wars fought on American soil combined. The battlefield, on the west bank of the Tennessee River just north of the Mississippi line, has changed little since the two armies clashed there.

General Albert Sidney Johnston, the Confederate commander, was wounded on the afternoon of the first day of the battle and bled to death from a severed artery. Before he died, Jefferson Davis regarded Johnston as the finest general in either army. Lee and Grant achieved their fame later. Without Johnston's leadership, the South lost the battle and, three years later, the war. He remains the highest-ranking American officer ever killed in battle.

Before Jeff's father died as a hero in Vietnam, he took Jeff with him to Shiloh. When Jeff and Sam were Boy Scouts, they camped and hiked there with Troop 1. They loved the place, returned on their own nearly a dozen times, and learned all there was to know about the battle. They went again with Troop 1 when Jason and Eric were Scouts.

On his trip in November, Sam returned to familiar sites on the battlefield—Fraley Field, where the Confederates launched their attack at dawn on a fateful Sunday morning; Shiloh Church, the tiny house of worship that gave the battle its name; Hornets' Nest, where the fighting was so fierce the musket balls sounded like angry hornets; the deep ravine where General Johnston breathed his last; and Bloody Pond, which turned crimson from the blood of wounded soldiers who made their way to it in search of water. Thirty-five hundred soldiers died in the battle, an equal number on each side. Four times that many were wounded. An unknown number later died as a result.

As dusk approached, Sam walked along the path winding through the battlefield's national cemetery, which sits atop a high bluff overlooking the river. Ancient white oaks and cedars standing among the graves cast shadows that stretched down the hill before disappearing at the edge of the bluff. Most of those resting here died on those two days in 1862, but others lost their lives in the two world wars, Korea, and the war that claimed Jeff's father. The graveyard was filled with soldiers who gave the last full measure of devotion to their country. Sam was the only living soul standing among the dead. All was quiet.

A small stone marker in the last row of graves caught Sam's eye. The marker contained but three words: Unknown Union Soldier. Sam wondered about the soldier. Where was he from? Did he live on a farm or in a city? How old was he, and how did he die? Did he fight bravely to the end, or was he a scared teenager who turned and ran and was shot in the back? If he had survived the war, would he have made his way home, married, and had children? How many future lives were lost when his was lost in a war against his fellow Americans? How many stories ended a century before they had a chance to begin?

Sam sat on the stone wall that encircled the cemetery, looked down at the river, and thought of all the times he'd come here with Jeff. The sun was setting behind him. The sky at the horizon beyond the river turned from blue to gray, then to rose and crimson. A barred owl called in the distance. Sam didn't call back; that was Jeff's job.

In the days after Jeff's death, before Marsha called and read Sam the letter, he had asked himself over and over: *What if?* What if the hurricane had veered to the west sooner and the Bar Convention hadn't been moved to Jackson? What if he and Evelyn had left the banquet ten minutes sooner or ten minutes later? What if they'd driven home a different way to avoid the unlit Natchez Trace?

But now he knew that none of that mattered. Jeff had a plan. He would spare his family and friends the agony of watching him waste away and die. If it hadn't been Sam, it would have been someone else.

Sam didn't want to leave this sacred place, but at the dimming of the day, when the sky grew dark and the air turned cold, he trudged slowly up the hill to the parking lot. "Taps," which a bugler played every night when he and Jeff were at summer camp with Troop 1, came to mind. *If God is nigh to any place on earth*, Sam thought, *surely it is this one.*

As he made his way out of the battlefield, he wondered if he would ever set foot here again. Before now, he'd always come with Jeff. After this trip, why come back? But then he thought of a reason. Jeff's son-in-law was a fine young man, but he had no interest in camping or the outdoors. When young Jeffery was old enough, Sam would drive to Oxford, pick him up, and bring him here. Sam would teach him how to build a campfire, show him the constellations, and tell him stories about his grandfather. And he would say that Jeff called him Jeff.

Sam had known he might not get back to his campsite before dark, so he'd already gathered firewood for the night. An Eagle Scout, even half a century after his days as a Scout, knows to be prepared. Once he had a good fire going, Sam retrieved his tin cup, filled it half full of Talisker, Jeff's favorite single malt, and settled into his camp chair. As always, for no good reason, he picked up a stick and began poking the fire. Jeff would have told him the fire was fine, to leave it be. Sam smiled and raised his mug. "To you, my friend," he said.

On the drive home the next day, the yellows and golds of the beeches along the Natchez Trace reminded him of the stand of beeches near the Pearl he and Jeff discovered the summer they met. Before the trip, Sam had made a playlist of a hundred of their favorite songs. Most were on the CDs Jeff had burned for their trip to the West with Jason and Eric a decade earlier, but there were newer ones as well. Great songwriters were still writing great songs. You just had to know where to look.

The playlist was in the order the songs were recorded, and Sam listened to it from beginning to end on the long drive home from Tennessee. When he was still north of Tupelo and heard the guitar intro of "Tuesday's Gone," he lowered the windows in the Explorer, turned up the volume, and sang at the top of his lungs.

The music of their lives kept Sam company for the next three hours. After he turned off the Trace and was almost home, he reached the end of the playlist. He smiled at the first notes of the last song, which was a perfect choice to end his journey. The melody was beautiful, the lyrics a late-in-life reminiscence about everything the writer has seen along the way. He remembers every single blade of grass and every tree, every town and hotel room, and every song he's ever sung on a guitar out of tune.

At the sound of these words, all the memories came flooding back. The day Jeff rang the doorbell, the king snake in Alice's desk, the night at the power plant. Jeff's toast at the rehearsal dinner in Charleston, their last night in the Ozarks, the wonderful times in Maine and Montana and all the places in between. All the time they spent together and all the campfires they shared.

Evelyn was waiting for him outside when he pulled into the driveway. Tears were streaming down his cheeks, but he was smiling. The music came to an end. It was John Prine's very last song. The title was "I Remember Everything."

# Acknowledgments

I am grateful to my publisher, Mike Parker of WordCrafts Press. I've enlisted Mike and WordCrafts to publish nearly all my books, and for good reason. He's a consummate professional, and I enjoy working with him.

I also thank my dear friend Michael de Leeuw, who has given generously of his time to review and improve the manuscripts of all seven of my books. My wife Carrie, the world's best wife, also made this a better book with her suggestions. She always does.

That's usually about all I have to say in the acknowledgments at the end of a book, but I have more to say at the end of this one. This is a work of fiction, but much of it is based on my own experiences. I've paddled the Upper Missouri, the Middle Fork of the Salmon, the Chattooga, and the Allagash, and I read the last fifty pages of *Watership Down* to one of my sons beside a campfire in a grove of beech trees beside the Pearl River.

The book is also based on wonderful times I've had with my friends as well as stories they've told me. Friends who contributed inspiration for the story include:

Blake Teller, nicknamed Blade because he was stabbed in the leg during an attempted robbery when he was in college—he was the victim, not the robber—is a recent president of the Mississippi Bar Association. When I sent him Sam's speech from the first chapter, he said he wished I'd sent it before he had to write and give his own. Like the fictional Sam, the real Blake is a great guy and a fine lawyer. Unlike Sam, Blake has never killed anyone, at least so far as I know. When I asked if he had, he said not that he could recall.

Blake and I have hiked together in Wyoming and canoed in Alabama, Georgia, North Carolina, and Maine. When we canoed Section III of the Chattooga long ago with friends Wilson Carroll and Bob Smith, all but one of us had children. Wilson, who was childless at the time and is much more like Jeff than Sam, was the only one who chose to run Bull Sluice instead of portage around it. His canoe capsized, his head barely missed Decapitation Rock as the current swept him past it, and he now has three grown children.

Tommy Louis and Roy Liddell have a great deal in common with Sam and Jeff. They are lifelong best friends born in 1960, they grew up in Jackson, and they love the outdoors. The three of us have enjoyed wonderful times together—camping, hiking, and listening to music by campfires.

Tommy and Roy are also law partners, and Tommy is an avid cyclist. Against his advice, another of their law partners, Bob Walker, went cycling alone at night and was killed in a hit-and-run accident. The driver panicked and fled the scene, but she didn't mean any harm and was remorseful. Bob's family forgave her and supported a lenient sentence.

One summer when Roy was in college, he and friends went on a long road trip to New England. When money was running low and they were about to head home, they found a handful of hundred-dollar bills in the car's glove compartment, compliments of one of their fathers. Like Sam and Jeff, they extended their trip.

Bobby Ariatti is my best friend. He and I have been to most of the places Jeff and Sam visited and have had some of the best times of our lives there. When I told Bobby that Sam kills Jeff in the book, I said not to get any ideas.

Though the story of Sam and Jeff's rescue of a parrot named Mr. Kelly is fictional, it was inspired by a real parrot of the same name. He was owned by Bobby's priest in Cape Charles, Virginia, and lived from 1926 to 1992. I know that because Bobby sent me a photo of his tombstone. Most dead parrots, I'm confident, don't get tombstones.

The real Mr. Kelly really was owned by a sailor before Bobby's priest bought him and, like the fictional one, really did speak fluent profanity. When another priest asked Mr. Kelly if he wanted a cracker, the bawdy bird responded with a familiar profane suggestion consisting of two words, the first having four letters, the second one three. Bobby's priest shrugged and, like the woman who owns Mr. Kelly in the book, blamed the sailor.

Tom Hamrick is a dear friend and longtime client of mine. Like the two main characters in the book and my friends Roy and Tommy, Tom was born in 1960. He was a freshman at Millsaps and a member of Kappa Alpha when the Easter flood ravaged Jackson in April 1979. Tom didn't save a profane parrot, but he helped save the power plant, working side-by-side with inmates and watching as a pickup truck toppled down the berm into the plant. Like Sam, he worked all night but still made his eight o'clock class the next morning.

Tom served as my Scotch consultant for the book—I know a little about Scotch; he knows a lot—and also as the model for Sam as a history buff. Tom is a gentleman and a scholar and knows more history than anyone I know. After I told him that Jeff nick-named Sam Britannica and claimed that Sam kept the family's encyclopedias in his bedroom, Tom told me his family had two sets of encyclopedias when he was growing up. The *Britannicas* resided on bookshelves downstairs, but Tom kept the *World Books* in his bedroom.

The fictional Susan mentioned briefly as one of Sam's former girlfriends is based on a real Susan, my high school girlfriend. Her last name was Eskridge then; it's Frazier now. Like the fictional Susan, the real one attended Millsaps. She graduated in 1981. Also like the fictional Susan, the real one is funny, brilliant, and loves John Prine. She and Tom knew each other in college.

When I told the real Susan that a fictional Susan makes a cameo appearance in the book, she offered to tell me what Millsaps was like during the years the fictional Sam and Susan were students there. I asked her instead if she wanted to review the manuscript. She did, and her suggestions were excellent. She didn't suggest I add dogs to the story, but she had just lost her dog Gracie, so I added Rory and Josey. Dogs make everything better.

Susan boarded a flight from Nashville to Memphis many years ago. After she was seated, John Prine came walking down the aisle and sat down beside her. She was just twenty-one but already a big fan. She had him right there in her sights and could have asked him anything, but she was young and nervous and blew the chance.

Nearly thirty years later, Susan was given a second chance. A friend who was also a friend of John's wife, Fiona, arranged for Susan and her date to meet John and Fiona in their suite after a show in New Orleans. Susan's friend had told Fiona about the flight long ago, and Fiona had told John. He greeted Susan at the door and said, "You may not remember this, but we sat next to each other on a flight once."

I also love the music of John Prine. His songs have kept me company for nearly fifty years. After he died of COVID in 2020, a friend asked me to share my thoughts about him. I wrote a long essay and posted it on Facebook, which led another friend to introduce me to Episcopal priest David Elliott. David has loved John and his music even longer than I have and is the inspiration for the fictional David Eldridge in the book. The real David has taught classes about John, used his songs in sermons, and spent time with him backstage. Unlike Susan and David, I never met my songwriting hero.

David hasn't been a priest since Moses parted the Red Sea, but nearly. He's in his mid-eighties but still priesting. I sent him the chapter in which the fictional David meets with Sam for the first time and asked for his thoughts. He had one suggestion. I had David sitting behind his desk when Sam first came to see him. David said he never sits behind his desk when he meets with someone—he didn't when he met with me—so I put them in chairs facing each other in front of the desk. I offered to make the David in the book more fictional by changing his name, but the real David said to leave him as is. I think he likes his fictional namesake. So do I.

Carrie and I have friends a generation younger than we are who had their third child in the entrance lobby of Baptist Hospital in Jackson. The father caught his son before his head hit the floor, and the boy is thriving. Security cameras preserved the incident for posterity, but when I gave the mother the option, she preferred that I not expand their fame by disclosing their names.

Jeff's Halloween prank was inspired by my delightful mother, who loved tricking the neighbors into giving her treats by pretending to be three feet tall. I was blessed to have wonderful parents.

I named the elementary-school teachers Sam and Jeff tormented with a bird and a snake in honor of Martha Cheney and Frances Gregory, my excellent teachers in the fifth and sixth grades at Joyner Elementary in Tupelo, Mississippi. The real Mrs. Cheney, however, had two sons who were Boy Scouts with me and would never have been afraid of a king snake.

Two Facebook friends I've never met and live far from Mississippi, Gary Chard and Paul Decker, provided helpful information about places I've never been that Sam and Jeff visited on their 1978 road trip. Gary has lived in tiny Monroe, Maine, for fifty-five years. I've been to Maine but never to Beals Island or Sandy Spring Pond in Baxter State Park. Gary suggested both for the book.

Paul is a Boston lawyer and a scholar of the Civil War. He's been to all the battlefields the boys visited on their 1978 road trip, and he shared detailed information about them with me. Of the five battlefields, I've been only to Gettysburg, but Paul knows far more about the battle than I do. I've offered to give him a tour of Shiloh if he makes a pilgrimage to the South. I was inspired to have Sam visit Shiloh in the epilogue by going there with Carrie and friends in November 2024 and seeing the grave of an unknown Union soldier in the last row of the cemetery.

The Waffle House story Jeff tells in a Waffle House in Colorado is a true story. My friend and former law partner David Kaufman once ordered pancakes in a Waffle House. The waitress's response as quoted by Jeff is exactly as David quoted the real waitress's response to me.

Carrie and I have hosted concerts in our home for a decade. Many gifted artists have played for us and our friends. Two of our favorites are Andrew Duhon of New Orleans and Jason Eady, who grew up south of Jackson but now lives in Texas. Andrew inspired me to create a character with Down syndrome named John with his beautiful song "Till I Met John." https://www.youtube.com/watch?v=d_6gHaHPKxM. I stole a thought for the epilogue from Jason's moving song about D-Day, "French Summer Sun." Listen all the way to the end, and you'll hear what I stole. https://www.youtube.com/watch?v=dGevzDkqhVk&t=29s.

Writing these acknowledgments is a useful reminder that, like Jeff, I've had a wonderful life and, like Sam, I'm a rich man indeed.

Brooks Eason was born in a home for unwed mothers in New Orleans three years before the fictional Sam Thompson and Jeff Freeman were born. Brooks and his wife Carrie live in Madison, Mississippi, with three rescue dogs and a fearless orange tabby cat. Over the course of his nearly seventy years, Brooks has lived in four homes less than half a mile from the Natchez Trace, including the one in Tupelo, Mississippi, where he was raised by the wonderful parents who adopted him as well as the one where he and Carrie live now.

Brooks has three children and five grandchildren. He practiced law for forty years before retiring to a life of walking dogs and writing books. In their spare time, he and Carrie host house concerts and dance in the kitchen. *I Remember Everything* is his seventh book.

Also Available From


# WordCrafts Press

*27 Words*
  by KL Collins

*Canelands*
  by Gerry Harlan Brown

*A Song I Heard the Ocean Sing*
  by Laura Mansfield

*King of the Lake and Other Stories*
  by Kira Marie McCullough

*The Filbert Ridge Miracle*
  by Tamelia Aday


**www.wordcrafts.net**